About the Author

Lexie Winston has been an astronaut, rock star, princess and time traveller. In her dreams. But none of the dreams have lived up to what becoming an author has been like. She gets to live in a world of pure imagination, and her heroines get to do the things she's always wished she could.

When not writing books, Lexie is a mother of two gorgeous teenagers and the wife to a patient and understanding man. They live in Western Australia and are lorded over by a black toy poodle. She loves camping, reading and if her iPad was stolen, her world would explode. (It has the kindle app on it.)

And check out my website at lexiewinston.com

And you can find all my links at
https://linktr.ee/LexieWinston

Also by Lexie Winston

Glorious Gluttony

Gangs, Guns, and Glory

Galaxy Circus

(Sci-Fi Reverse Harem Series)

Apprentice

Stagehand

Whisperer

A Night Most Wicked - Galaxy Circus Novella

Broken Promises

(Dark Poly Romance Series)

Secrets Kept

Lies Untold

M.I.T.H.O.S

(Contemporary RH)

Spies Like Me

Coming 2022

SUPERFICIAL GIRL

Part 2

LEXIE WINSTON

First published by Neighpalm Publishing in 2022

Superficial Girl - Part 2: Neighpalm Industries Collective

Mobi format: 978-0-6455261-0-3
Print: 978-0-6455261-1-0

Cover design by Lexie Winston
Edited by Inked Imagination
Proofreading - Elemental Editing

❀ Created with Vellum

Content Warning

Please be advised there is drug use and attempted rape in this book. There is also a small amount of dub-con.

Chapter One

Jacinta

I fly home from Hawaii the next day, accompanied by everyone except Harlow and the boys. I offered Alex, Shane, and Jace a lift, but they already had flights booked, and Shane needed to stay another night, so I kissed them all goodbye midmorning and headed to the airport.

The flight home is uneventful. I actually get to sit down and read for the first time in ages. I'm reading a new author to me, Kerry Keller. Who doesn't like a good paranormal academy book?

"What are you reading?" Cole asks, sliding onto the sofa next to me. The rest of my family is watching a movie in the back of the plane, but I really wanted to read this book. He's got a coffee in one hand and the kindle I used when we read

Spencer a story last night. It has a *Paw Patrol* skin on it that, according to him, his son picked.

I feel a slight blush heat my face but quickly shake it off. I've got nothing to be embarrassed about. "It's a reverse harem paranormal romance."

"Reverse harem?"

"Ah, yeah. Usually, it's a relationship with one woman and multiple men. Sometimes the men are involved with each other as well."

"Oh. So… like your relationship with the guys." There's no judgment in his tone for a change, which is nice.

"Yeah, I guess. I've been reading this genre for a while. Jilly put Nana and me onto them when Nana was curious about her relationships."

"You have to recommend a good starter book."

"You want to read one?" I can't keep the surprise from my voice.

He shrugs. "Yeah, why not? I like paranormal romance. I read *Twilight*, and I really liked the books *True Blood* was based on."

"Huh, you like vampires." You could knock me over with a feather. I would never have guessed. "I would have picked you as a Tom Clancy or James Patterson fan."

"Oh, I do like them, but I love supernatural stuff, and vampires are sexy. All the blood drinking is sexy." It sure is. I'm looking at Cole in a different light. I don't like to judge a book by its cover, but I've judged people a few times based on the books they read. If he's open-minded enough to have that variety on his virtual bookshelf, maybe I'm as guilty as he is for making assumptions.

"What are you reading at the moment?" I nod at his kindle, and an excited gleam enters his eyes.

"I've found this Aussie author Matthew Riley. He writes these fast-paced, high-impact, action thrillers. This one is set in an ice station in Antarctica, and there's a government conspiracy and orcas and mutated elephant seals. It's really good."

He's so animated as he tells me about the books, hands flying and leaning forward in his enthusiasm. I do love a man who reads.

We settle down and spend the rest of the flight keeping each other company while we immerse ourselves in our books. I also make sure to fill him in on everything that happened with Ash and the plan going forward. He's supportive and assures me that it should still help our family, which gives me an unexpected burst of comfort. I shouldn't care about his approval, but I have to admit that it feels nice to have him agreeing with me, validating that I've made the right choice.

I don't return home once we arrive back with the others.

"Aren't you coming?" Dad asks, leaning against the door of the limo. Nana, Poppy, Emma, and Molly are already in it, and Cole and Hope are waiting back with me.

I shake my head. "No, I've got plans this week. I'll see you down in New Orleans this weekend."

"Oh, okay." He sounds disappointed. "I feel like I barely see any of you anymore. With the boys and Harlow gone, and you and Hope so busy, I'm feeling a little lost."

"Aww, Dad, I guess it's hard when your kids grow up. But you'll have two new ones to shower with love soon, not to mention two grandchildren."

He pouts ever so slightly. "Doesn't mean I don't miss my others."

"Thanksgiving is coming soon. You'll get to spend the weekend with us all, then there's Christmas and two whole weeks with us at the cabin. We'll skate and ski and play games. You'll be sick of us by the end."

"Never." He gives us both a kiss and waves goodbye to Cole before he hops into the limo.

"Right, have fun, stay safe, and be careful," Hope warns me. "Our family won't want you doing something that makes you unhappy. We can come up with another solution."

"It's fine. *I'm* fine. I'll do anything for my family.

You know that. I don't want Dad or Poppy stressing. Didn't you notice how stressed the two of them looked this weekend?"

"The sex hotel wasn't well received by some of the shareholders. Despite the really good press, some of them were saying it's basically a brothel. Diamant Unlimited had a buying frenzy over the weekend, snapping up shares," Cole explains.

"Well, as long as the family holds the majority, we're fine," Hope says.

"There's a push to have someone other than a family member on the board. Someone who's independent of the Summers to hold them accountable."

"Maybe I should change my name to Bucătaru, then I would count as a non-family member."

Hope and Cole chuckle. "It doesn't work that way," he tells me, and I shrug.

"I know, but I can dream."

Hope leaves, and Cole and I hop into another car with Riku and Simon in the front to head to the hotel where I'm staying this week.

"Where do you live?" I ask him, watching the scenery pass us by.

"I was renting an apartment, but a suite at the hotel was a part of my salary package, so I gave it up. One day, I'd like to buy a house for Spencer and me."

"Do you have him very often?" I ask.

"Not as much as I'd like. Hayden travels all the

time for work, and she takes him with her. We have joint custody, so I'm supposed to get him every second week, but it doesn't always work out that way. I actually think it would be better if he stayed with me. It would be a more stable life than the one she's providing him. It's the one thing we fight about all the time."

"I'm sorry. That must be difficult for you."

"I've considered taking her back to court and challenging the agreement, but I don't because I'm grateful our split is reasonably amicable, I don't want to jeopardize that. Not to mention now that I'm living in the hotel, I'm sure that would go against me."

"But why? Doesn't Hayden live in hotels when she's traveling around the world? It would be no different than that except it would be the same room every night. And you have an apartment suite, don't you? So it's not like he won't have his own space."

He looks thoughtful, mulling over what I just said. "Yeah, you're not wrong. Maybe I'll speak to her down in New Orleans. Now that she has a new boyfriend, she might want to spend some child-free time with him."

"Why did you split up?" I casually ask even though I'm burning with curiosity. There's something that just makes me insatiable when it comes to learning about him. The more he tells me, the more I want to know. While we're getting along and having one of our most civil conversations, I want to take advantage of that.

Cole's face is pensive as he thinks about it. "We had a whirlwind romance that involved parties and socializing and being seen, but when she got pregnant, I wanted things to change. I wanted to provide a more stable family life for my child, and, to be honest, the parties weren't my thing. They were fun to start with, but in the end, I was doing it for her. She loved to be the center of attention, so when she found out she was pregnant, I had to beg her to carry him to term. That was the start of things going wrong. She didn't want to ruin her model body, which I understand, but she did it for me. I had to constantly nag her to eat properly and to not exercise too much. Spencer was born a month early because she had been starving herself, so I honestly expected the absolute worst about what she might be like as a mother, but she changed once he arrived and held him. She fell in love. I guess it didn't hurt that it only took her a few weeks to get back into shape. And thanks to those extra curves due to the pregnancy, Victoria's Secret made her an angel, and she's never looked back. Hayden's not a bad person, she's just self-involved. By the end of the pregnancy, our marriage was mostly over. I'm almost positive she was seeing other people in that first year of Spencer's life while I was very much a stay-at-home dad during that time. I could work from home, so I raised Spencer, and she continued to model. It was only when he became a cute accessory that he became important to her. That's when we got a divorce."

The car pulls up at the hotel as he finishes telling his story. "For what it's worth, you seem like a great dad, and I can tell Spencer thinks the sun shines out of your ass. I mean, he's clearly delusional, but I wouldn't want to tell him anything different."

Cole smiles. "Oh, I think I'm growing on you, Jacinta Summers."

"Yeah, like a fungus." I grin and hop out of the car. "Thanks for the company. I'm heading out to a club tonight with Ashton. I want to grab a shower and maybe a quick nap before that happens."

"Okay, well, call me if you need anything. I'll keep a close eye on what the media is saying. Like Hope suggested, we may need to sow a few seeds ourselves."

"Will do, and say hi to Spencer for me."

We part in the foyer when I head for the elevator and him to the bar. Riku catches up to me as we enter the elevator.

"What happened to Simon?" I ask, peering out before the doors shut.

"Your dad decided on the weekend that you probably need only one permanent guard, so I've reassigned him." Riku's standing close enough to me that our arms brush one another, which gives me this sort of tingly feeling that I can't look at too closely right now. Unfortunately, I get distracted by another much less welcome feeling.

"Oh, okay, well, I'm glad I've still got you." I bite my lip with worry. Having security makes me feel safer when I go out. Doesn't stop all the other issues, but it is one less concern. I'm thankful that Riku is still going to be with me. "I'll message you when I'm ready to leave. Ashton's going to come here, and we'll take my car to the club."

He puts his hand on my arm, stopping me in front of my door. "Are you going to be okay? You sound like you don't want to do this."

"Oh yes, it's fine. I'm just tired. A nap and a shower, and I'll be fine. You may want to nap too. We've got a busy week. We have a thing on Wednesday and Thursday night too, then we fly down to New Orleans on Friday."

"I'm assuming Lord Lavington will be coming with us?" he asks, and I suddenly feel a little guilty. Fuck. Although Riku was around when we were talking about it, I'm not sure he knows the full story. After he shared his feelings with me, I really didn't get a chance to fill him in. I was reeling from everything he said, and I had to hurry off to my spa appointment with Hope.

Well, no time like the present. I proceed to tell him the plan, and his face stays blank while I'm talking. He takes my keycard from my fingers and swipes it through the reader before heading into the suite to check it out. I allow him a few moments to look around before I follow him in. He's on the other side of the room, looking behind a curtain, when I walk in and place my handbag on the coffee table.

"Are you okay?" I ask. He hasn't said anything about the plan. Is it too much for him now? Has he decided that I'm not worth this extra trouble? I guess it's hard enough for him to share me with Alex, Shane, and Jace. To have to watch me with Ash when he can't or won't do anything in public may be pushing him too far.

He suddenly spins and strides toward me like a panther stalking his prey. It's all I can do not to run from his soul-deep stare when his eyes meet mine. Before I can kick my fight or flight instincts into gear, he gathers me in his arms and kisses me. *Hard.* A take no prisoners, leave no doubt to how he feels kind of kiss. I become putty in his arms. There's just something about all of my guys that make me feel safe and secure and comfortable letting them take the lead. For so many years, I've led Neighpalm Couture with a single-minded focus, not giving an inch in a professional capacity. Having the complete opposite in my personal life is life changing.

I'm breathless and shuddering when he pulls away. "As long as I have a place somewhere in your life, you could add a hundred men, and I'd support you," he tells me fiercely.

"Oh no, it's not like that with Ash. It's all pretend," I protest, and he gives me that serene smile of his.

"Of course it is, but if something were to happen with him, I wouldn't be upset or surprised."

"Yeah, I'm not so sure Alex would agree. It seems there are some unresolved feelings there, even if they did get some closure. It would probably become messy. Better to be strictly friends with him." I'm not sure whether I'm telling that to Riku or myself, but I'm sticking to it.

Riku has a disbelieving smirk. "Okay, whatever you say. Come now, climb into your bed and have a nap. I'll order you some food when you get up." He tows me into my bedroom by the hand and pulls back the covers on my neatly made bed. I sit down, and he slips off my shoes before dragging my leggings down. I'm left in my panties and the big baggy shirt I'd slipped on to be comfortable during the flight. I reach up and undo my bra, sliding it off through the arm holes, before climbing under the blankets. Riku goes to pull them up, but I put a hand out to stop him.

"Climb in with me?" I ask. "Just hold me while I nap. I always feel so safe in your arms." The smile slowly slides across his face again, with a hint of pride shining in his eyes, like he's pleased that's how he makes me feel. He nudges off his shoes and goes to climb in, but I shake my head. "Strip, I want you to be comfortable too."

He removes his dress pants and T-shirt, leaving him in a pair of tight boxers, and oh my... Riku is all long and lean with abs for days. I swallow as he slides in next to me, gently rolling me over so he can wrap his arms around me from behind. He pulls the covers up over us, and his body heat instantly makes me feel hot. His hand cups one of my boobs as he gets comfortable.

"Is this okay?" he asks.

"More than okay," I reply as I close my eyes and revel in the feel of having him in my bed. Apart from the other night with Shane and Alex, I haven't had a man in my bed in years. Any sex I partook in was one-night flings with me leaving not long after the climax. I hadn't realized how nice it would be to cuddle.

Riku nuzzles my neck and kisses me just behind my ear as his dick hardens against my ass. Neither of us mention it. We both know it's a forgone conclusion eventually, but not now. No, when we make love, I want to have enough time to really enjoy him because I'm almost certain Riku is going to blow my mind.

Chapter Two

The week is a drug and alcohol fueled blur filled with parties and appearances. My only constant is the underlying guilt that stays beneath the surface of my mind. Having to do this, being out in a world that wants nothing from me other than the superficial girl they believe I am, is making me grab that little baggie more than I ever wanted to. It awakens all of that insecurity that I spent years of therapy and thousands of dollars trying to heal. What can I say? Trauma is one determined motherfucker.

I tried to use alcohol as a crutch instead, but it didn't help. It made me paranoid and jumpy, so I reverted back to the coke usage, helping myself to more from the stash at Willow Castle. Unfortunately, it's now Thursday night, and I'm finally out. I don't have time to return to Willow Castle prior to tonight's outing with Ash.

We're going to another private party for some random celebrity, but this will be at a private residence. I'm not sure why Cole has us going to this one. Maybe there will be media out front? It's all superficial and fake, but I'm surprised to admit I'm enjoying Ashton's company. He's not as big of a douche as he portrays. I guess, much like me, he has a facade he presents to the public, but when we're in private, traveling to and from these events, we have had some interesting and insightful conversations. When we started this, I never thought we'd end up friends, but he's slowly wormed his way under my skin. His love for his sister is obvious when he talks about her, and someone who loves like that can't be all bad.

"Ash, why the playboy act?" I ask him once we're firmly entrenched in the back of the limo once more. Riku is riding in the front with the driver tonight, and I've poured us both whiskeys on ice. He seems to drink as much as I do at these things, and I'm almost certain he's been popping pills as well. Seems we may be two peas in a pod, self-medicating to get through life.

"To start with, it was to piss off my grandmother, mostly. I hated her dictating to me, and it was my way of giving her the finger. If I couldn't embarrass her with my sexuality, then I could embarrass her with my public womanizing. But the stupid old cow is old school, so she expects that kind of attitude from men. And by then, people had come to expect that kind of behavior from me. I was the party boy lord, and I was always invited to things. My popularity and reputation made it so that I could avoid the estate for as long as possible."

"Oh, that reminds me. If there's no money left in the estate, how do you afford your lavish life-style?" Because there has been no hesitation in splashing his money around. He won't actually let me pay for anything even though I can definitely afford it. He just picked up my hand and gallantly kissed me on the back of it, saying, "Now, what kind of gentleman would that make me?"

A smug, satisfied smile spreads across his lips, and his eyes light up with mirth. "My money, fair question. Well, my mother was an extremely wealthy woman. It seems the Lavingtons have a habit of encouraging their sons to marry for money. And when she died in childbirth, my grandmother and father were furious to discover she'd changed her will while pregnant with me. I inherited everything that was hers. She had discovered that my father started cheating not long after she revealed that she was pregnant. Her lawyer informed me that she had started divorce proceedings, but she died before she could finalize them."

"I'm so sorry, Ash. I know what it's like to have shady relatives."

"Ah yes, Count Bucătaru. I read that story. It was riveting, if somewhat unbelievable."

"Yeah, but I can assure you it was all true."

"They really found all those guns and drugs stashed in the house?"

"Yes, there were drugs stashed all over the house, not to mention my grandfather's body. The house is riddled with secret rooms and passages for staff. We found him in one of those."

He leans forward, totally absorbed with the story. "But not your father?"

I shake my head. "No, which leaves him as the only remaining loose end. Who knows if we'll ever find out what happened to him?"

He leans back, taking another sip of his whiskey. "So is that where you're getting your coke from?"

The mouthful of whiskey that I just swallowed goes down the wrong way when I gasp my surprise, leaving me sputtering and coughing. Ash hands me a napkin before taking my glass from me. I widen my eyes, feigning surprise. "I think you must be mistaken. I don't…"

Ash holds up his hand and rolls his eyes. "Save it, Jacinta. I know what someone on coke or uppers looks like. It's just like looking in the mirror. Why don't we cut the crap and come clean with one another?"

"Fuck off, Ash, like you haven't been using to get through the parties," I snarl, going on the defensive.

"Hey, hey, no judgment here. I'd just like to know what you're using in case you OD while on my watch. I only think that's fair."

I sigh and shrug. "Fine, it was coke, but I'm out now. I haven't been back to the house."

He runs a hand across his chin. He has a rakish look to him tonight since he didn't bother to shave, and the sprinkling of black stubble gives him a daring, slightly bad boy look. He hands me back my whiskey.

"No problem, I've got a hookup at the party. I'll take care of you." I breathe a sigh of relief. I wasn't sure how I was going to fake the appropriate Jacinta behavior and not give myself away by running screaming from the room. "But do you mind me asking why?"

"Why what?" I throw back the rest of my whiskey and hold my glass out for a refill. He complies, his brown eyes locked on mine like he's trying to work out a puzzle.

"Why does Jacinta Summers, heiress to the Neighpalm Industries fortune and now Countess Bucătaru, wealthy beyond all comprehension, need coke to make it through a party filled with shallow, superficial, insignificant people?"

I start to disagree, but the raise of a single pompous eyebrow stops me in my tracks.

"Fine. Jacinta Summers, heiress to the Neighpalm blah, blah, blah, suffers crippling anxiety and nerves at the thought of facing a room full of people who may be plotting to kill me or my brother or any of my siblings for something as petty as money. Not to mention the self-loathing."

"Really?" He can't hide the surprise in his voice.

"Yeah, ever since the kidnapping. I was fucking useless, Ash. First, Harlow was dragged into all that drama because my cousin was obsessed with her, then my uncle, or whatever he was, tried to kill her in Hawaii to stop that obsession and get his son back on track. When that didn't work, he resorted to killing his son. He kidnapped us all, including Harlow, because she was plan B if plan A hadn't worked, all because he wanted drugs and money and whatever! If he had just asked, Jax and I probably would have given him some. It's not like there's not enough to go around."

The dam has broken, and there is no stopping the flow of our family soap opera. Should I be telling him all this? I have no idea, honestly, but it's kind of cathartic to get things off my chest even though that doesn't solve anything. I'm not foolish enough to think this relief will be long lived. "Then Harlow managed to get free and sent me for help while she stayed behind to protect my brother. My brother, something that should have been my task, right? But no, I just ran like the coward I am. Then Harlow and he were forced to fuck at gun point for Peter's sick fucking games, and Jaxon was shot. I almost lost my twin because I wasn't strong enough to stay and help." Tears are streaming down my face now. Ash puts his drink down and comes over to my side, putting his arms around my shoulders and drawing me into him.

"Shhh, it's okay. Let it all out. I've got you." I sob into his shirt, making a mess of it, but he doesn't complain once. He holds me and rubs my back until the sobs finally stop.

I pull away. "Oh God, I'm so sorry." My face flames with embarrassment, but he just pulls out a bunch of napkins, passing them to me to wipe my face and blow my nose.

"Please don't apologize. It will dry. It sounds to me like you'd been holding that in for way too long. I have no words because if I said something along the lines of don't be stupid, I'm making light of your feelings, and I don't want to do that. I know the mind can be cruel, and the insidious whispers can be loud some days. Drowning them out with drugs is a perfectly reasonable solution to me. Hence why I have the hookups. So don't worry, Jacinta, I'll take care of you."

He puts one arm around my shoulders again, and I lean into him as we drive the rest of the way to the party. The silence between us is peaceful and relaxed, and I appreciate that he didn't try to negate my feelings. Instead, he reinforced that I'm legitimately allowed to feel the way I do.

"Call me Jazzy. All my friends do."

"Whose party is this again?" I ask him a little while later as the limo pulls up to a mansion that has lights blazing, with lots of cars parked out front and music pounding through the open doors and windows.

"Some movie exec," he tells me as he holds his hand out to help me from the car. A few flashing lights blind me, and I hold my hands up to shield my eyes.

"A Neighpalm one?" I ask, frowning, and he grins cheekily.

"No, the competition."

"*Jacinta, are you and Lord Ashton an official couple now?*"

"*Lord Ashton, have you given up your playboy ways for Countess Bucătaru? Is this a new way to infuse money into the Lavington estate?*

"*What does your grandmother think of the relationship?*"

Behind the gates of the estate are a few reporters whom I hadn't noticed on the way in. Ashton just smiles and waves before grabbing my hand and giving it a kiss. A valet takes away the limo, leaving Riku to follow us up the stairs.

My grip on Ashton's hand tightens as nausea rushes over me. All the sinister, self-deprecating thoughts are practically screaming at me over the sound of the party.

"Jacinta, Jacinta!" I look to see who's calling my

name, but I can't find anyone I know as we push our way through the crowd.

We stop in the living room, and Ash gazes around, looking for someone. He must see whomever he needs because he waves a hand and points to the back of the house. "Hey, babe, just wait here for me for a moment." He waves Riku over. "Riku, can you keep an eye on her while I'm gone? I'm just going to grab us some drinks, then we'll see if anyone we know is here." I appreciate the fact that he doesn't call them friends.

Riku is quick to nod, and we find a space of blank wall to lean against. I can't stop my foot from tapping, and I know from the copper taste in my mouth that I've chewed through my lip.

"Hey, don't do that." Riku reaches up a hand and frees my lip from my teeth. "He'll be back in a moment, don't worry." I'm perfectly fine with him misinterpreting my stress. I'm not about to explain that I'm nervous he won't find me any more coke.

"Jacinta, hi! I called you. Why didn't you wait?" Selena Cross is suddenly in my face, and she's dragging along Evangeline, who mouths, "Sorry," to me. "Who's this? Are you cheating on Ash already? I have no idea why he would have chosen you over me."

"Selena!" Evie gasps. "Sorry, she's rolling again, and she tends to lose all social filters." Evie has always been a bit too nice. Selena, the bitch, doesn't have any social filters when she's *not* out of her mind on drugs.

"God, Selena, you're so oblivious. This is Riku, my bodyguard. He's been everywhere I have for the last month. Ash has just gone to get us drinks," I tell them. And I swear if he doesn't return soon, I'm going to have a full-blown meltdown.

"Well, aren't you delicious? How would you like to guard my body?" She simpers at him, running her hand down his front. A burst of uncontrollable anger flows through me. How dare she proposition my bodyguard? I'm about to smack her hand away when Ash returns and gets between us.

"There you are, love." He kisses me hard on the mouth, which is the first time he and I have done that. Up until now, we've kept the physical touches to hand holding and hugging. To say I'm surprised is an understatement. The anger completely drains from me as he passes over a bottle of something pink. "Here, I got us a drink, but they are doing shots in the kitchen. Some of our friends are there. Shall we make our way to them?"

"Hey, Ash, how are you? We missed you at Lazlo's yacht party this weekend." Selena runs her hand up and down his arm, and the anger quickly returns.

"I'm a popular man, Selena. I was attending the opening of Neighpalm Luxure in Hawaii. I've got to put the little lady first, after all." He thickens his posh accent, and Selena eats it up, giggling.

"You're so silly!" She goes to touch him again, and I step between them.

"Shall we? Maybe if we find a spare closet between here and the kitchen, I can give you a quick blow job to get this party started."

Oh my god, what the fuck is wrong with me? I cannot believe I said that. But Ash chuckles and smacks me on the ass.

"Lead the way, babe."

We push our way through the crowd, Selena and Evie with us and Riku following behind. We pass a bathroom, and Ash pulls me into it, winking at the girls. "We'll catch up in a minute." Selena glares at me, but Evie pulls her away, and Ash and Riku exchange a nod.

Closing the door behind us blocks out some of the noise, and I can take a semi-normal breath for the first time since we entered the party. I lean against the door and take a long pull of my drink. It's sweet and tastes like cherries, and before I know it, half is gone. While I'm doing that, Ash uses the lid of the toilet as a table for us, making some lines from the baggie he pulled out of his pocket. I scrunch my nose up, and he rolls his eyes when he hands me the straw. "We can't be picky. Plus, I bet it's the only thing this toilet has been used for since the maid cleaned it before the party."

He's probably not wrong, so I place my drink down on the sink, take the straw, and inhale, one in each nostril, before passing the straw back to Ash.

The chemicals burn the inside, and it instantly starts to drip. I grab a piece of toilet paper and dab at the liquid. Ash does his two lines and tucks the bag, straw, and his card back into his pocket.

"All good?" he asks, and I take a couple of deep breaths in and out, feeling the coke take effect. A slow smile spreads across my lips as everything finally starts to feel good again.

"Yeah, I am now. Thanks."

He nods then reaches out and grabs me. Pulling me to him, he slams his mouth down onto mine. A surprised squeak escapes my mouth before he slides his tongue into it, tasting and teasing, and his hand grips my ass, making it easier for him to grind against me. As shocked as I am, I'm all in, returning the kiss with equal enthusiasm. My fingers run through his hair, messing it up.

Suddenly, he pulls away and looks me up and down. "Perfect, you look like you've had a quick fuck in the bathroom."

I wipe a finger over my lips, seeing how my lipstick is smeared in the mirror, but he pulls my hand away before I get it all. "Leave it. Let people think whatever they want. It's a good cover."

"Right, a cover, sure." I'm slightly dazed as I reach for my drink, and Ash gets his smug playboy grin firmly in place before he opens the door.

Chapter Three

Jacinta

In the kitchen, we find a group of people. Matthew is there, surrounded by a group of guys who might be slightly familiar, but I can't put names or TV shows to their faces. To my surprise, Chase and Anna are there, but the couple is definitely giving him the cold shoulder. They are chatting with Selena and Evie when we arrive.

"Oh yeah, my man Ash!" Matthew holds his hand up for a high five. "Getting some early action. Jacinta, I had pegged you for a cold fish, but you really aren't, are you?" He leers at me while Ash smacks his hand down.

"Shut the fuck up, man. That's my girlfriend you're talking about. Have a little respect."

Matthew chuckles and winks. "Sure, *girlfriend*." He waves a hand at the dude bros behind him.

"We've got a pool running for how long it's going to last."

"You're a fucking pig, Matt," Anna spits at him.

"Yeah, and you're a best friend stealing whore, so we can't all be superheroes like Chase here, can we?"

The three of them are still arguing when I start feeling light-headed and woozy. I grab hold of the kitchen counter as Chase tries to take a swing at Matthew, but Ash and Riku jump in between them.

"Whoa, okay, I'll go." Matthew holds up his hands, looking at me with a glint in his eyes as he blows me a kiss. "I'll catch you later, Countess."

He and his group of sycophants leave the kitchen, and Anna claps her hands. "Excellent! Now that the trash has gone, let's do some shots."

I feel a little dizzy and like the heat in the house has suddenly been turned up. I peel off the light cardigan I had on over my strapless top and throw it on the counter.

"Well, don't you look gorgeous tonight?" Evie raises her glass while eyeing me. I've got on a corseted, red satin, strapless bodysuit and a pair of skinny jeans tucked into some long boots.

"Thanks, babe, you look pretty good yourself. I recognize that dress," I fire back, draining the rest of my pink drink and looking around for another.

"A Jacinta Summers original, of course. When I saw it, I just knew I had to have it."

I smile at her compliment but can't seem to find

any more of the pink drinks. "Ash, honey," I call, running my hand down his back to get his attention. He spins around, surprise on his face before he recovers.

"Yes, snookums?"

"Where did you get that drink from? It was really yummy, and I want another one." He frowns and peers around the kitchen.

"I'm not actually sure. Matthew handed them to me when I first arrived. But there's a blue one over there."

I pout a little but step forward to grab one out of the tub. Unfortunately, the move isn't as smooth as I wish it was. Chase catches me when I stumble, which should be at least a little embarrassing, but all I can do is giggle.

"Shit. That drink has gone right to my head." Chase smiles and helps me upright again. "Actually, I might use the bathroom first." My head is really spinning now, and I'm starting to panic, thinking that maybe Ash's coke wasn't a good batch.

"You want me to come with you?" Ash asks, and I shake my head.

"No. I've got Riku. You stay and be with our friends." I lean up and give him a kiss, nipping him on the lip. Fuck, now I'm feeling horny as hell, like I could get down on my knees and blow this man. Actually, what would be even better is if I had a dick in each hand, swapping between them. Would Riku be up for that? "But don't go too far, alright?" I wink at him, and he gives me a strange look.

"Okay, babe, be safe."

I wave my hand and stumble away from them, Riku, my faithful shadow, just a little bit back from me.

I'm greeted by familiar faces and acquaintances from various Neighpalm represented bands. The elite of California is quite incestuous when you think about it. A giggle escapes. *Incestuous, that's a funny word.*

I weave my way through the crowd until I find stairs leading up. I'm sure there's a bathroom up there somewhere, and maybe I can get a breath of fresh air. I'm so fucking hot. Fanning myself, I walk up the stairs. On the landing, I hear a commotion, but as I go to turn around, I'm grabbed, and a hand is slapped over my mouth as I'm dragged backward into a nearby room.

I try to scream, but it's easily muffled by whoever is covering my mouth. Suddenly, it hits me. The coke wasn't bad. I've been fucking roofied! Dread infuses me, and I stop, my fight-or-flight response completely broken.

"I've got you, you stuck-up bitch, and while my guys are keeping your bodyguard occupied, I'm going to see what all the fuss is about. The good thing is the Molly and Rohypnol are going to keep you begging for more, and there's no chance you'll remember it in the morning."

Vomit surges up in my mouth, but it can't go anywhere thanks to Matthew's hand, so I have to swallow it back down. I struggle a little more, but my body becomes deadweight as he throws me onto the bed and rips down the bodice.

"Well, I've got to say, Jacinta, your tits are some of the nicest I've seen in ages, and all real. How about we cover them with my cum to start with?" I hear the zipper come down on his fly as tears well up, overflow, and run down my cheeks. I try to call out, but all I can do is mumble, and no one is going to hear that over the noise of the party.

Ashton

I watch, smiling, as Jacinta wanders away from the group in need of a bathroom. Riku stays behind her as her silent, reliable shadow. She's so cute, but what a lightweight. That one drink barely contained any alcohol, and she's hammered enough to be stumbling.

Which, now that I think about it, is weird because I haven't seen her stumble all week despite everything we've been putting into our systems.

"Don't you think, Ash?" Selena's voice grates on my nerves, but it drags me back to the conversation.

"I'm sorry, what?"

"We were just talking about next week's polo match and the afterparty. I'm sure you and Jacinta will have lots to celebrate if your team wins."

"Oh yeah, sure. Will you excuse me? I'm just going to make sure she's okay."

"Don't be silly. She has her bodyguard with her. She'll be fine." Selena tries to hold me back, but I push past her and into the living room where a lot of the party revelers are.

There's a commotion next to the stairs, and my heart rate picks up when I find Riku surrounded by the four guys that were with Matthew earlier.

"Where is she?" I ask as Riku takes a swing at one of them.

"She went upstairs. Go, I'll take care of these guys," he yells. I skirt around the fighting since Riku seems to have it all in hand, and I see Chase dive in to help. I race up the stairs to the landing, but the first room is empty. The next one has a couple on the bed, so I back out, murmuring apologies, until I catch sight of a flash of red out of the corner of my eye.

Slamming the door fully open, I find Jacinta on the bed, with Matthew's dick hanging out above her as he strokes it.

"Oh hey, Ash, I thought I'd take your girlfriend for a spin since you've already had a go tonight."

I see fucking red.

Jacinta isn't moving, so I'm guessing the drink he gave me was roofied. Fuck, I am so stupid, but I can kick my own ass later. I run at the guy, tackling him to the side. We go down in a heap of limbs, and I start to punch his face in, losing all track of time. He's a bloody, unconscious mess by the time Chase pulls me off him.

Riku is on the bed with a barely conscious Jacinta in his arms. "I'll call the police," Chase says, and Riku nods.

"Thank you." Chase leaves to do that while Riku waves me over. "Hold her, please. I'm calling the Summers' lawyer. He'll meet you both at Jacinta's hotel along with the family doctor. He can take blood samples so we can prove he drugged her." I wince, and he raises an eyebrow. "What?"

"She may have snorted a little coke earlier this evening as well." I look down at her, and it's like she's not there. The lights are on, but no one's home. This is not going to help with all her issues.

He sighs deeply. "Yeah, I kind of thought that might be the case. Alright, you take the car and the driver, and I'll call another for when I finish up with the police. Once they are done here, they'll probably follow me back to the hotel."

I bend down, help pull her bodice back up, and scoop her into my arms. Her head lolls onto my shoulder, bringing with it the smell of vomit. She groans, and I figure I'm probably going to be covered in puke, but I don't care. It's my fault this happened to her because I was stupid enough to take an open drink from someone. But fucking hell, giving someone a roofie is so fucking cliché.

I head down the stairs, Chase making a path through the crowd. Evie runs up to us and puts Jazzy's cardigan over her face.

"The press is still outside," she warns me.

"Fuck, is there a back way?"

"Yes, through the kitchen. There's a path that'll take you to the garage down past the pool. That's where all the cars and drivers are parked and waiting."

"Thank you," I say to Evie, then I change directions, heading where she pointed. If I might have kicked one of the guys that Riku had taken care of, well, I'm not sad about it in the least.

She groans again in my arms, and I tighten my hold on her. She barely weighs anything, so it's easy to carry her and still pay attention to our surroundings. "Hang in there, sweetie. I'll take care of you."

"Ash?" she slurs.

"Yeah, baby, I've got you. I'm so sorry I let you out of my sight."

"Riku?" I can barely hear her voice.

"He's fine. Matthew's friends waylaid him so he couldn't follow you, but damn, girl, you should see that man fight. He's like a ninja warrior or something," I say lightly. "He's just fine. He's going to see that Matthew is taken away by the police and charged."

"Couldn't stop him," she mutters, still limp in

my arms, then her head rolls back a bit like she's trying to look me in the eye. "Didn't want that."

"Oh no, of course you didn't. Don't you worry, we'll get you home and cleaned up. The doctor is coming to look at you."

For the first time, she struggles in my arms. "No, no doctor, coke." She's barely comprehensible, but I think I get her meaning.

"We have to, baby. They need proof of what he did to you."

"Don't want family to know," she says, and I finally understand what she's getting at.

"Don't worry, the doctor can't tell anyone anything without your permission. We can say he can tell them about whatever Matt gave you but not the coke." The halfhearted struggling stops, and she goes limp again.

"Okay, trust you." We get to her car, and the driver jumps out and opens the door.

"Is everything alright?" he asks, and I shake my head.

"No, Jacinta isn't feeling well. We need to get her back to her hotel for the doctor to see her." Thankfully, the driver doesn't blink. I guess he's paid well enough not to react in any way. I slide in behind her, pulling her back onto my lap, and he closes the door before hurrying around to get in. Before I've even got us settled, the vehicle is moving.

"So hot," she complains and tries to push me

away, but she's still not coordinated enough, so I push the button for the AC and reach forward, grabbing a bottle of water from the mini fridge. "Here, sweetie, have some of this." I coax her to drink, only allowing her to take little sips.

I have no idea how to deal with a situation like this, but so far she's staying sort of responsive, and I guess that's all I can hope for.

"Can you pull into the parking garage and bring us to the private Summers elevator, please?" I ask the driver, pushing the intercom switch.

"Of course," he responds. Other than that, the drive back to the hotel is silent, punctuated by slight moans and groans from Jacinta.

"Are you okay?" I ask stupidly. Of course she's not.

"Body is on fire. I'm so hot." She starts to pull at her clothes, reaching for the button of her jeans, but she still doesn't have complete motor function. Her efforts end with sobs with frustration.

"Please help me," she begs.

"Okay, okay, stop, you're going to hurt yourself." I grab her hands just before she accidentally smashes herself in the face. I move her off my lap and arrange her so she's lying across the seat. I put a pillow behind her head before I reach for her jeans. Flicking the top button, I drag the zipper down, swallowing deeply. Any time I've imagined getting Jacinta Summers naked, it did *not* look like this.

I realize I can't do anything with the jeans until I remove her boots, so I slide down the zippers on each of those and pull them off her feet, throwing them to the side, followed by her socks. Jacinta's dainty toes are painted blood red, looking sexy as fuck, and I want to slap myself once more. *Inappropriate much, Ash?*

Slipping my hands in the band of her jeans, I peel them down her legs, marveling at the fact that she got them on in the first place. They are skintight with absolutely no room for anything else but her legs. They join the shoes in the pile, leaving her in just the bodysuit. She looks amazing, all pale skin and dark hair and deep red satin. I feel my dick rapidly harden and want to punch myself in it, but I'm only human. As I watch on, hoping she's cool enough now, my mouth drops open when she slides her hand south.

"It aches so much," she whines, and I want to punch Matthew all over again. There's no way this is just Rohypnol. He had to have given her something like Molly to get this kind of reaction. He wasn't leaving anything to chance.

I pull her hand away, and she cries out. "Need it!"

"No, baby, not like this. When we get back to the hotel, you can have a shower and use the showerhead or something."

"It hurts. Please, Ash," she begs, and I feel myself beginning to waver until my phone rings.

"How is she?" Riku demands as soon as I answer.

"It's not good, man. He must have given her Molly as well as Rohypnol."

Jacinta's next sob sounds so loud in the back of the car.

"Fuck," he growls. "Well, take care of it."

I just about drop my phone when I hear those words. "Huh?" I ask, sounding stupid to my own ears.

"Look, man, you're the only one who can help her at the moment. She would be mortified if the doctor arrived and she started begging him for help. Take care of her."

"But doesn't that make me as bad as Matthew?" I ask, not even believing I'm considering this.

"Fuck no. She likes you. She tries to hide it because she thinks that five men are one or two too many, but I can see it. I see you watching her when she doesn't think you're looking. You're in deep now, so look after our girl."

"Alex will have my balls."

"No, he won't. He will hug you and thank you for looking after her when he couldn't." Jacinta moans again, thrashing her head back and forth on the seat, her hands reaching for me before they go back to pulling at her clothes. "Help her," he orders before hanging up.

"I'll help, but you need to keep your hands to yourself," I tell her. Miraculously, she leaves them where I place them above her head. "God, I hope you don't hate me in the morning," I whisper as I place my phone to the side and slide down onto the floor, adjusting my rock-hard dick inside my jeans. "Because I was just starting to get attached."

Chapter Four

Jacinta

My body aches like it never has before, experiencing a pulsating heat that is most definitely unnatural. My nipples are so peaked they hurt, and my clit throbs in time to my heartbeat. Pressing my thighs together, I try to ease the ache, but it has no effect. Sobbing, I mindlessly claw at my bodysuit, listening to myself beg Ashton to help me. He pulls my hands away and pushes them above my head.

"I'll help, but you need to keep your hands to yourself," I hear him tell me, and I quickly sob out my agreement. "God, I hope you don't hate me in the morning." That's the last thing I consciously understand before I'm too far gone to care.

His fingers flick open the clasps of my bodysuit, and it slides back up my body. He pulls down my thong, and just the sensation of his finger running over my mound has me crying out. Spreading my legs, he slides them over his shoulders and flicks his tongue over my clit. My orgasm explodes out of me, my body going tight with the convulsions, my scream echoing around the limo.

"Is everything okay back there?" a voice sounds out, but I don't care. I'm too busy panting from the exquisite sensations rolling through my body.

"It's fine," Ash replies through gritted teeth.

"More," I beg, reaching for his hair. Although the orgasm helped, it didn't even take the edge off. I'm right back where I was, aching and desperate.

"Fuck, I'm going to hell." His voice is low, and his stubble tickles my waxed pussy lips. Swiping his fingers through my release, he slides them deep into my channel before latching his mouth back around my clit. Sucking and fucking with his fingers, he draws orgasm after orgasm out of me until I'm hoarse and breathless and exhausted. I don't know how long it takes since the car stopped a while ago, and I lost track of time not long after the second orgasm.

"Stop, I can't take any more," I rasp, pushing his mouth away, and he draws back, sliding his fingers out of my punished pussy and wiping his mouth on his shirt.

"Thank fuck." When I look down at him, he's frowning, his mouth turned down with worry. "Let's get you covered and up to your room. We both need a shower before the doctor arrives." He fiddles with a couple of buttons on his shirt before pulling it over his head and sliding it over my bodysuit, so I won't flash the driver when we get out of the limo. We both look like a mess, me with no pants and him with no top, but our drivers are paid very well for their discretion.

He opens the door and slides out before reaching over and pulling me into his arms. Before I know it, we're in the private elevator. When we get to my door, he somehow manages to get my keycard and maneuver it through the reader without ever letting me go.

I share this suite with Hope, but thankfully, she's not here tonight. Without interruption or interference, he carries me in the direction of my bedroom and straight through it to my ensuite.

Carefully, he lowers me onto the closed toilet, helping me sit. My body is a quivering mess, partly from the drugs and partly from the unending, mind-blowing orgasms he gave me.

"Okay?" he asks before letting me go. I nod, staring down at my hands, too embarrassed to look at him.

He lets go to open the glass door to the shower and turn it on. The bathroom fills with steam as he waits for it to get to a good temperature. "Okay, hands up," he orders, and I follow his instructions, still not looking at him. He strips his shirt off of me before doing the same thing to my bodysuit. I hunch in on myself, trying to cover my boobs with my hair and my pussy with my hands, but he snorts. "I think we're past all of that, don't you?"

He toes off his shoes and rids himself of his jeans, leaving him in a tight pair of black briefs that are straining at the seams with his undeniably large erection. He bends down and helps me up, supporting me into the shower. I gasp when the hot water rains down on my still oversensitive skin, the sensation almost painful, but Ash pulls me into him so we're skin to skin. With a little encouragement, I rest my head against his chest while he starts rubbing his hands up and down my back.

We stand there in silence as the tears stream down my face, the evidence being washed away with the shower. My body starts to shudder as my sobbing grows harder.

"It's okay, baby. I've got you," Ash croons, his English accent gentle and soothing. We just stand there until I've run the gauntlet of emotions—scared, embarrassed, then finally angry. *So fucking angry.* Having no outlet for that right now, I let my mind drift, completely exhausted from it all.

Finally, I shift against him, needing to put some space between us, but he won't let me go, so I heave out a sigh and stay where I am. I didn't really want to move. There was just some weird part of me that thought I should, like that was the reaction I was supposed to have, but there's no part of me that truly wants that distance between us. I register something tickling my face, so I rub my cheek back and forth across his pec.

"Do you shave your chest?" I ask, unable to hide the amusement in my voice.

"I wax, actually," he grumbles a little defensively. "My father was a hairy beast, and I inherited it. I hate it, so I got rid of it."

"Huh." We're silent for a moment longer. "Laser is a better option," I suggest, and he chuckles.

"Is that what you did to your pussy?" I pull away to glare at him. He holds his hands up in defense, laughing, before gesturing for me to sit down on the built-in seat, which is not a bad idea because I'm still not super stable.

"Come on. After what we just went through, I think we're good enough friends that we can talk about those kinds of things." He winks and reaches for the soap and a sponge before lathering it up and starting to wash my body.

Another wave of embarrassment hits me, and I duck my head, but he grabs me by the chin and lifts it. "No. You shouldn't be embarrassed. None of this was your fault. If anything, it was all mine. I took the drinks he offered without thinking twice. And please don't be embarrassed about any of the rest of it. I was totally up for what we did. I hated the fact that it was nonconsensual. You had the choice taken out of your hands, and for that I hope you forgive me."

He sounds so sincere, and there's a crease of worry between his eyebrows. "While I hate how it happened, I can't thank you enough for helping me. It was unbearable. Not having control of my actions was scary, and I never want to be like that again."

"It probably didn't help that it was quite a cocktail of drugs streaming through your system. We're going to blame them all on him by the way." He finishes washing my body and hands me the showerhead to rinse off, keeping a close eye on me while he washes himself to make sure I don't fall. "Come on. Riku will be back soon, and the doctor should be arriving as well." He climbs out and wraps a towel around his waist before grabbing another huge one that he wraps around me. Once more, he picks me up bridal style and carries me into the bedroom, sitting me on my bed.

He digs around in my drawers, finding the big shirt I'd stolen from Shane, then he slides it over me before helping me into some panties.

"Turn around. I'll dry your hair," he says, gesturing for me to move.

Bemused and exhausted, I do as he asks. He uses the towel to rub the dampness out of my long locks before disappearing back into the bathroom. When he returns, he's got a comb in one hand and my leave-in conditioner in the other. Sitting down behind me, he applies some of the cream to my hair before combing out the knots, braiding it, and securing it with a band at the bottom.

"Scoot down."

"Thank you. Where did you learn to do that? An old girlfriend?"

He scoffs, returning the things to the bathroom. "Hardly. I've never cared about any of them enough. Alex was the only one I loved, and although he's had different styles, Fabio locks was not one of them. I used to do my sister's hair for her. The old battle axe nanny she had would always yank at the knots, and she would cry, so I took over. I'm just going to run down to my room and get a change of clothes. I'll be back shortly."

"No!" I can't stop the words from flying out. "Please don't go." Panic has my body tight with tension as I try to sit up in the bed. "Don't leave me," I beg, but before he can respond, the doorbell to the suite rings.

"That will be Riku. I'll just let him in." The panic slowly subsides as I nod and slide back down under the covers. It doesn't take him long to return, and he brings my bodyguard with me. Riku's cheek is bruised, and his lip is split.

"Oh my god, what happened?" Once more, I'm struggling to sit up. He rushes over to help me, putting a pillow behind me to lean against. He sits down next to me, and I reach up with my hand.

He grabs it and kisses it. "I'm okay. How are you? I've been so worried. I failed you. Won't be surprised if your dad finds another company after this."

"Fuck that. Riku got jumped by four of Matthew's mates, and he still managed to kick their asses. It allowed him just enough time to get at you. Don't worry, mate. I got there before he did anything, well, anything truly evil."

"Matthew messed with the wrong fucking family. He's going to wish he'd never heard of the Summers by the time I'm done with him," I growl, anger infusing my being. "Did the police arrest him?"

"Yes, charged him with assault and attempted rape. There's an officer waiting downstairs to take your statement. He's giving you a chance to see the doctor first so you can be examined. He was thinking we might have needed to do a rape kit."

"No, he didn't get that far thanks to Ash," I explain as the doorbell rings again.

"That should be the doctor and Forrest," Riku says.

Ash disappears, returning with Dr. Casey, our family's private physician, and Forrest.

"I swear you Summers are going to be the death of me," Forrest complains, wringing his hands together. "I really need to start bringing one of the junior partners along with me. I'm getting too old for this shit."

Grimacing, I apologize to the man who has really earned his firm's retainer over the last few months.

He waves a hand at me. "Rubbish, none of it

has been any of your fault. Now, how about we let Dr. Casey examine her? I want to get your version of the story, Lord Lavington, if you don't mind."

"Not at all." Ash follows him out into the living area, but Riku hesitates.

"I'm okay. You can go," I assure him, and he follows after the other two.

"Well, missy, it's been a while since I've seen you." Dr. Casey sits down on the bed next to me, placing his bag at his feet. His hair is a little grayer since the last time I saw him, but apart from that, he hasn't changed a bit. He still has kind eyes and a jovial smile. "Forrest said that you had been in trouble. Roofied?" the doctor asks, his eyes creasing with his worry.

"Yeah, something in my drink," I confirm, my voice low with shame. "I feel so stupid, and Ash is blaming himself."

The doctor pats my hand, the familiar gesture still giving me as much comfort as it did when I was younger. "No one is to blame but the person who drugged you. Don't you dare blame yourself. Now, did he get very far?" he asks.

I shake my head. "No, Ash got to him before he could do anything."

"So I won't need to do a rape kit?" Again, I answer no. "Okay, well, I'd like to draw some blood, so we can get it tested for exactly what he drugged you with, then I'd like to give you an IV with electrolytes to help flush the remainder of the drugs through your system. Maybe two bags."

"I'm flying to New Orleans in the morning." Yeah, alright, I'll admit that probably shouldn't be my first concern after I narrowly escaped being raped, but it's some semblance of normalcy. I need to keep my schedule, if only to ensure that I don't completely fall apart again.

"I'll return and remove the drip before you have to leave, I promise, but this will help you feel better." With that said, I don't have anything else to argue. With quick, efficient movements, the doc takes care of everything he mentioned. "Okay, I'll get this blood tested and let the police know the results."

"Doc, I'm assuming this is all falling under doctor-patient confidentiality?" I ask, and he gives me a gentle smile. That makes me feel a tiny bit better. At least I know for sure that the knowledge of what drugs Matthew gave me, as well as the ones I put into my system myself, will be kept private unless I give permission for it to be disclosed.

"Of course, Jazzy, but I'm sure your family would like to know so they can help you through it."

"I'll tell them, but in my own time." He looks a little unhappy about that, but he doesn't argue, respecting my right to decide who knows about what's happened to me. After a little more small talk, he leaves.

After he does, Forrest escorts the detective in. It's the same man we had dealt with during Harlow's stalker drama. He takes my statement in a professional and sympathetic way, assuring me the charges should stick, so Matthew won't be going anywhere anytime soon. Apparently, he had more Molly and Rohypnol in his pocket when he was arrested.

Once he leaves, Riku and Ash return, the latter now wearing sweats instead of a towel. He must have run to his room while I was distracted. "Oh good, that will help you feel better in the morning." He nods at the drip in my arm.

"And I've got the next bag," Riku says, holding it up. "I've changed them out before, so the doctor left me to do it. I also know how to remove it, so you and I will be playing doctor and patient in the morning." He winks and wiggles his eyebrows suggestively, and I manage a small smile. It's kind of ridiculous to see that expression on the normally serious man.

"I'm going to get going," Ash says, starting to back out of the room. "Again, I'm so fucking sorry for everything." He won't even look at me, directing the words to Riku instead.

"Stop!" I shout, and he freezes, frowning. "Are you still coming to NOLA with us?" I chew on my lip, hoping he says yes.

"Do you still want me to?" he asks hesitantly.

"Yes, absolutely. Please don't go. Stay, both of you. I don't want to be alone." I feel so vulnerable admitting it, but if they leave now, I'll be scrambling for more drugs quicker than you can say addict.

They exchange a glance.

"Please," I whisper, realizing I'm not above begging.

Like they are sharing some kind of telepathic mind link, they move at the same time. Riku strips off his jeans and shirt, leaving himself in his underwear, while Ashton removes his shirt but leaves on his sweats. When I raise a brow, he mumbles, "No underwear."

They climb in on either side of me, Riku being careful of the drip in my arm. I roll over to face him, leaving Ash at my back, keeping his hands to himself.

"Hold me," I demand over my shoulder. He slides in behind me, wrapping himself around me, and I pull Riku in closer so he's wrapped around my front with my drip arm over him. "I just need to feel safe," I mutter quietly.

The silence is awkward for a moment, then I brush my hand against Riku's smooth, defined pec. "Ash waxes his chest," blurts out of my mouth, breaking the tension in the room. Behind me, Ash groans and buries his face into my hair.

"Big mouth."

It's with a small smile on my face that I snuggle down, their warmth and strength helping me recover from one of the most horrible nights of my life.

Chapter Five

Jacinta

Our flight to New Orleans is uneventful. The three of us are using one of the smaller jets in our fleet, the big one having taken the others down a few days ago. I feel a little guilty that I haven't been there for Jace, but I'm sure Nana, Emma, and Molly have him all sorted. That helps soothe the quiet voice that says I'm somehow letting him down.

Once we get to the plantation, everything is a flurry of movement and organization to get ready for the next day's show. A runway is being constructed, and chairs are being placed out for the attendees with a section for photographers, and that's just the outside. Inside the mansion, the ballroom has been turned into the dressing room.

Racks of clothes and semi-naked men and women run around for final fittings.

I take one look at the flurry of people and promptly turn around and walk back out. My chucks are quiet on the wooden floors of the old house, and when I finally make it outside, I gulp in a huge breath of air.

"Are you okay?" A hand on my shoulder has me squeaking in surprise and whirling around, but my heart rate slows when I realize it's just Riku with Ash behind him. Of course he followed me out. I can imagine he's going to be a little overprotective for a while in light of what he sees as his failure.

"Yup, they look like they have it under control. Me getting involved is just going to confuse things." I've exited out one of the back doors on the lower floor, and I can see the sweeping staircase leading down from the ballroom in front of me. The path to the natural arbor looks cool and inviting despite the workman constructing the runway.

"Shall we go for a walk and get some fresh air?" I suggest.

The three of us spend the next hour wandering the grounds of the plantation. Farther along the natural arbor are the old slave houses, which have long since been turned into guest accommodations. We find an old stable house, which looks like it's been converted into guest lodging as well. They use this place as a wedding and function venue, so it makes sense.

The three of us don't talk much during our walk. I think we're all lost in our own thoughts.

"Where are we staying?" Ash finally breaks the silence as we head back toward the main house.

"I'm not sure what was planned, to be honest. Let's find Nana. She'll know what the plan is."

When we get back to the ballroom, it looks like the frenzy is starting to settle down. There aren't as many people here, and we passed quite a few returning to their rooms as we walked back.

I spy Nana talking to Jace, Alex, and Shane through the crowd, so I head in their direction. A few people say hi on the way through, but I don't stop. I can feel the anxiety prickling at my consciousness, the urge to run growing stronger, but the way Jace's face lights up when he sees me holds me on my path.

"There you are, my sweet granddaughter." Nana is all smiles when we reach them, giving me a hug and a kiss before greeting the guys.

"Lord Ashton, how nice of you to join us. Has that dragon of a grandmother kicked the bucket yet?" Nana asks pleasantly, bringing a cheeky smile to Ash's face.

"You are looking lovely as usual, Mrs. Summers, and not yet, but we can only keep hoping." He kisses Nana on the hand, and she twitters like a fool. Handsome men truly are her weak spot.

"Please call me Grace. I mean, you may be my

grandson soon if the gossip columns are to be believed."

The two of them laugh, and I roll my eyes, turning to Alex, who I realize has a slightly hurt look.

"Hi." I pull him away from the group, wrapping my arms around him and hugging him tight. "Don't be upset. Let me explain when we get a quiet moment. Remember, we did go over what was going to happen." I pull back and look him directly in the eyes, wanting him to see that I'm genuine.

"I'm trying, I promise. It's just weird. I'm not jealous, just sad. Sad for Ash. I'm perfectly content with Shane and Jace and you. I wouldn't change that for the world. I just wish Ash was free to have the same for himself. He deserves happiness, especially now that I know he's protecting his sister."

"Okay." I kiss him before rejoining the others, giving Shane and Jace their own kisses and hugs.

"Isn't this wonderful?" Nana beams at the group of us, and the guys all shuffle awkwardly while I roll my eyes again.

"How about you leave your meddling ways until we're less occupied? Where are we staying? I had a rough night, and the three of us just really want to grab some dinner and call it a night."

Nana's grin drops, and her mouth dips down in concern, making the slight wrinkles on her face deeper. "Is everything okay? You are looking a little pale. Paler than normal."

"Nothing you need to worry about. Just a little hungover."

"Again?" I hear the surprise in her voice.

"Sometimes alcohol is needed to deal with the morons that attend those things."

She shakes her head. "I have no idea why you're suddenly Miss Life of the Party." Her gaze slides to Ash. "I'd blame you, but this started before you. Just be sure to take care of one another. Your grandmother's approval is not worth the effort the two of you are putting in." Neither of us miss the disapproval in her voice, and I steel my nerves against the guilt that's waiting for me to weaken. She doesn't know it, but I'm doing this for her—for all of them. I can survive a little grandmotherly disappointment if it keeps my family and their legacy intact. "We're all staying in town. Molly and Emma have already left, and we were just about to. Didn't you check in when you got to town?"

"No, we came straight here, but you seem to have everything under control."

"Yes, it's like Jace has been doing this all his life." Nana tucks her arm into his, giving him a squeeze.

"Aw, Grace, only because I had your amazing expertise, not to mention these two and Emma and Molly." He nods to his two boyfriends. Alex puffs up at the praise, but Shane just smiles.

"That's awesome. So we'll head out and see you all back at the hotel, maybe?"

"We're all having dinner together tonight. Brad booked a private room to celebrate Jace's first show," Shane shares as we leave the ballroom and head downstairs to the cars.

A feeling of utter dread fills my stomach, and I stumble on the stairs. Riku puts a hand out to steady me.

"All?" I ask, and Nana nods.

"Family and these guys, Cole, and of course Ash and Riku are welcome. Brad wants to talk about security arrangements for the coming months with you."

I sigh with relief. That I can handle, mostly.

"Okay, well, great. We'll check in and see you all at dinner."

The private dining room is noisy, and it looks like we're the last to arrive. I talked things over with Riku and Ash, and I've decided to tell my family what happened. It's bound to hit the media eventually, and I want to be involved in seeing Matthew pay. If his money somehow greases palms and he escapes the justice system, like many seem to do in LA, my big brother Declan is the perfect solution to seeing him pay permanently.

By the time I've been kissed and hugged by all

my family members, Ash has been reintroduced to everyone. I grab a fork and tap it against my glass—just water for me tonight. My body wouldn't be able to cope with anything more.

The tinkling sound gets everyone's attention, and the room quiets down, everyone looking at me.

"Could you all just take a seat for a moment? I have something to tell you." My family and friends do as I ask.

"You're not announcing your engagement, are you, Jazzy?" Oliver calls laughingly. "I read you were having Ash's baby and were running away together to Romania to live in your house there."

"Ah, no. Riku, could you just make sure that the staff gives us a few moments?" With a nod, he disappears to do that.

"What's this about, Jazzy?" Dad asks, and I take a big breath. A warm hand sliding into mine has me looking down. Ash is now standing just behind me, a silent support and warmth at my back, giving me the courage to tell them.

"Please let me finish before any of you say anything. I just need you to remember I'm okay."

"Fuck this shit." Jax jumps to his feet. "What's going on?" he demands.

I tell them what happened the previous night, obviously leaving out that I snorted the coke and Ash's stress relief in the car. Everyone remains quiet through the whole thing, but the minute I finish, the room bursts into sound.

"I'll fucking kill him," Shane growls, slamming a fist down on the table.

"Get in line," Kai snarls at him, getting to his feet.

"Why wasn't I called last night?" Cole asks Riku.

Harlow and Hope crowd closer, wrapping their arms around me as the rest of the family continue to express their outrage. I shudder as their individual scents flood my nostrils, bringing comfort to my ragged soul. The urge to cry hits me, but I hiccup, holding the sob in. Both of them coo words of comfort, stroking my back.

"I'm okay. Ash got there in time," I assure them, pulling away. "I'm angry more than anything else. He was an asshole. We caught him feeling up his best friend's girl. How many women did he drug and rape that were too scared to say anything because he's famous? He has to pay." I raise my voice so the rest of the family can hear me.

"Of course he will pay," Poppy says. "He was arrested, yes?" He looks to Riku, who nods and tells them about what happened after I left.

"He was supposed to be going in front of a judge today or tomorrow. Detective James said he would call me when he'd been seen, but I haven't heard from him yet."

"What are the chances he'll get bail?" Thomas asks, and Riku shrugs.

"The detective said it could go either way depending on which judge he gets."

"No matter what happens, he's done in Hollywood." Declan has his phone out. "I'm just going to call our legal team. He has a morality clause in his contract, forbidding basically anything that can bring the company into bad repute, and he's breaching it. We're usually lenient with smaller matters, but there's absolutely no scenario where drugging and attempting to rape someone could ever be excused. I'll speak to the writers. He's done. We'll just write him out. In the likelihood that he does get off for any reason, I'm going to ensure no one will ever represent or hire him again. Here or anywhere else in the world." He leaves the room to make his calls.

"I'm going to check if the story has broken yet. If not, I'll issue an appropriate press statement if that's alright with you, Brad?" Cole has his phone out, tapping away on the screen.

"Yes, as long as that's okay with Jacinta." Dad looks at me, and I quickly nod. As much as Cole and I clash, I trust him to have my back for this.

He leaves too. One by one, my family comes over to check on me. I'm surrounded by love, and I remember why I'm doing all of this in the first place, protecting them in any way I can. Alex, Shane, and Jace are last, and the three of them crowd around me in a four-way hug, but Alex is especially subdued. There are no pervy quips or sassy smiles. He fusses over me while Shane and Jace watch on. Shane's expression is stony, and somehow I know he's blaming himself, which is ridiculous because he wasn't even there.

"Shane," I quietly say once Alex has finished his examination. "Shane, don't blame yourself. They had everything planned. They got past Riku, and he's trained for this." He turns his glare on Ash, and I step into his line of sight. "No. Don't blame him either. He's the one who saved me then beat him to a pulp. Look at his knuckles. That's from wailing on Matthew."

"If Matthew comes near you again, I'll do just as bad," he growls, and Jace and Alex add their agreements.

"Okay, but for now, let Dec destroy his career and Forrest make sure he goes to jail for a long time."

"I shared a few more things that I know about Matthew with Detective James. He was getting a warrant to search his house. He should go to jail for a long time," Ash assures all of us, and Shane loses the edge of his glare.

"Come now, let's all have a nice dinner." Nana raises her voice above everyone, gesturing to the table, but as we all move to take seats, she stops me.

"Please make sure you talk to your therapist about this, Jacinta. You know you can talk to any of us, but I know you don't like to burden us with your problems. None of us feel that way, of course, but use your therapist. You've been through a lot in a short period of time. Promise me."

"Of course, Nana," I promise, kissing her on the cheek, even though it's been weeks since I actually spoke to her.

Dinner was a slightly subdued affair for our family, and I retired to bed shortly after it, making sure Riku and Ash leave the doors to their adjoining rooms open.

When I wake up from a nightmare, screaming, both of them come running like the room is on fire. Once I assure them I was just dreaming, they climb into bed with me. It's only after that that I sleep like a log, dream free for the rest of the night.

Chapter Six

Jacinta

Breakfast is delivered to our room, and we eat together before getting dressed. Riku is a morning person, so he's able to hold a conversation, but Ash struggles to function before his second cup of coffee. It amuses me to no end to watch the two of them interact over food.

"What do we have planned for today?" Riku asks, pulling back the curtains to let the room fill with light. Ash shrieks and flinches like a vampire in the sun, and I dissolve into a heap of giggles on the couch.

"Shut it," he grumbles as his eyes adjust to the light. Riku is busy gaping at him, his mouth wide open. "In the last two weeks, when have you seen me up before lunchtime?" he asks my shocked bodyguard.

I get myself under control and think back. Actually, now that he mentions it, I haven't been out of bed early on any morning after one of our outings. Ash had moved into the Neighpalm Hotel when we started this plan so it was easier for us to return home together each evening. It perpetuates the idea that we're spending every moment together. Nobody has to know that he's been going to his own suite each night.

"Okay, yeah, you're right, but shit, man, I expected your skin to start smoking or something." Riku chuckles as he drinks his coffee and steps out onto the balcony.

"Ha-ha." Ash's sarcasm is thick, but he gets up and follows Riku, grabbing his sunglasses and pack of smokes on the way. He doesn't smoke often, but he still has one occasionally. He says he needs it to relax. I almost feel sorry for him, but then he adds that a morning blow job would do the same job just as nicely, but he isn't getting that anytime soon. All guilt disappears after that.

Before I can join them, there's a knock on the door. I peer through the peephole and feel a tingle inside my stomach when I see it's two of my... boyfriends? Can I call them that? I desperately want to call them that.

Shaking my head, I open the door. "Hi, come on in. We're just having coffee and deciding what we're doing today." I close the door behind them, and before I can lead them outside, they surround me, one to my front and one at my back.

"Are you okay?" Alex lifts my chin so he can see my eyes. I guess he's looking for the honesty in them.

I shrug. "Mostly. I know in my mind that none of it was my fault. I never led him on or anything. I could barely stand the guy. So yeah, I will be just fine as long as none of you treat me any differently. I'm not fragile or scared of intimacy or anything like that. Promise me?" It's my turn to look at his reaction now.

I can see the doubt in his eyes, but he nods. "Of course." I turn my head to look back at Shane. "And you? You're not still blaming yourself. You weren't even there, for fuck's sake."

Alex snorts in the wake of Shane's silence. "Oh no, but he's been through the gauntlet of whom to blame. Riku for not being there, Ash for getting you the drink, Cole for coming up with the stupid plan of you being seen as a party girl princess, us for not being there... Everyone but the actual person responsible. Jace and I finally managed to calm him down after turning the tables on him and giving a bit of his famous punishment. We firmly straightened him out."

Color me intrigued. I raise an eyebrow. "Oh?"

Alex's sexy lips turn up in a wicked grin. "Yup, and we filmed it. I'll show you later," he promises before giving me a kiss. I moan as his hands come up to cup my ass, pulling me against his hard dick. Shane still hasn't said a word, so I reluctantly break away.

"Are we good?"

He sighs. "Yeah, we're good. I'm sorry I'm making this about me."

"No, you're not. I completely get it. I feel the same way about what happened to Jax and Harlow. You don't have to explain yourself to me at all. Anyway, I do have to tell you something. I was hoping to get the three of you together, but I'll have to tell Jace later. I didn't share one of the details with my family." I drag them over to my bed and pull them down so that they are lying on it. I'm perched between them, facing them. The low rumble of Riku's and Ash's voices can be heard from outside, and the acrid smell of cigarette smoke occasionally drifts through the open door.

"Is he still smoking?" Alex grimaces, but his attention doesn't drift from me.

I clear my throat. "Look, this is uncomfortable for me to admit, and it's probably going to hurt you, but I need to be honest." Both men's muscles coil in tension. They suddenly have a wary light in their eyes, and I feel like such a massive bitch. "Matthew stacked the deck in his favor, or he tried to, anyway. Along with the Rohypnol, he dosed me with Molly. I was hurting big time, and, well, Riku told Ash to help me out."

They both frown, and I get the feeling they are

not quite understanding what I'm telling them. I'm trying to figure out how to explain it better when I hear a sound behind me.

"Basically, what Jazzy is trying to tell you is she needed an orgasm, and I helped her out." Ash's voice is light, but when I turn to look at him, I can see he's braced for the fallout.

Comprehension fills Shane's face. "Yeah, okay. Thanks, man. That couldn't have been an easy decision."

Ash shrugs. "Riku made me. He wasn't there, otherwise I would have let him do it."

Alex has been quiet, and I can see him working through it in his mind. When he suddenly figures it all out, he leaps off the bed and throws himself at Ash, fists clenched, knocking me over in the process. I tumble to the floor as Shane leaps after him. Having rolled off the side of the bed, I can't see what happens, but when I get up, Shane has hold of Alex, and Riku is standing between them and Ash with his hands held up.

"Hey, man, think about it. She was in pain, and he helped her. Don't make a liar of me. He was worried about you and wasn't going to do it. I told him you would be fine when you stopped and really thought about it."

Alex relaxes in Shane's grip, and Ash heaves a sigh of relief. "I'm sorry, Alex. I hated not having her consent, but it was awful seeing her like that, so I won't apologize for helping her."

Alex nods, his jaw clenched with tension, and I feel so bad for him. This can't be easy. All of us can see he's still half in love with Ash, and I would say the feeling is very much mutual if the way Ash looks at him when he thinks no one is watching has anything to say. But Ash, for all of his other faults, seems to respect Alex's relationship with Shane and Jace and is no homewrecker. He told me he never ever wants to be anything like his father, a womanizing piece of crap who didn't care who he hurt in the process.

"Okay, well, now that that's settled, shall we finish our coffee and decide what we're doing today?" I push up off the floor, and Alex gasps, pulling himself out of Shane's arms. "I'm sorry. I'm such an ass." He fusses over me while the other three discreetly take themselves out to the balcony.

"Are you okay?" I ask him once we're alone, and he sighs and dramatically throws himself back on the bed, draping a hand over his eyes.

"No... Yes… No. Aghh!" Alex screams quietly.

I climb onto the bed and sit down on him, my legs on either side of his waist, then pull his hand away. "Talk to me."

"I was jealous, but I don't know who I was jealous of, and now I feel like a complete asshole." He looks miserable as he admits this, and I grin. "No, don't grin at me, bitch! Poor Shane and Jace. I'm completely happy with them, but Ash was my first love, the one who got away, and now that I know it was for a noble reason and not because of something materialistic, I feel like such an asshole for giving him an ultimatum."

"Have you talked to them about it?" I ask him, and he shrugs.

"Yeah, extensively, and they completely understand. Both of them have said if he ends up in your harem, they won't be upset if something happens between us."

"Whoa there, cowboy. My *harem*? Who said anything about a harem? That has been all you guys."

"Please, who's in denial now?" Alex sasses me, and I groan and collapse down on him. He wraps his arms around me and rolls us so he's on top. "Face it. You, Jacinta Summers, have a harem, or a potential harem, so why not embrace it?"

"Nope, nope. *Ixnay on the aremhay.*" I try to pull away, but he just chuckles and kisses me until there's a knock on the door.

"Look at that! Saved by the bell." Alex lets go of me. I get up, but he stays where he is, his hands behind his head, posing for whoever it is at my door.

Peering through the peephole, I'm a little surprised to see Cole with Spencer in his arms.

"Hi," I say as I open it.

"Hi, Jazzy, hi! Mummy brought me with her, and Daddy is going to spend the day with me while she's busy." Spencer races into my room, but he skids to a halt when he sees Alex on the bed. "Who are you? Did you tuck Jazzy into bed last night? Have you seen her tigers?" He throws himself onto the bed and bounces up and down while Alex looks on with a delighted smile on his face.

"Well, hello there. I'm Alex. Who are you?"

"I'm Spencer. My daddy is Batman. Jazzy is my best friend."

"I'm sorry. He was eating Fruit Loops for breakfast when I picked him up from Hayden," Cole apologizes while Alex gets up on the bed and grabs Spencer's hands. The two of them bounce together, Spencer madly giggling the whole time.

I wave my hand. "Don't worry about it. There's nothing more pure than happy children. What are you guys doing today?"

"I'm not sure, but he demanded a visit when I arrived. Hayden must have told him you were here. Apparently, you're all he can talk about—you reading him a story and the baby tigers."

"Come on, the others are having coffee on the balcony. Let's have one."

Alex has turned on the TV, and he and Spencer are discussing the merits of *Paw Patrol* versus *Bluey*, both of them settling cross-legged on the bed.

"He'll be fine. Alex is basically just a big kid."

The other three greet Cole, and Shane hands me a coffee before pouring one for Cole while Ash lights up another smoke. "Where's Jace?" I finally get a chance to ask Shane.

"He's gone out to the plantation with Emma and Molly for final preparations. Alex needs to head out after lunch, but we were hoping you'd like to play tourist with us this morning."

"That sounds like fun. Ash, what about you? You want to come play tourist?"

Ash blows out a stream of smoke and shakes his head. "No, I've got a call with my sister this morning. We speak every Saturday."

"That sounds nice. What about you, Cole? You and Spence want to play tourist with us? We should get beignets and have a carriage ride. I bet he'd like that."

"Maybe for a little while. He'll probably get bored quickly, but then we can find something else to do."

We leave Ash to do his thing while the rest of us head out to explore New Orleans. First, we head to Cafe Du Monde for coffee and beignets. Spencer and Alex giggle when they get covered in powdered sugar, which is *totally* an accident, of course. Next is a carriage ride through the French Quarter and down Bourbon Street. After Spencer starts to rub his eyes, universal kid code for being tired, Cole brings him back to the hotel for a nap. Alex, Shane, Riku, and I have gumbo for lunch, and afterward, Alex insists we go pay our respects to Anne Rice.

After Alex places a bunch of flowers at her tomb, we wander around the cemetery for a little while, looking at the different tombs and mausoleums. It's kind of creepy, but Alex keeps us entertained with wild, made-up stories about the residents of each tomb.

"Look, this one's open!" Alex calls out. He hurries ahead a little bit since Shane and I are perfectly happy wandering hand and hand, taking our time. Riku decides to give us a little privacy, taking a business phone call and telling us he'll wait in the car.

Shane groans as Alex disappears inside the white-washed building. "Shit, we're going to have to go after him."

"Go into the tomb?" I hesitate, but Shane doesn't let go of my hand, dragging me after him.

"Come on. If we don't reel him in, he'll be a menace."

We enter the tomb hand in hand, and I wrinkle my nose at the dank and moldy smell. It's dark inside with the only light coming from the open doorway. I gaze around once my eyes adjust. It's neglected, the large double stone casket caked in dust, and I can see puddle stains on the concrete floor from where the roof must have leaked during the last rain. Alex is standing on the other side of the casket, wiping it clean with his hands before clapping them together to remove most of the dust. He then wipes what remains on his shorts and leans over to read the inscription, running his finger along the etched words.

"*Together forever in eternity*. Isn't that romantic?

Together beyond death. We should have a custom casket made for us, so we can all be interred together when it's time." His eyes sparkle with delight when he grins at the two of us.

"Ah, yeah, sure, if you count two bodies rotting inside as romantic. Could you imagine what it would be like with all of us? No thanks." I shudder, and Shane chuckles.

"Yeah, that's a visual I didn't need."

Alex groans. "Ugh, now I need brain bleach. Here I was thinking how sweet it was, and you had to ruin the moment."

"I'm sorry." I'm not really, but he has this sad little boy pout on his lips that always tugs at my heartstrings.

The pout disappears, replaced with a wicked grin. "Oh, I can think of a way to make it up to me." He nods at Shane behind me, who crowds in, the heat of his body warming my back.

"Jacinta, you made Alex sad. I think it would only be fair if you made it up to him, don't you?" A shiver runs down my spine as Shane brushes his lips across my neck and moves me forward until my legs lean against the casket. Pressure between my shoulder blades has me bending at the waist, my torso sprawled across the hard surface. Gentle hands roll me to my back, and I hear Alex draw the zipper of his shorts down.

"Be a good girl. Suck his dick, and I'll give you a reward." Shane's growl is like a taser to my senses, and I shiver again as I open my mouth and stick out my tongue, licking the tip of Alex's dick like a lollipop. He groans when I feel Shane's hands running up my legs, dragging my dress up then pulling my panties off. Once that's done, he nudges my legs to widen my stance and licks a path from asshole to clit. My mouth drops open in pleasure. Alex surges in, filling it, and Shane holds up three fingers.

"Suck them, Alex," he orders, and Alex takes them into his mouth, forcing his cock farther down my throat. I gag slightly, breathing through my nose as I try to wrestle my gag reflex under control. I swallow, and Alex gasps. Shane removes his fingers and slides them into my pussy as he flicks his tongue across my clit. I'm suspended between the two of them, a prisoner to their erotic ministrations, their plaything to use at will. Alex and Shane thrust in time with one another, and I'm lost in the sensations. Grunts and groans fill the dark space, and I feel my orgasm curling inside me. The taste of Alex is salty and bitter as he leaks precum into my mouth, but I lap at it, enjoying pulling sounds of pleasure from him. Just as I feel my muscles tighten in anticipation of what's to come, they stop and pull away. I whine, needing to somehow convey my frustration, but all it does is draw a dark chuckle from them both.

"You didn't think it would be that easy, did you?" Shane asks.

"I want to watch our boyfriend fuck you," Alex whispers in my ear as Shane drops his own shorts and fists his dick in his hand. "I want to see your cunt stretch around him as he fucks you until you can't walk. Then, when he's done, having filled you with his cum, I want to shove my dick deep inside you, using him as lubrication while I fuck you full of my own cum."

I shudder at the picture that builds in my mind, and together, they roll my pliant body until I'm back on my front. A sharp slap to my ass has me squealing in surprise.

"Be a good girl and keep sucking Alex's dick while I wreck your pussy." Shane pushes my head back on Alex's cock, and he doesn't stop until I have my nose against his pelvis, forcing me to swallow around him.

"Fuck yes. You should feel her throat, babe. It's amazing," Alex rasps as I feel Shane line himself up. Another slap on my ass, then he thrusts home. Luckily, Alex has pulled free, or I might have taken a bite of his dick as I shout out at the invasion. The two of them chuckle, then they set a punishing pace, spit roasting me between them. I'm a sobbing, sweaty mess, and it feels fucking amazing. I love being used for their pleasure, treated like their dirty princess. The two of them keep talking, sharing naughty, filthy words the whole time. Finally, Alex pulls free, fisting his dick.

"Hurry up, Shane. Fill her with your cum. I

want a turn too." Alex moves around behind me, and when I turn my head, I catch sight of them kissing before Alex bends down and runs his tongue around my puckered asshole. He pushes a finger in, setting all the sensitive nerves on fire, and I feel myself fly over the edge.

Screaming, I orgasm hard, gripping Shane's dick tight, my muscles doing their best to keep him deep inside. He shouts, and I feel his dick pulse inside me.

"Look at that, Shane. I can't wait to get into this hole too and see our cum dribble out of it," Alex croons as we ride out our orgasms. He places kisses on both of our mouths, whispering words of encouragement, and it's not long before he has Shane pulling out, demanding his turn.

I expected him to thrust deep, but he rolls me over again and drops to his knees and pushes Shane's cum back into my pussy with his tongue. The aftershocks of my orgasm turn into the slow build of another.

"Can't waste perfectly good cum," he tells me, licking his lips as he gets back to his feet. Shane tucks his dick back into his pants then occupies himself with grabbing my hands and holding them over my head.

"Fuck her, Alex. I want to hear her screams fill the tomb again," he orders, and Alex lifts my legs, wrapping them around his waist.

"My pleasure." He impales me on his length,

and my mouth falls open in a silent scream. They are both so thick, and my pussy is still tight from the last orgasm. "So hot and wet, it feels fucking amazing." Alex's eyes roll back in his head in pleasure, and he grits his teeth. "Not going to last long."

He starts to thrust back and forth, looking like a god lost in rapture, but I soon lose sight of him because Shane leans over me and wraps his lips around one of my nipples. He bites and sucks, alternating between the two, until they are so sensitive, I'm pleading for him to stop. The orgasm that rocks through my body is even more powerful than the first one, and I find myself screaming before I go limp with the sensations, my body unable to support itself. Alex grunts and seats himself deep as I feel him fill my womb once more.

Shane rights himself and caresses me, whispering words of praise in my ear as he gently kisses me. "Such a good girl, taking all of our cum."

"Don't want to move. Want to keep her with our cum inside her," Alex says as he drapes himself over my body. His mouth finds mine, giving me a kiss that curls my toes, his cock still throbbing deep inside of me. "Want to keep her filled with our cum all the time," he mutters, almost to himself, and Shane chuckles again. I feel wrung out and used in the best possible way, and I almost cry out in disappointment when Alex pulls himself free of my body, but his cock is quickly replaced with his fingers. I'm fighting my mind, still not quite able to make coherent thoughts, when I finally tune back into Shane and Alex talking.

"Hurry up and put these back on her." I see Shane pass my panties over to Alex, who grumbles as he removes his fingers and pulls them back up my legs. That's when the faint voices finally hit my ears, and my heart races in panic.

"Fuck!" I scramble to stand up, and Shane's hand on my back helps me. I groan as all my muscles protest after being flat on a hard surface. Shane comes around to my front and helps straighten me out as Alex gets his clothes sorted. Finally, he brushes his hands through my hair, turning my freshly fucked look into something a little less bird's nest. He pulls back and smiles.

"Perfect," he tells me, kissing my nose and pulling me to my feet. The voices are louder now, and Alex puts his arm around me and tucks my head into his shoulder.

"Act like you're crying," he whispers as the three of us step out of the mausoleum. When we pass the people, I keep my head averted and loudly pretend to sob, but as soon as we round a corner out of sight, we stop.

"Holy shit! That was close." I smack Alex on the shoulder, but he and Shane are grinning.

"But it was fun." Alex is unrepentant, and I can see Shane isn't any better.

I wrinkle my nose when I feel their cum drip out

of me. "It was, but now I need a change of undies or a shower."

Alex grabs me by the hand and drags me in the direction of the entrance. "If we hurry, I can shove that all back into you on the ride home." I shudder at the thought of Alex's fingers in me while Riku watches. What are these men doing to me? I don't recognize these reactions. I've always enjoyed sex, but it's never been like this before. Does it somehow become *more* when feelings are involved in the act? Whatever it is, I don't hate it, and I find myself smiling just as wickedly as Alex.

"Shane, can you drive?" I ask, and when he catches up with me, I can tell his mind has gone where mine did.

"Poor Riku." He shakes his head, but he doesn't sound sympathetic at all. In fact, he sounds like he can't wait.

Chapter Seven

Jacinta

When the sun sets and it's time to head out to the plantation, Riku goes down to bring the car around to the front while I step into Ash's room. He looks great in dress pants and a button-down shirt, but seeing him in jeans and a tight T-shirt is devastating.

"Hey, are you ready?" he asks, putting on his watch and shoving his wallet into the back pocket of his slacks.

"Do you have any stuff?" The words burst out as my anxiety rides me hard. Ash's eyebrows jump in surprise.

"Now? It's Jace's debut. All of your family will be there."

"Yeah, I need it."

He shakes his head. "Oh no you don't, babe. It's

fun and everything when we're partying, but you don't need it to get through the day. Nobody is judging you, and even if they are, there are plenty of people who love you and accept you for who you are."

Anger wells up in my chest, adding to the anxiety and fear, and all of a sudden, I'm fucking fuming. "How fucking dare you? You don't know me. You don't know anything about me. Don't you fucking dare tell me how to feel." I spin around and storm back into my section.

"Babe!" he calls, following after me.

"Fuck you." I grab my handbag. There will be someone backstage with coke. I don't need Ash. He can kiss my ass.

The car ride is tense, and as soon as we get to the plantation, I hop out and make my way to the ballroom, leaving Ash to do whatever. I don't care. Riku follows, but I stop him at the entrance. "You can guard from here. Otherwise, you'll be in the way." He's already noticed my bad mood, so he doesn't say anything, but he does raise his eyebrows.

My anger is still fueling me as I enter the chaos of the ballroom. Although this many people would usually be enough to freak me out, my head of steam has me moving through the crowd toward the bathrooms on the other side.

Pushing through the door, I find exactly what I was looking for. Two underwear-clad models are bent over the sink, snorting coke. They blanch when they see me.

"Please, Ms. Summers, don't fire us," one of them pleads, rubbing her nose.

"If you move away from it and leave right now, I won't say a word, but if I catch either of you snorting again in one of my shows, I'll have you blacklisted," I tell them, tapping an impatient foot with my arms crossed.

The one with the straw drops it and backs away. The other one looks at the remaining lines, uncertainty showing clear on her face. "Should we clean it?" she asks, and I huff impatiently.

"I can imagine you've got a dress to put on or hair and makeup to attend. Get your asses out there, and I'll deal with it."

"Okay, and thank you," she says, and they both sprint out.

Not making the same mistake as them, I lock the door and proceed to snort the remaining three lines. One line just doesn't cut it anymore. My nostrils burn, and as I ditch the straw into the garbage and make sure the bench is wiped down, I feel the drip down the back of my throat as I pocket the little clear bag they left behind. Coke lasts an hour or two in my system, so I'm good for a while, but it's going to be a long evening. I'm sure I'll need the rest of it. I straighten myself out as the coke floods my system with confidence, and I unlock the door and step back out into the chaos. I weave my way through the dressers, makeup artists, and hairstylists until I find Jace.

"There you are! Oh God, I'm so nervous." He pulls me in, giving me a tight squeeze.

"Hey, it's going to be awesome. You look like you've got everything under control." I squeeze him back before pulling away. "I just came to wish you good luck before I found my seat."

"Well, how do I look?" a voice behind me asks, and I spin around to find Alex. Holy shit, he looks incredible. He's wearing a suit Jace designed, and it's like it was made especially for him. It has small, flamboyant embellishments that make it perfect for Alex. The cravat and morning coat are stylish and reminiscent of old-world Hollywood, though as he dips his top hat, he almost smacks us with the cane in his hand.

"Whoa," Jace cautions him, holding up his hand, but I just giggle.

At a loss for words, I press a finger to the corner of my mouth to make sure I'm not drooling. "Wow, you can keep that when we're done, so long as you take me out somewhere wearing it."

"Jace will have to make the guys matching ones, so we can all take you out." He wiggles his eyebrows as the show's director starts calling instructions to everyone.

"Okay, good luck. It's going to be amazing." I give them both a kiss before heading out to find my seat. Emma, Molly, and Nana join me as I cross the room.

"How are you today, Jacinta?" Emma asks, tucking her arm into mine.

"I'm great. We spent the day playing tourist, and I had a blast. What about you? How is my brother or sister treating you?"

"I feel healthy as a horse, though poor Molly has dreadful morning sickness. Hits at exactly the same time every morning without fail. She feels rotten for about an hour, then she's good again."

"Oh no." I look at the woman in question. She grimaces, but there's still something about her that exudes joy.

"Yeah, you can practically set a clock to it. Pretty sure it's a boy. A girl wouldn't be so cruel." She rubs her stomach affectionately as we all laugh.

"While it's just the four of us, I want to talk to you about the designs Rowena brought to us."

"Oh yes? What were they like?" I ask her, and the three women exchange a glance. Now, it's my turn to grimace. "That bad?"

"No, actually, they are amazing. She sketched a full maternity range and a variety of children's clothes, ranging in age from infant to ten years old. She worked her ass off." Molly grabs a phone out of her bag and hands it over after a couple taps.

I scroll through the sketches, thoroughly impressed with everything. The maternity clothes are stylish yet comfortable and don't make the model look frumpy or dowdy. The kids' clothes are fun and full of color. "Wow, these are gorgeous."

"Yes, we want to offer her a show, just like Jace, but wanted to check with you first," Nana adds. "She's here tonight, and we'd like to give her the good news at the afterparty at the hotel."

"Absolutely, I agree. But you guys don't need to run things past me."

"Yes, we do. This is still your baby even if you've stepped back." Molly squeezes me on the arm. "The new intern we hired is here too, so we'd like you to meet her as well, but let's get through the show first."

"Oh great, yes. I'd love to meet her. She certainly has an impressive resume and interviewed well. When does she start?"

"Monday, and she's dying to meet you. You're her idol, apparently." Nana chuckles, but I shrug.

"Shit, I hope she isn't disappointed. Come on, let's get out there."

I gasp when we step out into the backyard. The runway looks amazing. Fairy lights are threaded through the natural arbor, and spotlights have been set up along the path to give the audience a good look at the clothes. Three rows of seats line either side of the catwalk, and they are filled by celebrities and important people in the fashion industry. People call their hellos as the four of us pass. We smile and wave but don't stop. The other three find their seats, but I can see Shane amongst the photographers at the end of the runway, and I want to say hello.

Shane

Alex and I headed out to the plantation not long after we got back to the hotel in the afternoon. Jacinta pleaded that she wanted a nap, and after a panicked phone call with Jace, we decided he needed some moral support.

Once we got there, we tried to calm him down, but Alex's flamboyant enthusiasm just made it worse, so I pulled them into one of the bedrooms upstairs and used a sweaty sex session to settle them both.

Now, the three of us are watching the sunset over the plantation from the top balcony, taking a moment for ourselves to have a celebratory drink before the real mayhem begins. I hand them both a bottle of beer before raising my own.

"Jace, Alex and I were perfectly content in our relationship, happily loving one another and occa-sionally inviting another person in. We had set our sights on Jacinta becoming our permanent third, but then you stumbled into our life. What thought would be a hot and steamy fling quickly became so much more, and the two of us couldn't be happier having you as our third permanent." A lump in my throat makes me swallow before I can get the next bit out. "We love you and wish you all the luck tonight," I finish.

Alex takes over, putting down his raised beer and digging in his pocket for something before pulling out the ring we had made for Jace. It matches the ones that Alex and I both wear, our initials engraved on them. We've added his to ours and are both hoping he will accept this one.

Alex clears his throat, all serious and slightly nervous all of a sudden. Gone is the flamboyant act that he wears as armor, replaced with someone who, like many others, is scared of rejection.

"Shane said everything perfectly. We do love you, and our life is so much better for having you in it. Will you wear our ring?" He holds out his hand.

Jace gasps, slapping his free hand over his mouth, eyes widening with surprise. "Oh wow, gosh yes, yes please, yes, yes, yes." He flaps his hand much like Alex would, and I smother the chuckle that wants to slip out. It's not often that Jace is like this. He puts his beer down and throws himself at Alex, who grunts in surprise as he catches him. Jace kisses him like he's drowning and Alex is the air he needs to live. Watching them is fucking hot, but I want my bit of sugar too. Growling, I step up behind Jace, sandwiching him between Alex and me like we love to do. Grabbing his chin, I angle his head so I can kiss him too. When I pull away, we're all breathing heavily.

"Love you." I nip at his ear as Alex slides the ring onto his finger. Alex passes us our beers again, and we clink them together.

"To us." Jace sighs, admiring the ring on his finger.

"To you, precious, and may your debut be an amazing success."

A couple of hours later, the seats are full, and I'm in the camera pit, but as I scan the crowd, taking in who's here, my eyes lock on a gorgeous sight. Walking toward the pit is Jacinta, wearing a siren red, fitted dress that hugs her gorgeous curves. I see all the admiring and envious eyes tracking her path and feel my chest puff up because I know I'm who she's heading for. Riku trails close behind her. I know he felt like he failed her the other night, but from the way Ash explained it, the attack was well thought out and calculated, and they had done everything they could to counter him. People start to approach her a couple of times, but he shakes his head, stopping them in their tracks. He has a 'don't fuck with me' aura tonight instead of his usual 'blend into the background' thing.

I make my way to the edge of the roped-off area, and when she gets to me, she leans over it and hugs me tight. My camera gets stuck between us, causing her to pull back.

"Whoops." She giggles, and I'm about to laugh too when I notice something.

"Shit, Jacinta, your nose is bleeding."

"What?" Her hands fly up just in time to stop the drop of blood from dripping onto her dress. She catches it on her finger and stares at it.

I dig around in my pocket, knowing I've got a lens cleaning cloth she can use. Pulling it out, I hand it to her, and she dabs daintily at her nose. Riku has now joined us, and he's staring at the blood on the cloth. There's something on his face that says there's deeper meaning to this, something that catches my eye.

"I guess all the stress is getting to me," she says faintly, pinching her nose. "I'm going to see if Nana has a wet wipe. She usually does. Good luck tonight, Shane." She kisses me on the cheek and rushes away before either of us can say anything.

"Is that normal?" I quietly ask the silent body-guard as we track her path to her seat.

He grunts. "No. Not that I've noticed."

"You really think it's the stress?" I ask, pushing a little. I can see that he's weighing something in his mind.

"No, I think she's using. I've suspected it for some time." He lowers his voice so that only the two of us can hear.

"Coke?" I ask, and he nods.

"Yeah. Every time she has to appear in public, it's like there's a personality change. She dreads it and worries, then all of a sudden, she's the happy life of the party. You've known her longer than I have. Have you noticed anything off?"

I quickly shake my head. "No, I never would have suspected her of being on the gear. She's never displayed that kind of behavior before. In fact, her company policy says that anyone caught using during a show will never be hired again."

"She really wasn't happy about this plan of Cole's, but she agreed to do it because she'll do anything for her family. Hope was shocked when she discovered Jacinta agreed," Riku shares with me.

"Jacinta has always been a homebody, preferring her books and horses to parties. But you're right. If he played it so that she was helping her family, she would do just about anything. I bet she's also racked with guilt about what happened to Jax and Harlow."

"Yes, she told me she felt useless." Riku's words confirm what I had expected.

"Well, if her nose is damaged, she's been relying on it to get through all the public appearances. Has she been speaking to her therapist?" I ask him, and he yanks on his ponytail in frustration, huffing.

"She says she is, but I very much doubt it."

"Alright, so what do we need? An intervention?" I ask, trying to come up with some way to help her.

"Addicts don't like to be confronted, but it's usually the best thing for them." He sounds like he's speaking from experience, but I don't push for answers about it yet. He'll share when he's ready.

Spotlights illuminate both the staircases and the balcony, interrupting our conversation. The emcee for the night steps out, and the crowd hushes as he starts to introduce Jace's line.

"Shit, I'll talk to you after, okay? Just watch her." I push my way back into the middle of the crowd of photographers. I want to be in the right place to take the best photos I can for Jace's first show. Unfortunately, I don't think this situation with Jacinta and the drugs is going away that easily, so, right now, I need to focus on what I can control.

As the music starts to pump out of the speakers, Riku makes his way back to where Jacinta is sitting. She's in one of the back rows, so he stands directly behind her. She startles slightly at the heat of him at her back, but she relaxes when she realizes it's him. He puts his hand on her shoulder, and she leans her head against it. It all happens so quickly that no one would have noticed unless you had been staring at them like I had. Riku may be the best person to help her at this stage.

Chapter Eight

Jacinta

Jace's debut show is a hit. The designs are gorgeous, and everyone raves about them at the afterparty. The coke I stole from the models is long gone by the time I stumble into bed. I got another nosebleed while I was dancing with Alex, and his eyes narrowed with suspicion, so I feigned exhaustion and took myself off to bed.

I wake up the next morning with only Riku in my bed. I'd still been pissed with Ash and locked the door between our rooms. I feel a little guilty about it now because I know he was just looking out for me, but still. There have been a lot of things outside my control lately, or rather, throughout my entire life. For someone else to try to take this away from me, decide when I need a little help to get by… It just wasn't his place to comment or his decision to make.

We return to LA with the rest of the family on the big plane after breakfast. The crew had worked hard to dismantle the show, and all the clothing racks had been delivered to the plane while we'd partied and slept. There's a subdued attitude on the plane, everyone having had too much to drink or not enough sleep from the previous night. Most of the men retire to the theater to watch a movie, but Dad and Poppy stick with the rest of us in the lounge area.

"Those babies in there better be girls," Hope grumbles, her arm covering her eyes as she lays across a couch. "I'm so sick of all the testosterone in this family."

"Hey," Dad complains even though he has a grin a mile wide. It's what always happens when the subject of the babies comes up.

"Present company excluded." Hope lifts her arm and blows Dad a kiss. "You and Poppy are always the exception."

The two of them chuckle.

"Are you going to find out what you're having?" I ask the two women.

Emma shrugs. "We haven't really talked about it."

"I know what I'm having. It's a devil spawn,"

Molly complains. She's only just returned from the bathroom, her morning sickness having hit like clockwork. Hope, Harlow, and I had quietly giggled under our breath at the shouted profanities when Dad and Emma tried to comfort her. They both returned with sheepish looks, allowing her to vomit in peace and quiet after that.

"I want it to be a surprise," Dad announces, and the two women look at him with raised eyebrows. "To me, it doesn't matter. I'll love them no matter what they are."

For a man who is socially awkward as fuck, sometimes he really says the right things. The two women melt into his side, cooing at him. He stands up and pulls them to their feet.

"I think that Molly should have a nap after all that. We'll be in the master bedroom for the rest of the flight."

I gag a little internally as the three of them disappear. Pretty sure a nap is not what's going to be happening.

Both Hope and Harlow look a little ill too, and a peal of laughter leaves Nana's mouth. "Now, remember this next time any of you want to disappear into a bedroom with one of your men."

"No problem with that here, Nana. I am one hundred percent celibate... unfortunately." Hope puts her arm back over her face, so she misses the calculating look on Nana's face, but Harlow and I don't. The two of us exchange a grin, knowing what's in store for our new sister.

"What are your plans for the week?" Harlow asks me, grabbing my hand. "I feel like I haven't seen you in weeks. You haven't been home at all."

Guilt racks me, and I grimace. "I know, and I'm so sorry. I promise I'll get back to the renovations soon. I'm coming home for a couple of days. I haven't seen Prada and Coco for ages. I need a break, but I have to be back in town on Thursday. Next week will be better, hopefully." I stopped all renovations on Willow Castle while I've been busy playing media darling, and I miss that peaceful chaos. Sure, the renovations were a lot to organize and deal with, but they were the kind of chaos that I could manage and make my own. I miss that kind of mess.

She waves me off. "I don't care about the renovations. It's not like the house isn't livable. We miss you, is all, and I worry about you. All the media attention you're getting, you hate that kind of shit, and I guess I just want to check that you're okay."

Hope sits up now, a little crease of worry between her eyebrows. We hate lying to her, but we agreed we wouldn't tell Harlow about the plan because we didn't want to worry her. Plus, we knew she would tell the boys.

"I'm fine. Ash is a blast. We've become really good friends, and at least people are focusing on me and him now, not everything else that happened."

Poppy's eyes narrow at my words, but before he can say anything, Jilly interrupts to ask if we want coffee. We all jump at it, except Harlow. She shakes her head and asks for peppermint tea. I guess she's feeling queasy too.

"Listen, do you want to go for a ride during the week?" I suggest to her, then I remember something. "Oh my god, I'm such a bad fucking sister. Your foal? Did he come? I can't wait to see him. What did you call him?"

"Yes, and he's gorgeous! I called him Jupiter. I'd love to ride, but the boys won't let me take the horses outside of the arena. They say there are too many variables when riding the paths, and they don't want me to fall. If there was just one of them, I think I'd stand a chance, but it's impossible to change their minds when they all band together."

I feel slightly disappointed. "Oh, I completely understand. Don't worry about it. I'll ask Dad if he wants to go. We haven't ridden together since Holden got shot."

"Shit, that feels like years ago," Hope murmurs.

"Yeah, it does. Oh hey, Harlow, would you mind if Cole brought his son out to our place and showed him the tiger cubs?"

"Cole has a son?" The blatant surprise in her voice makes me frown. Has it really been so long since we talked that I haven't told her this? Did she not meet him this weekend? But then I guess he did have a babysitter for the show and afterparty.

"Yeah, he's freaking adorable, and when I read him a bedtime story the other night, I told him about the cubs, and he begged to see them. I kind of said he could, but I thought I should ask."

"You read him a bedtime story?" She grins at me, and I shrug.

"Long story. So?" I ask, waving away the question.

"Yeah, of course he can. How old is he?"

"Three, I think. Why?"

"Did you know that Devil Spawn is actually a children's pony? I have a saddle and bridle for her if he wants to take a pony ride."

Hope's mouth comically drops open in horror. "You would let a child near that... that... that monster?" Hope and DS are not friends.

Harlow and I laugh. "DS loves kids and Jacinta. They'll be fine. Maybe Cole should just watch from the stands though," she suggests, giggling as Jilly returns with our drinks.

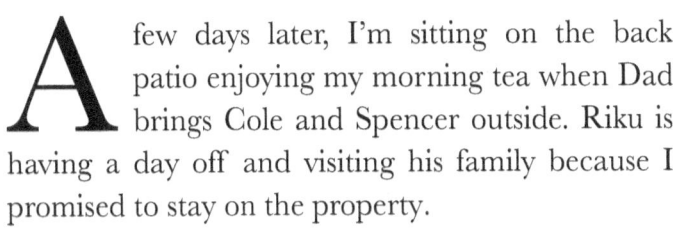

A few days later, I'm sitting on the back patio enjoying my morning tea when Dad brings Cole and Spencer outside. Riku is having a day off and visiting his family because I promised to stay on the property.

"Jazzy, your guests are here," he teases me. It's

been so nice to be home and just relax. I've only had one hit of coke, and that was when I went over to Willow Castle and had a tour of the zoo with Harlow. The place is a construction zone. The McCallister brothers are working hard, and they have a huge crew of people working for them. I thought I did pretty damn good for being surrounded by strangers.

"Hi, Jazzy, hi. We've come to see the tigers. Hi!" Spencer bounces up and down on the spot, one hand firmly in Cole's, the other waving wildly. "Brad said we can pet them."

I raise an eyebrow at my dad, and he shrugs sheepishly. He loves kids, and I can see that he's enamored with Spencer already. That kid will have him wrapped around his finger in no time.

"Well, hi there, buddy. I guess if Brad says you can, then you can. While we're waiting for my sister to come over, do you want some morning tea?" I gesture to the pile of cakes on the table, and his eyes widen like saucers.

"Yes, please." He pulls free and runs around to the seat next to mine. He struggles to pull out the heavy wooden chair, so I help him while Cole takes a seat across from me.

"Are you staying, Dad?" I ask as Spencer climbs up and licks his lips at the sight of all the lovely treats Mrs. Heyton prepared for him.

"No, I'll go call Harlow and let her know they are here. She said to let her know when they arrived. Hey, Spencer, after you see the cubs, would you like to have a pony ride?"

Spencer looks at his dad, the amazement on his face growing. "Can I, Daddy?" he asks.

Cole smiles, the gesture full of warmth and comfort that I wish I could experience for myself. Not that I am ready to admit that anywhere except to myself. The guy being a good dad turns me on, so what? Totally normal. Totally fucking normal.

"Sure can, buddy."

"Yes please, Brad," Spencer says politely, and Dad beams.

"Excellent. Come find me when you finish with the cubs, and I'll take you to meet DS."

"Thanks, Brad."

Dad leaves us, and I pour Cole a coffee, passing it over to him. Mrs. Heyton set the table with the good china, and the dainty cup looks funny in his big hand.

"What would you like to drink, Spencer? There's milk or juice or hot chocolate."

"Chocolate!" He grins and bounces up and down. "And can I have the pink one, please?" He points at the little iced cupcake with sprinkles on it.

"You have lovely manners," I say to him, pouring some hot chocolate into a cup and passing him the cupcake.

"Maybe not in that cup." Cole looks worried as his son grabs the delicate china.

"Nonsense, as Nana would say. Children need

to be trusted, and if it breaks, it's not a big deal, Cole. We've broken plenty over the years."

Spencer's chest puffs up with pride as he carefully lifts his china cup to his mouth and takes a sip. "Delicious." He smacks his lips before carefully placing the cup down. He shoves the cupcake into his mouth, and Cole groans.

"So much for those manners."

Harlow arrives about half an hour later, giving us just enough time to get a good sugar rush running through Spencer. He's been running around on the back grass for the last ten minutes, making plane sounds. He was disappointed to see that the pool was covered. Despite the day being cooler, he wanted to swim. I didn't tell him about the indoor one yet. I'll wait and see how tired he is after his pony ride. I distracted him by telling him the back lawn was where our helicopters landed. He was super impressed, and I sent a quick message to ask Kai if he would take him up in it this afternoon when he arrived home. The kid is so freaking adorable, I can't help but want to spoil him.

We walk to the tiger enclosure, his hand in Harlow's as they walk in front of us. He's listening intently as she tells him all about the tigers. She's great with him, and I can see now that the zoo will be a hit with elementary school children. She doesn't baby him, and she answers all his questions.

When we get to the cage, the cubs and Nyx are all in the play area. The cubs are rolling around, wrestling, and Nyx has put herself out of their reach. She's using one of the sunning platforms to have a nap.

"Wow, look how big they have grown!" I lean against the mesh, threading my fingers through the holes. My voice has the cubs stopping what they are doing and running over to us. Spencer squeals with delight.

"Look, Daddy, kitties!" He claps his hands as the cubs rub against the wire, trying to get Harlow's attention. Cole's eyes are just about as wide as Spencer's.

"Whoa," he breathes out as Nyx yawns and stretches before jumping down from her perch to stalk over to us. She stops in front of the two of us and sits down, putting her paw up on the wire in greeting. I reach out my hand, but Cole snatches it from the air.

"What are you doing?" he asks, and I shrug him away.

"Saying hello," I tell him, putting my hand up against hers. "Hey, pretty girl." She chuffs as I tickle one of her pads with my finger.

"Aren't you worried she'll hurt you?"

"Not with her claws. Nyx was declawed as a cub." I point to the top of her toe, showing him the lack of claws, and he blanches.

"That's horrible."

"Yeah, it is, and it usually doesn't end up so good for the animal in question," Harlow chimes in.

"Luckily for her, whoever did it knew what they were doing. Come on, let's go around to their den. You can help me feed them." Spencer grabs her by the hand, looking at her like she's the best thing since pink-iced cupcakes.

Chapter Nine

Jacinta

About half an hour later, we leave the cubs and Nyx. Spencer declared Nyx his best friend after she allowed him to hug her. Cole watched on, his body tight with tension, but Nyx just lay at his feet and let him do what he wanted. She's basically an overgrown house cat. The rough-and-tumble cubs were a bit much for him, but he still giggled as they pounced after the ball he threw for them. They all wanted to sit in his lap, but he was a little too small, and unlike Nyx, they have claws, so he watched them from afar.

We walk back across the grass to the stables. It's a gorgeous day, and the sun is shining. Jupiter, Harlow's foal, sees us and races around his paddock in excitement. In the next one are Prada and Coco. Coco races around just like Jupiter, albeit a little smaller. Prada ignores them both. We stop to give everyone a pat on the way past, and both colts settle.

When we get to the stables, Dad has DS all ready to go. "Here you are. How did it go with the cats?" he asks, and Spencer excitedly tells him all about it. "Wow, that sounds fun! Cole, do you ride?"

Cole startles at the abrupt change of conversation, but he nods. "Yeah, I do."

Dad grins. "Excellent. I had Josh saddle up a couple of horses. Why don't the two of you go for a ride while I give Spencer a lesson?" Dad suggests as Josh leads two saddled horses out of their stalls. I glare at Dad, but he continues to grin unrepentantly.

"But what about Spencer? I wanted to see him ride." Cole looks between the horse and his son.

"Nonsense. It will be better if you aren't there so he can concentrate. Harlow can video for you. Right, love?"

"Of course." She pulls out her phone and waves it around, coconspirator to our father. "You two should totally go for a ride. I haven't been able to go with Jazzy since I got pregnant. The guys won't let me leave the arena."

"What do you think, Spencer? Are you going to be okay?" Dad has already helped Spencer put on a helmet and is lifting him onto DS's back.

"I'm fine, Daddy."

"Once we're done, Spencer and I'll have some

lunch while we wait for you both to come back. Mrs. Heyton is making mac and cheese, Jazzy's favorite."

"I love mac and cheese!" Spencer claps his hands with excitement.

"Me too," Harlow says, rubbing her belly. "I picked the right day to come here."

"Well, I guess it's decided. We're going for a ride," he agrees, his eyes still clouded with worry.

"Come on, let's grab a helmet." He's already wearing jeans and boots, so he's good to go once he puts a helmet on. I swap out my sneakers for a pair of boots, slap my own helmet on my head, and then I'm good too.

Dad, Harlow, and Spencer have disappeared into the arena, so it's just us, Josh, and the horses now.

"Thanks, Josh." I smile at him as I take the reins from his hands.

"No problems. Don't stress, Mr. Chambers. Brad taught all of his kids to ride. Spencer will be begging you for a pony by the time he's done." Josh tries to reassure Cole as he hands him the other set of reins, but I think any parent would be alarmed by the idea of their child begging for a pet.

"Just call me Cole, man, and that's what I'm worried about. There's no room for a pony in an apartment," he mutters, and Josh laughs.

"Hey, Jazzy. How's Hope? I haven't seen her

since your birthday party." Josh tries for subtlety, but I can't help the grin that crosses my lips.

"I think she avoids this place like the plague since a certain set of brothers moved in. I don't think Nana will stand for it much longer though." There's no sense in sugarcoating it. I like Josh, and he deserves to know there might be some competition.

"Well, tell her I said hi next time you see her."

"I will. We shouldn't be gone too long," I tell him, and he tips his hat.

"As long as I get some mac and cheese before you come back, I'll be happy. So take your time." He wanders in the direction of the arena. I'm sure he's gone to cheer on Spencer. Josh is a great guy and freaking handsome too. Maybe he's just what Hope needs as a distraction. She always blushes when he's around. I'm rooting for him to be part of Hope's happily ever after.

I did see them talking privately at my birthday. I'll have to remember to ask her what that was about. Fuck, I'm such a bad friend, so completely wrapped up in my own shit that I haven't taken the time to make sure she's okay. As much as Nana thinks she's matchmaking, Hope has some deep-seated resentment for the McCallister brothers, and I'm not sure that's a place she can easily come back from.

The ride is peaceful and exactly what I need to reset myself. Cole knows when to be quiet and just take in the serenity. We do that for the first half of the ride, but curiosity gets the better of me eventually.

"So where did you learn to ride? You look like you're at home on the back of a horse." We're riding Western today, and he's had no problem no matter what pace we travel at.

"My parents have a ranch in Wyoming. I grew up riding horses."

"Oh wow, okay. So what made you go into PR and not ranching?"

He grins. "I have four brothers and a sister. There are enough of us that I didn't have to, and the whole reason I went into PR in the first place was to help the ranch. It wasn't doing very well, so we decided to turn it into a dude ranch to generate some extra income. We built some rustic cabins, and now people pay a fortune to come play ranch hand for a week. We even have a large lodge now for corporate retreats." Huh, that was *so* not what I had thought. His accent doesn't say country boy at all. He laughs at what must be a stunned look on my face.

"I try to get back a couple of times a year. My brothers have kids that are all a little older than Spencer, and he loves going to see his cousins. He's finally getting to an age where he can really enjoy it."

"That sounds awesome. Well, I'm sure the

riding lessons with Dad will help when you get out there."

His smile drops into a frown. "I'm not sure when that's going to happen next. When I picked him up this morning, Hayden told me she's been offered a movie role, but it's filming in Australia for the next year."

"Oh no, Cole. What's going to happen with Spencer? She can't possibly take him as far away as Australia, can she?"

"That's the weird thing. She didn't even bring up that possibility. Hayden wants him to stay here with me. She leaves after the new year, so instead of me having Christmas with Spencer because it's my turn, she wants him with her, then he'll come to me when she leaves. She says she doesn't have the time to be worrying about him as well as concentrating on her new career."

"Well, that's bullshit." The words fly out of my mouth, and Cole chuckles ruefully.

"That's what I said too, but it's what she's like. She's only a mom when it's convenient for her. I also think that the new boyfriend might have some-thing to do with it."

"No matter the circumstances, this is wonderful for you, Cole." I reach out and grab his hand, squeezing it.

"Yeah, but what happens when she finishes and comes back?" He rubs a hand across his chin. "I think I'm going to take her to court for full custody, and she can have visitation rights. I would never keep Spencer away from his mother, no matter what, but I want to keep his life as stable as possible."

"If you need representation, Forrest has a great family lawyer on his team. We can arrange for you to see him."

He stares at me for a moment, wrinkles creasing his brow as he really studies me before shaking his head. "You are not the person I thought you were, and I really want to apologize for making assumptions. That would be great if you wouldn't mind."

I'm a little surprised at his outburst, but I appreciate the apology. I shrug. "It's okay. I'm used to being judged."

"Well, even though I'm guilty of it, it's still bullshit. I should have known better than to jump to conclusions. I guess Hayden made my walls bigger than they need to be because she's an expert at appearing one way when she's actually another." I'm not surprised by his words. It kind of explains why he's been the way he has with me, not that I'm excusing his behavior.

Maybe I'm willing to let him off the hook too easily, but an apology is more than I've ever gotten from most of the people I surround myself with. It's really only ever been my family, and now Riku and the other guys, who have cared enough about my feelings to recognize and admit that they have wronged me in any way. Maybe I should make him work harder for some kind of forgiveness, but as someone who's made some awful assumptions herself, I know how much of an internal battle it can be to rewire your brain. If he's willing to look at me with fresh eyes, I'll take that as enough.

When we finish up our ride, we look after our mounts and return them to their stables, saving Josh some work.

"Let's wash up. I'm sure Mrs. Heyton saved us some lunch," I say as we walk back to the house.

"That's if Spence didn't eat it all. Mac and cheese really is his favorite." We enter the house from the back patio and grind to a halt at the sight in front of us. Dad and Spencer are on the sofa with the TV on in front of them, the channel set to show some cartoon, and they are fast asleep. Spencer's head is resting on Dad's lap, and Dad's leaning back on a cushion. He's snoring quietly.

"Aw, that's so freaking cute," I whisper to Cole, who looks torn. "Leave them be for now. We can go eat, then we'll wake them when we get back." I drag him to the kitchen. In the oven, I find two covered plates of food, so I pull them out and set two places at the island. Grabbing us both a beer to go with it, I gesture for Cole to take a seat.

We dig into the food, and he groans with appreciation. "This is amazing," he says, swallowing. "I'm going to need to get the recipe from Mrs. H."

"And I'm sure she'll give it to you. She loves it when people appreciate her food. Listen, would you like to take Spencer for a swim after their nap? I've arranged for Kai to give him a ride in the helicopter when they come home, but they won't be back until a little later this afternoon."

"It's a bit cold to go for a swim. I wouldn't want him to get sick."

"We've got a heated one downstairs, and there are spare suits for you. I'm not sure if we have anything that will fit Spencer, though if I know Dad, that will soon change. Maybe he could go in his underwear, then we can throw them in the dryer when we're finished. There's a hot tub down there, too, and a sauna," I singsong, remembering his groans when he got off the horse.

"Sold. I can't believe how sore I am. I used to live on horseback growing up."

"You're welcome to come out and ride whenever you want. There's always a horse or two that needs exercise. Josh and Dad will welcome the company. Chuck would be happy for you to ride some of his too."

"I'm not sure how much time I'll get now that I've got Spencer."

"Bullshit. You can just bring him with you. You saw how fat DS is! She's a spoiled pony, and she could do with regular exercise. There's plenty of room here at the house. Just come home for the weekend now and then. The both of you can get on the helicopter at the end of the day with the boys and go back with Dad the following Monday. It's good for kids to grow up around animals and to get plenty of fresh air, and he won't be getting that living at the hotel with you." I quickly add an excuse at the end, so it doesn't seem like I want him there. I have enough boyfriends, or that's what I'm going to keep telling myself.

He's staring at me now, but I can't decipher what the look means. He's obviously weighing things in his mind. "I'd like that, and I'm sure Spencer will too," is all he says, and we eat the rest of the meal in silence, which is more comfortable than I ever thought it could be between us.

COLE

When Spencer and Brad wake up, he's thrilled to learn his day is not over. Jacinta leads us downstairs into an epic game room and through a door to an indoor swimming pool. Spencer wrinkles his nose at the smell of chemicals, but he starts stripping off his clothes as soon as he can, tossing them on a bench seat along one wall.

"Hey, hey, slow down, buddy," I warn him. "You can't go in until I'm ready."

"Hurry, Daddy, hurry!" He bounces up and

down on his little feet, naked except for a pair of *Paw Patrol* underwear.

"See that door over there?" Jacinta points out. "That's a change room/bathroom. In there is a box of spare suits and towels. Help yourself and grab both of you a towel. I'll hang with Spence until you get back."

As I hurry away, she moves his clothes and lifts the lid of the bench seat. When I hear his shout of joy, I turn around. She's pulling out some pool noodles and what looks like something inflatable. Sitting back down, she starts to blow it up as he bounces next to her, clapping his hands. My son has been filled with more joy today than I've seen in a long time, and no matter what else hits us in the near future—custody proceedings, Hayden's new boyfriend, me shifting my view of Jacinta and whatever comes along with it—I'll keep the memories of how he's smiled today in my mind forever.

I rush through getting changed and grab us both towels. When I return, she's halfway done blowing whatever it is up.

"Hey, how about we swap? I'll finish while you get changed."

She shrugs sheepishly. "I wasn't going to go in." Before I can reply, the door opens, and Brad dashes in, heading straight for the pool.

"Cannonball!" he shouts and throws himself into the pool, sending up a huge splash of water that hits us all. Spencer squeals with laughter as Jacinta shrieks.

"Me too! Me too!" Spencer shouts, running at the pool. I lunge for him, but I'm not quick enough. Thankfully, Brad is there to catch him after Spencer throws himself into the water with great enthusiasm. When he comes up, he wraps his little arms around Brad's neck and looks at Jacinta. "Did I get you?"

She groans. "I guess I have no choice now since I'm already wet. Thanks, Dad and Spencer." She glares at her dad before smiling at my son. "I won't be more than a moment." She stands up and heads for the changing room, glaring again at her dad. "You're such a child." He chuckles as she disappears. She's already a better sport than Hayden ever was. Her reaction definitely wouldn't be to change and join in the fun with him. Hayden would never yell at Spencer for something like this, but she'd definitely get a good sulk going about her hair or her outfit being unexpectedly splashed.

"The thing about Jazzy is you have to convince her to do the things she really wants to." Brad tosses Spencer up in the air. "And we all know she really wanted to go swimming. Right, bud?"

I finish blowing up the raft and snort when I realize it's an eggplant emoji. I bet this was Oliver's choice. Throwing it into the pool, Brad helps Spencer swim over to it and climb on while I sit down on the edge.

"Hey, Cole, that's the sauna and hot tub over there." Brad points to a glass door on the other side of the swimming pool. "I bet your muscles are sore from the ride. Why don't you go have a soak? Me and my new best buddy here will be fine without you."

I give him a wry smile. "Why do I get the feeling you keep trying to get rid of me?"

Brad grins widely. "Nope, just enjoying having a child around again. It's nice to let your inner child out occasionally, and what better time than when you're with one?" Brad holds his fist out to Spencer for a bump, and Spencer indulges him, whooping when Brad chucks him into the air again.

"Okay, but he's not a very strong swimmer. Hayden doesn't like to get her hair wet."

"Don't worry, if he spends enough time with us, he'll be a fish come summer," Brad assures me, so I haul myself to my feet and head in the direction he pointed. Pushing through the glass door, I enter a tiled room with a hot tub built into the ground. There's a large wooden room on the opposite side which must be the sauna.

Stepping into the hot tub, I press the button, and the jets roar to life. Groaning, I sit down on the seat and lean back against the molded sides. Oh yeah, this is just what I need. I close my eyes and let the jets soothe my aching muscles. If my family could see me now, I would never live it down.

I crack an eye open when I hear the door, but I

quickly sit up when I see who's there. My mouth instantly gets dry, and I feel the blood rush into my cock as I take in the sight before me. Jacinta is wearing a bikini that doesn't leave much to the imagination, and I have a very good one. There's only a couple of triangles and string over her full breasts and another couple of scraps of material tied together with string to cover her bottom half. The rest of her gorgeous creamy skin is on display. My eyes scan her curvy body and long legs before coming back up to her head. Her nose is wrinkled, and she's scowling.

"Someone replaced all my bathing suits with things like this. I'm not sure who, but I plan on killing them when I find out. How am I supposed to swim without worrying about falling out of this?" she grumbles as she moves forward and climbs into the hot tub with me.

I say a little prayer of thanks to whoever fucked with her swimsuits. I really don't mind if she falls out of them.

She sinks down into the water, groaning much like I did. "I'm not getting enough riding in. I'm more sore than I've been in a long time." She sits down next to me, and I can feel her brush against me just slightly, her skin soft and silky, and my dick practically shouts with joy. Thank fuck for bubbles. Otherwise, there's no way I could hide my reaction.

"Yeah, this is magic. No wonder you all still live

at home." We both lean back, and when Jacinta closes her eyes, I turn my head to watch her.

She smiles slightly, and it occurs to me that I see this all the time—a semi-smile that dimly shines. Does the woman truly smile? I don't know why, but I'm hit with a desire to make her do so.

"Well, all these perks don't hurt, but I think the main reason is we all come from broken homes, so we cling as long as possible to the one place we all felt safe and the people who made us feel that way."

"Yeah, I can see that. I was blessed with my family, but not everyone is, which is one of the reasons I get so mad at Hayden sometimes. She loves Spencer, I know she does, but it's the wrong kind of love."

She reaches for my hand under the water and gives it a squeeze. "Well, now that he's going to live with you, it's your chance to give him what he needs."

"Yeah, I guess I should start looking for a house, but I don't know where to start."

"Why don't you include him in the decision making? Ask him what he would like in a house," she suggests, not letting go of my hand, and I can't deny how good it feels to hold hands with this woman.

I chuckle. "I bet if I asked today, the list would include tigers and a jaguar, ponies, and a swimming pool."

She giggles. "Yeah, maybe give it a few days.

Though you're always welcome to bring him back whenever he needs an animal or pool fix."

We spend about twenty minutes in the hot tub, but I eventually feel a little guilty, so we join Brad and Spencer in the pool. Spencer's shrieks of joy are music to my ears, and I don't stop grinning the whole time. It's even better later when the helicopter touches down, delivering the rest of the Summers home, and Jacinta tells Spencer he gets to have a ride. I'm pretty sure his eyes were stuck wide open in surprise the whole time we were in the air.

When it's finally time to tuck him into bed that night, he's exhausted, but he can't stop talking about his day and his new best friends Brad and Kai who let him sit in the front of the helicopter.

I can't believe this family managed to make my son so happy in just one day. It's about more than just the things—exotic cats, pools, and helicopters. It was about their genuine happiness in making a child happy. They barely know me, and God knows they don't know my son, so why do they care so much about being so kind to us? I want to be worthy of their regard. Something says I *need* to be worthy of it because the Summers are people that you want on your side, people who will always try this hard for others.

And, after seeing her interact with my son more than once, I'm ready to admit how badly I misjudged Jacinta Summers. I have so much to make up for.

Chapter Ten

Jacinta

My time at home was a blessing, but now I need to get back to my charade with Ash. Things have been a little awkward between us since he ate me out in the car, then the whole fiasco with the coke at the line launch. We don't really have the same easygoing camaraderie that we once had. There's this sense of awareness that wasn't there before, and neither of us know what to do about it, but I promised him I would attend his polo match and the subsequent afterparty, so I drive myself back into town.

This is a major event on the LA elite calendar, so I'll know lots of people there. Despite things being a little awkward between us as well, I'm kind of glad that Riku will be with me. After the situation with Matthew, he's aware that I'm still using coke, though he hasn't confronted me about it or tried to pin down just how much I've been using. My bloody nose at Jace's launch didn't help either.

I need to be more careful. Maybe I can get my hands on some Adderall or Ritalin so that I don't have to snort so often. I'm hoping a week of mostly not using it has helped my nostrils recover a little. I can't afford to be caught with a nosebleed this weekend. I managed to secretly get some more coke out of the safe at Willow Castle this week, so I know I'm using good quality stuff. With it all packed into a secret compartment in my handbag, I'm good to go.

Although I'd be more comfortable wearing jeans and boots to the polo match, it's a somewhat dressy affair, so I find myself putting on makeup and heels. I'm wearing black satin, wide-legged pants, with a fitted, turquoise half-sleeve shirt. I have a black wrap with me even though the day is sunny, so I'm hoping I won't need it, but it might be cool in the shade.

"Are you ready?" Riku calls from the living area just as I finish snorting my first hit of the day. I dab at my nose with a tissue as I feel the chemical drip down the back of my throat and the sting in my nose.

"Won't be a second," I call back, then I toss the straw I used back into the drawer and wipe off the sink.

Smoothing my hair down, I check everything one more time, assuring myself I'm ready to go. I go through the bedroom, grabbing the bag that contains my change of outfit for the afterparty and my handbag, before meeting Riku in the living room.

"Hi," I say to him somewhat shyly. He actually took a couple of days off, so I haven't seen him since before Cole and Spencer visited. I'm still a little unsure of where we stand. He made his intentions clear in Hawaii, but we haven't really talked about it since. Is he still interested? Or has he decided I'm just a job and we should keep things professional? Has the revelation about my continued coke usage pushed him too far away from me?

"Are you ready to go?" He takes my garment bag and looks closely at me. "You look a little flushed. Are you okay?"

"Yeah, fine." I try to breeze past him, but he grabs my arm and spins me around.

"Did you use again?"

"What? I don't know what you're talking about," I argue, but he just shakes his head and drops my arm.

"Do me a favor, Jacinta. Don't lie to me. I am quite familiar with all the tricks of addiction." He doesn't sound mad, just disappointed, and that may be even worse.

"Addiction? I'm not addicted. I just need a bit to

get myself through these public engagements. My anxiety and nerves and fear are just too much to do this without it." I'm trying to convince him my words are the truth, but I can tell he doesn't believe it.

"You know, it's funny. I used to tell myself the same thing with alcohol. Just a little drink before I did something because it helped block out the horrors I had seen in Iraq, but one turned into two, which turned into three, and before I knew it, I was drunk and in no condition to save a kitten out of a tree, let alone someone's life. Simon is the one who put me straight. Got me into AA and consistently seeing a therapist."

While I feel for Riku, I truly do, I don't fully see the connection between our circumstances. Clearly, he had much more trauma to deal with than me, so I can see how he wasn't able to stop himself from getting addicted to alcohol. Regardless of that, I'm glad that he shared something of himself with me, and I don't want to turn his effort at connecting with me into a fight. "Oh wow, I'm so sorry that happened to you. I didn't even know you were in the military."

"Maybe we can both share our experiences with each other one day. It helps to have someone else to talk to about what you went through, especially someone who isn't personally involved. I learned that through my therapist. Coke, however, is not the answer."

"Oh, I can stop at any time." I wave my hand at him, trying to keep the moment as light as possible between us. "I can! I didn't touch it all week at home." My mind tries to remind me that there was that one time, but come on, one hit surely doesn't count. If I was an addict, I would have needed a lot more than that.

"But you were comfortable, Jacinta. You weren't doing anything that caused anxiety and fear, but the minute you have to go out in public again, you're reaching for it. You need to join a group, and you need to see your therapist again."

"I'll make an appointment next week. Come on, we'll miss the start of the match." I'm done talking about this. I don't have a problem. I will be fine. I survived the start of my life with my monstrous mother, the drama with Harlow's stalker, and all that shit with my family and the kidnapping. I can beat a little baggie of white powder. He's underestimating me, which I really don't appreciate, but I don't want to talk about this with him anymore. He'll understand I'm telling the truth when he sees it.

I hear him sigh deeply behind me, but at least I know he's following me out.

In the car, I start to pour myself a drink, but I stop. "Shit, I'm sorry. You should have said something earlier. I would have gotten rid of all the alcohol, and we wouldn't have drunk in front of you." I put the bottle and glass back down, but Riku shakes his head.

"It's okay. I've got it under control. You having a drink won't trigger me. If it did, following you around these last few weeks would have turned me into a stumbling drunk again."

I feel the color drain from my face as it suddenly occurs to me what I've been putting him through. "Oh my god, Riku. How can you ever forgive me?"

He comes over to my side of the limo and puts his arm around me, pulling me into his side. A warmth rushes over me that has nothing to do with the coke in my system. The fact that he's not outwardly rejecting me now that he knows is a huge relief, but, like I said, I can stop at any time, so he has nothing to worry about.

"Being an alcoholic is a me thing. It shouldn't stop everyone around me from having fun. I have enough control over my situation that it doesn't bother me anymore. Had I not been sober for three years, it might be a different thing."

"Okay, well, make sure you tell me if it ever becomes a problem. Have you ever been to a polo match?" I ask him, changing the subject, and I feel him shake his head.

"Nope, I can't say I have. I haven't really been around horses at all."

"Ha, don't tell Dad that. He'll have you up on one before you know it."

"Josh said the same thing. I think he gave Simon

a couple of riding lessons before I reassigned him, and he keeps trying to talk Doug and Clem into having lessons in the evenings."

"Are you still okay living with them? I'm sure Dad wouldn't mind if you moved into the house. God knows we have enough room."

"No, I'm fine. There's plenty of room over there, and none of us feel on top of each other. Doug and Clem go home most nights. They only stay out at the house if they have an early or late start, so most of the time it's me and Josh. We've discovered a shared love of first-person shooter games and spend a lot of time using his console and talking smack to one another."

I giggle at the picture that pops up in my mind —Riku and Josh in their underwear, controllers in hand, surrounded by empty coffee mugs and cheese ball wrappers. Somehow I don't think that's quite right.

"Sounds fun. Maybe you can hang out with me one night, and we can use our console. You can teach me to play. I never got a chance to when my brothers lived at home."

"I'd love to. It's a date," he promises, and I have something to look forward to this week.

The smell of horse manure and grass is strong in my nose as I swat a fly away from my face. A roar goes up from the watching crowd. Ash just scored the winning goal for his team as the timer runs down to zero. Shouts and screams go on around me, and I plaster a smile on my face when Selena grabs my arm, drawing my attention.

"Oh, he is wonderful. You can just imagine what he'd be like in bed when you watch him on his horse. I bet that man has stamina." She fans her face, and I can't miss the question in her voice. One I have no idea about.

"Stop it, Selly. Jacinta doesn't want to talk to you about her sex life. Leave her be," Evie protests.

"Come on, let's hit the bar while we wait for him," Anna suggests, dragging Chase in the direction of the clubhouse. "He might be a while."

"Oh, I'm sure he has a groom that does everything for him." Selena watches Ash on the field like a wolf stalking her prey. I swear if I wasn't around, she would be all over him. I'm pretty sure she'd love to be known as Lady Lavington. Well, she's out of luck because for now, he's all mine, even if it is mostly pretend. If I finally gave myself permission, I think I could make it all real, but there's still something holding me back. I think it's Alex and his prior relationship with Ash that makes me so uncertain.

The clubhouse of the polo team is a donated mansion. The grounds are the former dwelling of a polo-obsessed Wall Street millionaire. When he died, he donated the grounds to the private polo team he established, meaning for it to be their home base. The afterparties are always off the hook and full of debauchery. Bedrooms can be rented out so that revelers don't have to leave early or arrange transport, they can just stumble up the stairs.

The bar Anna and Chase drag us to overlooks the swimming pool lagoon in the backyard. It's surrounded by seating with fire pits dotted here and there. The sun is setting, and those pits will be lit by the staff soon enough.

"We should grab one of the pits as home base for the night and have some pizzas from the restaurant brought out to us," Anna suggests as Chase waves down a bartender.

"What is everyone having?" he asks when he gets to us.

Selena flutters her eyelids at him. "We'll take two bottles of Dom and half a dozen glasses."

Anna wrinkles her nose. "Not for me. I'll have a margarita, and Chase will have a whiskey and Coke."

"I'll have a margarita too," I tell the guy and raise an eyebrow at Evie, who shakes her head.

"I'll have champagne with Selly."

"Oh, and put it on Lord Lavington's tab," Selena adds in, and I scowl at her.

"No, don't do that. I've got this round." I pull my credit card out of my pocket and hand it to the guy who quickly makes our drinks before tapping my card and handing it back.

"Well, I guess you're loaded too. I should have ordered three bottles." Selena grabs the two bottles while Evie grabs the glasses, and they walk toward a pit in the backyard as I growl.

"Why the fuck do we continue to hang out with her?" I mutter loudly enough that Chase and Anna hear.

"Because every group has someone that everyone doesn't like but puts up with. We actually had two, but Matthew really fucked up," Anna says, and I blanche at the mention of him. "I'm so sorry about what happened. I can't believe he was let out on bail!" She reaches out to give me a hug, but I stop her.

"What do you mean? He was let out on bail? What the fuck? He's not here, is he?" I look around, and Riku must read the panic on my face because he comes over.

"Is everything okay?" he asks, looking between the three of us.

"Hey, man, I'm sorry. Anna thought she knew."

"Knew what?" Riku looks as clueless as I do, thank goodness. I would have hated to think he was hiding it from me.

"Matthew made bail," I tell him flatly, and he frowns, pulling his phone out of his pocket.

"Let me call Forrest and get to the bottom of this. Don't panic. We'll get it sorted." He leans in and gives me a distracted kiss on the cheek before walking away. Anna's eyebrows just about jump into her hairline, and I feel myself blush.

"Damn, girl, you have been busy. Don't worry, we won't tell Ash," she assures me, but I shrug.

"Ash knows. It's fine." I giggle at the look the two of them exchange, grateful for the momentary distraction.

"Well shit, now I need to hear all about this." Anna tucks my drink-free arm into hers and drags us after the other two with Chase trailing good-naturedly behind us. He really is a wonderful, down-to-earth man. I must see if I can talk to Declan about finding him a major role. Maybe the two of them playing opposite each other? That would be fun.

I'm completely on edge as I wait for Riku to return, but luckily, Selena distracts Anna with some salacious gossip the minute we sit down, so I don't have to tell her about my complicated love life.

When he returns, he pulls me aside. The others watch on with undisguised interest, but they are far enough away to not hear. "Yup, he made bail, but the minute he did, Forrest filed a restraining order against him. He's not allowed within five hundred feet of you, and Forrest is putting a rush on the case. He's not sure how he made bail when the police had drug evidence against him and the blood test results. I can put a tail on him, though, so we can make sure we know where he is at every moment. I already called Simon, and he said he'll have a guy on him within the next hour."

I breathe a small sigh of relief, but I still feel nauseous. If he ever comes near me again, I'm going to put my foot in his balls. "Okay, thanks. I appreciate it."

"Don't worry, sweetheart, I would do everything and anything to keep you safe. Especially since I failed the first time."

I desperately want to kiss him, but I can't do that to Ash, not at the moment. "When we get somewhere a little more private, I'll show you exactly how much this means to me," I tell him, and his eyes heat with lust.

"I'll hold you to that."

I return to my friends, and he melts into the background as we wait for Ash to join us. I quickly down my first margarita then grab one of the spare glasses, pouring myself some champagne.

Selena glares at me. "That glass was for Ash."

"He prefers Cristal, so I'm sure he won't mind if I drink some. Besides, I did pay for it." Other things overwhelmed me earlier, and for a moment, I forgot who I am. I don't need to put up with shit from her. I could make or break her career with one quiet word in my big brother's ear. She's already on his shit list, so it wouldn't take more than that, and as much as I've turned over a new, nicer leaf, I won't allow someone to walk all over me. Especially someone who would like to get her claws into my boyfriend… friend… whatever Ash is. I toast her before tossing it back, the bubbles tickling my nose and throat as they go down. Oh yeah, just what I need. I reach out and pour another one.

"Oh hey, slow down. The night is only getting started." Chase chuckles again, but he looks slightly concerned.

"Just one more, then I'll slow down. Just give me this," I plead, looking around to make sure no one else is paying attention, and his eyes soften.

"Of course. And again, I'm sorry."

"Dude, you don't need to apologize," Anna scolds him, and I put my hand on his arm.

"She's right. His actions are not your fault. Let's not even waste our breath talking about him anymore. He'll pay eventually. He's probably realizing at this very moment that his career is absolutely fucked, so I have to be happy with that."

Anna grins. "I received the revised script for this week. They are not even giving him any on-screen time. His death will be talked about by the rest of us, but that's it."

"Yup, and any offers he had on the table will be rescinded. I wish I could be a fly on the wall when he discovers his agent has dropped him too."

"Wow, remind me never to fuck with you or

your family," Evie says with wide-eyed wonder, and Selena squirms ever so slightly on the spot. I smile with satisfaction and slowly sip my glass of champagne as I wait for Ash.

Chapter Eleven

Jacinta

It takes Ash about an hour to join us, and when he does, he's not alone. He has Shane, Alex, and Jace with him. I jump up out of my seat in surprise, but I have to stop myself from greeting them as enthusiastically as I want. Instead, I go for a peck on the cheek and reluctantly introduce them to the other people in the group—not because I'm ashamed or anything like that. I just know Selena is going to set her eyes on one or maybe more of them, and that drives me wildly jealous. And, sure enough, I can see her eyeing them, but when the three of them sit down together and Shane wraps his arms around each of them, her eyes almost bug out of her head.

Smirking, I watch Jace snuggle into Shane and whisper in his ear while Alex chats with Anna next to him. I'm so distracted that I miss Ash, and suddenly, he's there in front of me, pulling me to my feet and kissing me like I'm the reason he scored the winning goal. I'm breathless, and my heart is pounding when he pulls away. He's smirking like he knows what he's done, but maybe I'm affecting him just as much if the bulge that's growing in his pants is anything to go by.

"My lucky charm," he declares, keeping his arms around me. "It's all thanks to you that we won."

I snort my amusement and roll my eyes. "Hardly. But it was a great match. You ride like you were born in the saddle."

"Ah yes, my British aristocratic upbringing was good for one thing at least." You can't miss the sarcasm in his voice. "The estate management degree that Grandmother made me get is pretty much useless, though, so cheers to that." He steals my glass of champagne and drains the rest of it before pulling back and wrinkling his nose. "Dom? Who purchased this pig swill? Darling, I thought you knew me better." I turn to look at Selena, and she blanches.

"Oh, that was what the bartender gave us when I asked for some champagne," she lies to him despite knowing we all heard her order it.

"Do you like my surprise?" he quietly asks me, nodding to the other three men.

"Yeah, I do, but why?"

"Because I know you've been spending all your time with me and haven't been seeing them, and that's not fair to them. They are being kind enough to deal with all my crap. It's only fair that they get to see you too. If you want, I'll cover while you sneak off to one of the bedrooms with them."

"Really?" I can't hide the surprise in my voice, and he grins ruefully, running a hand through his elegantly coiffed hair, giving it that well-fucked look.

"Yeah, babe. I mean, seriously, look at the three of them. I'd kill to swap with you." He sounds kind of wistful, and I know he has many regrets about how he and Alex ended things. I don't blame him. Aside from being absolutely delicious, Alex is also a wonderful person, and the other two shine just as brightly as he does.

"You know, I may just take you up on that," I tell him.

The drinks flow and the food continues to be served, but I touch very little of it as person after person stops by our fire pit to chat with Ash and congratulate him on the win. Halfway through the evening, Ash takes a phone call. He moves off to the side so he can speak privately, but my eyes follow him. I've somehow become low-key obsessed with this man, and our charade is no longer one on my behalf. This isn't going to end well. Someone is going to be hurt just like Alex warned me from the start.

I signal for a waitress to bring me another drink

as I watch Ash argue with whoever is on the phone before the color drains from his face. He looks at me with panic, but he smoothly plasters on a fake grin after hanging up.

Before I can ask if he's okay, loud music pumps out of the speakers as the DJ starts his set, and the patio area becomes a dance floor. Ash grabs my hand and tugs me into the crush of people. I let him, and we grind on one another as everyone else in our party joins us. Not far away, Alex, Shane, and Jace are dancing together, and between what I'm seeing and what Ash is doing, I'm all kinds of turned on.

Before I can act on Ash's suggestion, there's a commotion off to one side, and we stop dancing to watch Camilla Carlos push through the crowd. Ash's hand tightens on my waist, then he whispers, "Please forgive me, but if I don't do this, Edie will be married to the sheik within weeks."

He spins me around, then, to my horror, he gets down on one knee. Grabbing my hand, he looks up at me. The music stops, and everyone gathers around to watch. I can feel the insidious prickles of their stares and the echo of their whispers as Ash clears his throat.

"Jacinta Summers, these last few weeks have been nothing short of magical. I've fallen madly and deeply in love with you." He reaches into the pocket of his jeans, pulls out a black velvet box, and opens it, holding it out to me. The ring inside is a canary yellow princess-cut diamond. "Will you do me the honor of being my wife? Will you marry me?" Gasps happen all around us, and I swallow the urge to bolt off the dance floor. As horrible as this is for me, I can see his body is tense, his eyes pleading with me to say yes. Out of the corner of my eye, I can see Camilla recording the whole thing on her phone, so I conjure up a watery smile and nod my head.

"Yes, yes, of course I'll marry you." Ash stands up and sweeps me into his arms, kissing me like I'm his savior before pulling away and slipping the ring on my finger. Cheers fill the hushed air, then we're surrounded by people wishing us congratulations. Thankfully, Camilla gets pushed into the background by the excited crowd.

Everyone surrounding us makes me feel trapped, and I hold Ash's hand in a vise-like grip. All the voices and touching and being crowded has my stomach rolling with nausea, my senses freaking out, so I look for a way to escape. Seeing a gap in the crowd, I pull away from him. "I've just got to pee really quickly," I tell him through gritted teeth, and without waiting for an answer, I hurry away. Detouring past our fire pit, I grab my handbag and beeline for the inside of the mansion in search of a quiet bathroom to have a breakdown.

Before I can make it to the bathroom, Ash catches up to me. He's quickly followed by Jace and

Alex. They pull me into a nearby unused office, and just as Shane closes the door, Riku slips in too.

"What the fuck were you thinking?" I scream at him. "Did you think to run that by me? Or the guys? Can you imagine what it felt like to witness that?" I pound on his chest with my fists, so fucking angry at him on their behalf.

"Hey, man, what was all that about? It looked like you set her up." Alex sounds reasonable on the surface, but there's a hint of sadness in his voice that makes Ash hunch in on himself.

"My grandmother rang and told me if I didn't ask Jacinta to marry me, then my sister would be married to that sheik this time next week. She demanded it from day one, but I've been putting her off. She wanted me to propose a week ago, and I kept saying no, but I can't risk my sister. She won't hesitate to do as she promises."

"Fuck, man, I knew you said she was bad, but that's horrible. Did she arrange for Camilla to be here?" Jace is gobsmacked if the look on his face has anything to say.

Ash nods wearily. "Yes. I really am sorry, to all of you. If you give me a few weeks to try to sort everything out, we can have a spectacular breakup."

I drop my fists and step back. Ash sounds defeated, and after everything I've done for my family, how can I hold it against him that he was doing exactly the same thing? I shake my head and put my hand on his cheek.

"It's okay. We can do this. We won't let that bitch win," I assure him, and thankfully, the other guys also add their words of encouragement. Shane is the quietest, but I don't think it comes from a place of anger or disapproval. It feels more like he's trying to wrap his head around all of this, which is totally understandable.

"We have to go back out there. It won't look good if the six of us hide in here together just after you two get engaged." Alex opens the door. "We can talk about this more tomorrow. Let's just get this night over with. We need a happy, smiling, loved up couple, okay?" He's all business now, like he can see how much the two of us are struggling, so he's going to micromanage us. "I'll grab some champagne, and we'll toast you. That will give them something else to speculate about—am I really happy for my ex or putting on a brave face? Shane and Jace can be seen comforting me... a lot." He grins like he can't wait to play a role.

"Thank you." Ash's words sound like a blessing, then the three of them leave.

"Shall we go?" Ash asks, and I give him a shaky smile.

"I really have to pee. Just give me a moment."

"Okay, we'll wait here." He steps aside to let me leave. As I brush past Riku, he grabs hold of me. The way he looks at me, it's like he can see all the turmoil bubbling beneath my skin. It's all I can do to hold my impending meltdown inside. Gritting my teeth, I force a smile.

"I'm okay," I say to him, and he silently lets me go.

I hurry away to a nearby bathroom, closing the door behind me, and dig around in my bag for my coke. Trembling with an urgency like no other, I upend my handbag on the sink when I can't find what I'm looking for. My whole body is shaking, my breathing erratic, as I scramble around to find what I need. Panting, I pick up the bag, but my hands shake so badly that it slips. I watch on in horror as all the white powder falls to the floor.

Fuck no. I start to shake even harder, so I drop down to the floor and use my hands to try to gather it all up into a line, but there's lint and all sorts of things in it. Shuddering, I start to sob, leaning back against the cupboard. I need the hit. I need it like I need my next breath of air, so I reach for the straw and lean over. I try to pick out the worst of the dirt, and just as I put the straw to my nose and take a small sniff, the door opens. I wipe my nose with the back of my hand, the gritty feel of everything I just snorted irritating my nostrils. Suddenly, I sneeze twice. The second time, when I pull my hand away, there's blood-splattered snot on it.

Riku stares down at me, and his lips purse. "Oh baby, no." He crouches down and tries to take the straw away from me, but I fight him for it.

"No, I just need this last one. Just tonight,

please." I can hear the desperation in my voice. A flood of self-loathing and disgust rolls through me, but I can't stop myself. He quickly overpowers me even as I scream and pound against him. That's when Ash finds us.

"Hey, what's going on?" he asks, but I ignore him, continuing to hit Riku.

"That's enough, Jacinta." Riku's stern voice has me freezing before I sag against him, sobbing and shaking uncontrollably.

Ash must step farther in because the look on his face tells me he's seen the small pile of dirt-filled coke. "Oh no, Jazzy." He sounds so sad, but I just glare at him.

"Fuck you, Ash. You don't get to fucking judge. You, who are under your grandmother's thumb!" I scream at him, lashing out even though I know he doesn't deserve it.

He flinches at the direct hit.

I struggle to get out of Riku's arms, but they are like steel bands around me. "Let me go! I just want a little bit, just enough to get me through the rest of the night," I beg him, but he shakes his head solemnly.

"No, this ends now. You might hate me, but it's for your own good. You have a problem, Jacinta." He picks me up. "Can you gather all her stuff?" he asks Ash, pointing to my upended things. Ash pushes past us to do as he's been asked.

"What are you going to do?" Ash asks as he finishes.

"He's going to put me down and stop treating me like a fucking child," I snarl at the two of them, but they ignore me. My body is shaking too hard for me to really struggle against Riku, and it finally hits me that I'm truly powerless right now. "Please, it hurts," I beg, my anger giving way to desperation.

"Fuck, I had no idea it was so bad," Ash tells Riku.

"I think she's been using every time you've gone out, so almost nonstop for weeks now, minus the few days she was at home."

My anger builds up again as they continue to talk about me as though I'm not here. "Screw you two. You have no idea how I'm feeling."

"Hush now, Jacinta. Stop being a bitch. I think both of us have an idea about how you're feeling," Riku scolds me, and I feel a small wash of shame as I remember his own addiction problems. "Right. Come on. We're going home, and you'll have a shower and sober up. Then we're going to find you a meeting and come up with a plan."

"Please, I don't need a meeting! I can stop at any time. I'm not weak," I sneer, and he looks down at me with hard eyes.

"Jacinta, stop being such a bitch," Ash says wearily. "You're going to regret this."

By now I realize we're moving through the clubhouse, away from the music and the people, toward where we left the car and driver.

"Can you tell the other three what happened?" Riku asks Ash.

"No! Please don't." Somehow, telling the others makes it feel more *real*. Like maybe Riku and Ash are right, and I don't have as much control over this as I thought I did. There's something there, a truth that I don't want to acknowledge. If I can truly stop at any time, why should I be afraid of them knowing? I can just prove it to them... Can't I?

"No, Jacinta. They deserve to know. They want to be in a relationship with you, and you owe it to them to be honest." Riku is firm, and I can see there's no point in arguing with him. Fine, I need a target for all this poison bubbling up in me anyway. Screw them both. I thought they cared about me, but now I know the truth. The only people I can really rely on are my family.

Ash opens the car door, and Riku places me on the seat before retrieving my handbag from Ash.

"We'll see you back at the hotel, yes?"

"Yeah, I'll leave as soon as I've told the others."

"Don't bother," I call out. "I never want to see you again."

"But what about the engagement? What about my sister?"

"We can pretend in public, but stay away from me otherwise. And Riku, you're fired."

Riku snorts. "You're not my boss. Your father is."

"Just you wait until I tell him. You won't last five seconds." I can feel the old me, the pre-movie premiere me, rise up and take control. Bitchy, insecure, coke high Jacinta is fully in play now, and although there's a small part of me that's incredibly ashamed at what is coming out of my mouth, it gets pushed right down. "You'll never work in the industry again."

Ash and Riku exchange a glance, and Riku shoves me over, climbing into the back of the car with me.

"We'll see," he mutters as Ash closes the door and taps on the roof for the driver. I move as far away from Riku as possible. I just have to survive the trip back to the hotel, then I can raid my stash there.

Chapter Twelve

Ashton

I watch the limo drive away with mixed feelings. Sadness for Jacinta, because her head must be really mixed up to have become so dependent on drugs to get through public appearances, but also panic for me because of my grandmother's threat. I just have to hope she regrets what she said and will follow through on the charade.

It feels wrong to be concerned about myself in the face of this. Addiction is no joke, and with the way Jacinta was behaving, it's going to take a real slap in the face to make her admit her problem. But what Riku said is playing over in my mind... She's been using coke to help her get through all these events by my side. Is this partly my fault? If my grandmother marries off my sister, then this was all for nothing. I've added to the destruction of a girl

I've come to truly like and enjoy, and it might all be for fucking nothing.

Sighing, I head back to the party. I don't even make it back to the guys before Camilla has me cornered. "Lord Ashton, what happened to your new fiancée?"

I plaster on a fake smile. "Jazzy wasn't feeling very well, unfortunately, so she had her bodyguard take her home."

Camilla's eyes narrow in suspicion. "Is there a reason for her not feeling well? Maybe the reason for the quick engagement is that the pitter-patter of little feet could be gracing the Summers' mansion soon?"

Before I can answer, Shane pushes between us, ignoring the blogger. "Hey, come on, man. We've got a bottle of champagne to celebrate."

"Shane, how do you feel about Ash asking the woman you have been seen out and about with to marry him? Ash used to be hot and heavy with Alex. Surely you two aren't friends?"

"I can assure you that Ash and I are very much friends, and I couldn't be happier for him and Jacinta. As for Alex, he's also thrilled for the couple." Shane grabs me after giving his sound bite, hustling me away from the barracuda who is most definitely on my grandmother's payroll.

"Thanks, man," I say quietly, and he squeezes my arm.

"You looked like you wanted to punch her in the face. I thought that wouldn't be so good."

I snort at his dry words. "Ya think?"

"Where are Jacinta and Riku?" he asks, sounding concerned. "I thought we were going to play this up for everyone."

I scrub my hand through my hair and shake my head. "Fuck, man, it's all gone so wrong. I had no idea it was so bad."

Shane frowns and pulls me off to a quiet corner. "What do you mean?"

Before I can answer, Jace and Alex join us. Jace is smiling, but there's a hint of worry in his eyes. "Hey, what's going on? We're waiting to toast you."

"Where's Jazzy?" Alex is frowning. "And why do you look so stressed? You're newly engaged. You should be smiling, or people are going to think something is wrong. It's already suspicious that you both disappeared as soon as it happened. Luckily, they think you'd gone off to fuck."

I just stare at the three of them, unable to put my words together. It's hitting me again that I'm mostly responsible for what happened. I mean, I didn't put the coke in her hand. She was doing that before I came along, and she was partying a lot before I made the suggestion that she help me out, but I can't help feeling responsible. I thought she was like me, using to make the party more enjoyable, not using because that's the only way she could stand to be there.

"Ash!" Jace snaps. "Where's Jacinta?"

"Riku found her on the bathroom floor."

"What the fuck? What happened?" Alex looks around like he's searching for them. "Do we need to call an ambulance?"

"No. She'd dropped her coke, and she was trying to sniff it from the floor," I say flatly, and Jace's and Alex's eyes almost fall out of their heads, but Shane looks resigned.

"What?" Jace scoffs. "Jacinta using coke? I don't think so. She's fairly antidrug after everything she went through with her mom. Weed is about all she'll touch."

"No, Ash is right. Apparently, she's been using it to get through the public appearances. She had a bloody nose last week in New Orleans. He told me he suspected then that she's been using it every time they go out."

I sigh. "She and I had a fight before the show in NOLA. She had run out and asked if I had any, but I told her she didn't need to be using it because we would be surrounded by family and friends. She told me she gets anxious when we go out in public. It's been happening since the kidnapping. I guess I misunderstood how strongly she was feeling and how badly this was affecting her."

Jace's mouth has dropped open in shock, but Alex is still looking around. "So where are they now?"

"Riku took her home. She wasn't happy with

either of us when we told her it had to stop. I think he's going to tell her family tomorrow and stage an intervention. She fired him and told me she never wanted to see me again outside of public appearances. I don't know how to do something like that with her. I'm not that good an actor, and she was furious." I feel my whole body shudder. I can't believe I've fucked things up so badly. Not just because I'm worried about Edie and what is going to happen with her and my grandmother, but I think I've fallen a little in love with the feisty heiress. I want to be a part of whatever she's got going on. I want to be one of her men, and it has absolutely nothing to do with the fact that Alex is one of them. I can see how happy he is with Jace and Shane, and I'm incredibly happy for him, but I want my own happiness. With all these realizations, of course, comes an even bigger problem. If I'm publicly with Jacinta, she can never be public with anyone else. My grandmother would never stand for me being associated with Jacinta's unconventional relationship. Oh, sure, she'll love that I'm with a woman, an extremely rich woman at that, but the fact that the woman has more than one boyfriend will be scandalous, and I can't ask them to hide it for the next four years until Edie's of age. How did I ever think this could work?

"Hey, man, it's okay." Shane grabs my shoulder and squeezes, not realizing that my mind is going through more dangerous mental gymnastics than just handling Jacinta's unveiled addiction. "Between us and Riku, we've got this."

"And Cole," Alex chimes in with a cheeky wink, but Shane frowns at him, and it drops.

"As I was saying... Between the six of us, we'll get her fixed up, and while we're at it, we're going to find a solution for you. A way to get your sister out from your grandmother's guardianship. Jacinta, and the rest of us, can't go on as we have been. Shit needs to change if we want to be there for our girl and have a real future with her."

"You'd do that for me?" I look to each of them, searching for hesitation or indecision, but they stare back at me with nothing but confidence.

"Dude, you're a brother-boyfriend now." Jace smiles at Alex's words, his grin only growing wider with my automatic disagreement.

"No, it's not like that between us..." I break off as the three of them chuckle, and Shane shakes his head.

"It's okay. We're not blind. We wouldn't have agreed to the charade if we were opposed to it. We know how intoxicating Jacinta Summers can be. Face it, you're hooked."

I rub a hand over my jaw and heave out another sigh. "Yeah, I am. I can't believe how much her words hurt. It's like I didn't realize how much power she had over me until she used it as a weapon."

"It was the drugs talking. She didn't mean them. When she sobers up tomorrow, she's going to be incredibly ashamed, so we need to give her all the love and support she needs to deal with this." Alex puts his hand on my shoulder, and I feel a shudder run through me. Shit, that's not good.

"Come on, let's go. You should call Cole and tell him all about what happened tonight. I don't think Camilla saw any of the drug stuff, but I'm sure the speculation about her being pregnant will be on all the front pages tomorrow, along with your engagement." Shane is all business as he guides us toward the parking lot. I'd been dropped off here this morning and was hoping to catch a lift home with Jacinta, but I guess I'll be going with the guys. "I'll call Riku when we drop you at the hotel and see if he needs any help. Hopefully, she'll have sobered up by then and can see things more rationally."

He clicks the locks to his car, and it lights up. He and Alex get into the front, leaving me with Jace in the back. As the car pulls out of the parking lot, I drum my finger on the window and watch the darkened streets roll by. I jump when Jace takes my other hand in his and gives it a squeeze, but I squeeze back, thanking him for the comfort. Instead of removing it like I expected him to, he keeps his hand in mine. I should pull away, but the comfort is nice, so I leave it there, holding hands with my ex-boyfriend's boyfriend all the way back to the hotel.

Jacinta

I fume with anger all the way home. I'm so angry with Riku that I can't even look at him. How dare he suggest I have a problem? He doesn't know what it's like to have all those people looking at you, talking about you, and you can bet none of the things they have to say are nice. Nope, they are just trying to figure out how they can use me to get ahead in life. Not to mention the reason I have him. I mean, seriously, he's my bodyguard because I've already been kidnapped once! I can guarantee Peter isn't the only one out there who looks at me and Jax and sees a big-ass payday.

I grab the bottle of whiskey and take a long drink, not bothering with a glass. It burns as it goes down, and I cough a little, but I like the warmth in my stomach. It's the only part of me that actually feels warm, since the rest of me is frozen. Riku frowns, and I flip him off before taking another long draw. If I can't use coke to numb the voices, then whiskey is the next best thing.

It's more dependable than any of these traitors I'm surrounded by.

Even Ash is using me for his personal gain. The panic I could see in his eyes when he thought that I wouldn't follow along with his scheme… Shit, I'm a lot of things, but putting a fourteen-year-old girl at risk is fucking low. I'd never do something like that, and I'm hurt he would think that. A heads-up would have been nice. That's all I ever wanted him to understand, but no, I can't ever have someone just listen to me for fucking once.

When the car pulls into the parking garage at the hotel, I don't wait for Riku. I open my door and stalk toward the private elevator. I can hear him call my name, but I ignore him. He's got a lot of fucking nerve. I just fired him, so I don't have to listen to a fucking thing. Unfortunately, he catches up before I can get the doors to close. He can kiss my ass.

"Jacinta, don't be so childish," he scolds me, and I feel my anger explode.

"Childish? Fuck you, Riku. I fired you! Go away."

The doors to the elevator open, and I storm out, but my steps falter when I see who's waiting in front of my door. I turn to my ex-bodyguard. "Who are you now, my father? You called and fucking tattled on me?"

Cole is wearing a pair of sweats and a T-shirt, and his feet are bare, but he has his laptop in hand. He must hear my words because he scowls, showing none of the warmth that had filled our last interaction.

"Jesus, Jacinta, do you have to be such a huge bitch? For your information, Ash called me and told me that you all needed to speak to me." He looks behind us to the elevator. "Where are they?"

"Who gives a fuck? He can rot in hell as far as I'm concerned." My words are slurred, all the whiskey I had downed on the way back suddenly catching up to me. I stumble into the wall, bouncing off it before continuing to my door. I look down for my handbag and realize I don't have it. Fuck, I'm going to have to go down to reception to ask for another key. *Hang on, maybe Hope's here.*

I push past Cole and bang on the door, the noise echoing through the quiet corridor of the hotel. "Hope, let me in," I call out, hoping she'll hear it.

"Jacinta!" Cole hisses behind me. "Jesus, you're going to wake the whole floor."

"Pfft, no one is up here but us." I flip him off, not looking at him, and bang on the door again.

"Jacinta, I have the key," Riku's quiet voice says from behind me. Spinning around, I eye my bag in his hand.

"Of course you do." I snatch it out of his hand and lean against the door, digging around for my plastic keycard, but I go tumbling back when the door suddenly opens. Hope's cry of surprise makes me snort as I land on my ass. I start to laugh even though there's a sharp pain in my hip where it connected with the floor.

"Jacinta, fuck. What are you doing?" Hope

stares down at me, bleary-eyed, before looking at the two assholes with me. "What's going on?"

I laugh even harder at how confused she sounds.

"The other guys should be here shortly. Let's just move inside," Cole suggests as Riku bends down and grabs me under my arms, hauling me to my feet.

"Don't touch me." I push him away when I'm vertical again and stumble toward my room, banging into the sofa and another wall before I get to my door.

"Jacinta?" Hope sounds worried now, and I feel a little guilty, so I turn around and try to smile for her. With the way she flinches, I'm not sure I succeeded.

"It's fine. *I'm* fine, just a little too much to drink tonight. I'm going to have a shower and then go to bed. I'll see you in the morning," I reassure her before I push through my bedroom. I strip off my clothes, naked by the time I get to my bathroom, and it doesn't take long before the room is filled with steam from the shower. I step in just as Riku enters the bathroom. He leans against the sink, arms crossed.

"What are you doing? Come to look at the goods now that you've blown your chance?"

He shrugs, looking indifferent. "Nothing I haven't seen before." Damn him and his lack of reaction.

"Why don't you hop in, and I'll give you a farewell fuck? Then you can tell all your friends that you got to fuck the heiress." I know my words are hateful, but I can't stop them from flowing out. I've reverted to lashing out at anyone in the line of fire.

"I'm just here to make sure you don't kill yourself on my watch. I'll pass on the rest."

I run my hands over my body and moan when my fingers brush against my clit. "Are you sure you don't want to? I'll even get down on my knees and suck your dick if you want."

The door slams open, and Cole bursts in. He tears open the shower door and reaches in, twisting one of the knobs. I shriek as the water turns freezing cold.

"What the hell, Cole?" Instead of answering, he turns the water off and throws a towel at me.

"Get dry. You'll thank me in the morning." He storms out, not waiting for me to respond.

My teeth start to chatter, but my mind clears a little, and I feel my face blush with embarrassment. Nothing like frigid water to literally cool off a temper and whiskey buzz. Not looking at Riku, I wrap myself up and stumble back to my bed. Throwing back the covers, I climb in and pull them up over my head, not caring that my hair is wet. My eyes are heavy, but I have a sinking feeling that I just completely fucked everything up. Is there a way to come back from this?

My stomach starts to roll, and I struggle to sit

up. Suddenly, Riku is there, holding a garbage can, and I turn my head, expelling the contents of my stomach into it. Over and over, I heave, and the whole time I can feel Riku's hand on my back, rubbing it as he whispers soothing words. Finally, I'm done, and he hands me a glass of water so I can rinse my mouth before spitting it into the trash. I lie back on my bed with a groan, and the tears start to fall. I'm a fucking mess, and I think I may have ruined the best thing that ever happened to me. Muttering a quiet thank you, I roll over and try to sleep. I feel him get up to dispose of the grossness, and although I expect him to leave after that, he comes back and uses a towel to dry my wet hair. I don't talk to him since I wouldn't even know where to start, but just as I drift off, I feel him lean in and kiss my forehead.

"Don't worry, baby, we'll get you sorted out."

Chapter Thirteen

Jace

When we get to the hotel, the three of us accompany Ash up to Jacinta's room, following the directions Cole texted Ash. When we get there, Jacinta and Riku are nowhere to be seen, but Hope and Cole are both there. Cole is in his sweats, and Hope is wearing a pair of pajama pants and a tank top. Clearly, we've disrupted both their evenings, and I'm afraid it's not going to get any better from here.

"Right, now that everyone is here, will someone tell me what the fuck is going on?" Hope demands as Cole lets us into the room.

"Hang on, Riku needs to be here too. Let's just wait until he's done. Poor guy will probably need a drink by the time he gets out here," Cole mutters, sitting down at the table and opening up his laptop.

"He doesn't drink," Shane says as he takes a seat on the sofa, pulling Alex down next to him. He holds a hand out for me to join them, but I shake my head. I need to move. I go to the fridge in their kitchen area and open it to see what's inside. There's a six-pack, so I grab one for me and the other two and hold one up for Cole.

"Yeah, that would be great," he says as his fingers fly across the keyboard.

"Hope?" I ask, and she grimaces and nods.

"Why do I get the feeling this conversation will need something stronger than a beer?"

Ash sighs. "Because you're right." He'd gone straight to the balcony to smoke a cigarette, but he can still hear everything we're saying. "I'll have one, please."

I do the rounds, giving them to Alex, Shane, and Hope before I hand one to Cole, then Ash. Ash grabs my hand before I can go.

"Thank you. For before. You have no idea how much I appreciate it." I flush with the attention from the sexy British man and hurry away to grab my own beer, but a chuckle has me looking toward the couch. Alex is sitting there, and I instantly feel guilty, but my mischievous boyfriend just winks at me. He obviously saw what happened outside. There's nothing to stop them from seeing since the curtains have been pulled back.

I take a sip of my beer and join them on the couch. Hope looks like she's about to explode at any second, but the door to Jacinta's room finally opens, and Riku steps out. The guy looks exhausted. His normally sleek ponytail has strands hanging out of it, and he has bags under his eyes, not to mention his defeated posture. I jump up and grab a bottle of water from the fridge before bringing it back to him just as he takes a seat at the table with Cole. He gives me a grateful nod as I hand him the water.

"Great, everyone's here. Ash, you want to come in now?" Cole calls, and within moments, Ash is back inside, bringing the strong smell of cigarettes with him.

"Okay, so what the fuck happened?" Hope asks before Ash can even take a seat.

"Jacinta has a coke problem." Riku pulls the tie from his hair, finger combing it before tying it back again. This time, instead of the ponytail or braid he usually wears, he puts it into a man bun.

Coke? Seriously? I'm still not sure I can convince myself to believe it. I'm waiting for this to be some kind of morbid joke with a shitty punch line. When we were in Prague, she explained all about her mother and the meth-fueled rages and swore she would never touch drugs because of that. Has the kidnapping really affected her so much that she sought solace in something she swore she never would? And how did we not notice it? I feel sick with guilt that I hadn't looked beneath the facade she's been projecting and noticed what was going on below. Is it our fault? Have we rushed her, or should we have not given her space when it all first happened? Maybe if we had been there for her from the start, none of this would have happened.

"What? She's drinking too much Coke? How is that a problem?" Hope sounds annoyed, and if the situation wasn't so drastic, I'd be tempted to laugh at her question.

"No, not the drink, the white powder kind of problem," Alex chimes in, miming snorting, and Hope pales, speechless.

We all give her a minute, letting her process what has to be heartbreaking news, but then she starts shaking her head. "No way! Not a fucking chance. Drugs fucked up her mother, so she never touches anything harder than weed."

"She's been using it every time she has to make a public appearance. If I think back to the first event we escorted her to, that fashion award thing, then I'd say she was using alcohol to self-medicate before she found a source for the coke. She got blitzed, and we had to help her home. The coke use had to start after that because there was a visible change. She was terrified to go to that awards show, but after that, it was like there were two Jacintas. Everyday Jacinta, then bubbly, larger-than-life Jacinta."

"I saw her using on her birthday," Cole admits, and Hope whirls on him.

"Was this before or after you fucked her in the closet?"

Cole grimaces. "Same time. I didn't think anything of it. It was a party."

Oh snap! I knew there was something more between the two of them. I watch on with amusement as Alex's jaw drops open, and he waves a hand in Cole's direction. "You and Jacinta?"

"Yeah, but it was a one-time thing. She didn't even know who I was, just a stranger in a mask. It meant nothing to her." He keeps protesting, but I'm not the only one who notices that he didn't say it meant nothing.

"But did it mean something to you?" Shane asks what I was thinking even though Hope is still glaring at him.

"At first, no. It was a quick fuck in the closet, which we both enjoyed, but the more time I spent with her, the more I realized I misjudged her, and... I can't deny that I have feelings. More than I ever thought I would."

"Okay, this is good!" Alex claps his hands. "Let's lay it all out on the table. I think we've been pussyfooting around admitting to each other what's going on. Let the first official family meeting of Jacinta Summers' brother-boyfriends come to order."

The room is silent as we all stare at my boyfriend and the smug grin plastered on his face. Hope sputters a couple of times before clearing her throat. "Yes, well, okay, I'm happy you are all on the same page... sort of, but what about Jazzy? I just don't understand how it has come to this. Why has she been using coke?"

"She told me that since the kidnapping, she hasn't been able to escape the feeling of continuously being watched." Riku nods, confirming what Ash just shared.

"But that's nothing new. She's always been watched," Hope argues. "Why would that push her over the edge?"

Ash continues as I pace back and forth across the carpet. "But now she has all these doubts about everyone and everything. She second-guesses who wants things from her or is using her to social climb or get ahead in life. She's also worried about being kidnapped again. She feels worthless, like she did nothing to stop Peter and what Jaxon and Harlow both went through. It's kind of survivor's guilt, I think? Then all the ugly shit her mother said to her as a child is also playing a pretty big part of it."

"She hasn't seen her therapist in weeks," Riku adds, "despite what she's telling everyone."

"This is all my fault, my stupid plan to help Neighpalm Industries. I had no idea how much she hated the spotlight, and I also had no idea the lengths she'd go to for her family. I'm supposed to understand the family so I can protect you all and the company, but I didn't open my eyes to Jacinta until the truth was shoved in my face. I'm such a fucking idiot. She's part of the family I'm supposed to keep safe from all those vultures on the outside."

Cole sounds devastated, and Ash steps up behind him and puts his hand on his shoulder, giving it a squeeze before taking a seat in the chair next to him.

"Dude, I can share the guilt. I wouldn't have asked her to play along with me if I'd known the full extent of what she's going through. I just thought she didn't like media attention, not that it affected her mentally and emotionally."

"Stop, just stop!" Hope stands up. "There's no point in playing the blame game. Jacinta is an adult who could have said no at any stage, but she turned to drugs instead of talking to me or Harlow or anyone who would have helped. Let's put the blame where it firmly belongs, and that is on her. Those choices have been made by her, and now all we can do is help her get through the aftermath and road to recovery."

"I think we need to get her out of the city, away from all of this shit," I tell them quietly. My brain has been whirling while I've been listening to everyone. "I think she needs to start therapy again and maybe go visit her new holdings. She needs a distraction, something to work toward. She's always happiest when she's doing something. Willow Castle helped with that for a while, but staying at Brad's place is still too close to all the negative things that drove her to this point in the first place."

"That's actually a good idea." Riku rubs a hand across his chin. "She can join a narcotics anonymous group online, so we can get her away from all of this."

Shane and Alex are nodding. "Good thinking. Riku, you'll go with her?" Alex asks, and Riku nods.

"Yeah, she won't be able to get rid of me. I've been through this, so I know all the stages. It's probably best if you guys stay away for a while, but I'll let you know the minute she's good to see you again, I promise."

"What about Ash's grandmother?" I ask, because I can see how worried the man is.

"We can spin a story that will keep her occupied while I look into getting custody of my sister. Jacinta said that Forrest had a great family lawyer as one of partners, so I think it's time I tried again."

"That's a good idea. I'll set up a meeting for you." Hope sits back down and heaves out a sigh. "And all that leaves is to tell the family."

"Can you set me up a meeting too, please?" Cole's been quiet for a while, but he suddenly jumps in. "I need some custody advice as well."

"Yeah, no problem."

"Jacinta is going to hate telling everyone," Alex says quietly. "I think we should just see Brad for now, or maybe him and Grace and Howard. Harlow and the brothers don't need to know until she's in a stronger place and able to handle their reactions. If they don't handle it the right way, that worthlessness and self-loathing could spiral into even more dangerous choices. They'll forgive us for the secret once Jacinta is back to herself again."

"Agreed," Hope says. "Okay, I'm going to sleep with Jazzy to make sure she's alright. Just shut the door when you all leave."

With that, she waves bye to us and takes her leave. I finally stop pacing and collapse into her vacated seat.

"Alright, let's address the elephant in the room," Alex says, standing up as Shane wraps his arm around my shoulder and gives me a kiss on the temple. "All six of us are into Jacinta, right?" We all give him some kind of confirmation. "Excellent, and everyone is aware that no one is prepared to bow out?" Again, we all nod. "Good, so this is going to be a full-court press as soon as Riku gives us the okay. We will be there for her wherever, whenever, and however she needs us, right?"

"Absolutely, but I will have custody of Spencer, and if we can get Ash's sister out from under their grandmother, he will have custody of her, so whatever happens, we need to take both of them into account." Cole is finally all in. It took him a while to wrap his head around the fact that he was totally wrong about who Jacinta is, but I'm glad he's finally there. I think Jacinta would have been disappointed if he'd wanted out, not that she would have told us or acted any differently, but we would have known.

"Right, so we need a plan. Are we going to live

together, and where?" Shane asks next to me, and I snort.

"Good luck prying Jacinta out of her wing at her dad's place."

"We can't get ahead of ourselves. She's pretty fucking angry at me and Ash at the moment." Riku sounds so sad that my heart aches for him. He's been by her side this whole time, and I can't imagine how hard it's been for him. He's supposed to protect her from threats, but he's been unable to protect her from one of the most dangerous ones— herself. "We need to take this day by day. She may decide that a seven-way relationship is not what she wants. Let's get her addiction sorted before we make any decisions about the future."

We all reluctantly agree, knowing it was the drugs talking, not her, but that doesn't erase the wounds that her words inflicted. As much as we all forgive her in theory, the ones she lashed out at may need their own time to be ready to show that forgiveness in action, like trusting her with their hearts and taking the leap to fully commit. They'll probably need to hear from Jacinta herself that she truly doesn't believe in anything she said to them.

"Fine, but if you get the chance to knock her up, do it. I want to be a daddy, and I want her to be the mommy. I don't care if it's one of your swim-mers that gets the job done," Alex declares, and we all stare at him, speechless, before I pick up a pillow and throw it at him. I'm pretty sure Alex has a breeding kink or something. Yeah, I think we're all wordlessly agreeing to ignore any contribution he made in the last sixty seconds.

"Okay, so we all meet back here in the morning. We'll get Brad to come here, that way she can't avoid the conversation or escape it, and we'll go from there." Shane stands up and pulls me with him.

"All hands in!" Alex whisper-shouts and puts his hand out. The rest of us ignore him, and Ash, Riku, and Cole wave goodbye to the three of us as we take our leave. Shane and I hold hands while Alex grumbles all the way down to the car.

"Don't worry, babe. We've got this." Shane squeezes my hand before opening the door for me so I can slide in. "And if we fail, Alex will just knock her up so she'll have no other choice." I smirk as Shane teases our boyfriend who flips us both off as he slides into his seat.

"I'm going to be a great dad, just you wait and see."

Chapter Fourteen

Jacinta

My mouth feels like the Sahara, and my head is pounding as I roll over in bed. What the fuck happened last night? I bring my hand up to my face to shield my eyes when something hard bangs against my skin. I pry my eyes open, and they just about fall out of my head when I see the diamond engagement ring on my left ring finger. What the fuck?

I scramble through my memories of yesterday and groan when I get to the relevant ones. No, not the one of me agreeing to marry Ash, but the one of my complete and utter embarrassment in front of Riku and Ash and even Cole. Jumping out of bed, I stumble for the bathroom and hurl up what's left in my stomach. Which is nothing, really, because I'd already done this in front of Riku last night.

I'm sprawled across the bathroom floor, hanging on the toilet seat, groaning, when a pair of feet appear in front of me. I feel a small amount of relief at the fact that they are dainty, with toes painted a pretty coral color. My eyes scan up the body of the person in front of me, and I moan internally because she's got her hands on her hips and her lips pursed in annoyance. I wonder if anyone's told her she looks constipated when she does that. The foot in front of me starts tapping.

"No one has ever told me that I look constipated when I purse my lips, so thank you for the delightful start to my day." *Oh fuck, I said it out loud?* "Just a little?" she tells me, holding up her fingers.

"Kill me now." I lean my forehead against the toilet seat.

"Seems like you're giving it a good go yourself. Who knows what's on that seat that might kill you." Hope sounds conversational, but I'm pretty sure the beast is waiting to explode. "You bet your ass the anger beast is waiting to explode, but I'd like you upright and looking at me when it happens." Oh Jesus, I said it out loud again? What the fuck is wrong with me?

"Maybe your inner filter is broken because of all the *coke* you've been using!" She shouts that last little bit, and I try to slump even farther down, but she growls, scoops her hands under my arms, and hauls me to my feet. Then she turns on the shower, strips off my clothes, and unceremoniously shoves me in. I brace myself for the cold, but she's not as cruel as Cole was, so it's warm water that rushes over my body. Groaning, I slide down the tiles until I'm sitting at the bottom of the shower with the unrelenting pounding of water raining down on my head.

"Hope, I fucked up," I mutter.

"I'm sorry. What did you say?" Hope asks even though I know damn well she heard me.

"I fucked up," I say a little louder.

"You're damn right you fucked up. To be honest, I just don't know what to say. I don't know if I'm more angry or hurt that you didn't think you could talk about any of it with me. I'm certainly angry that you didn't talk to your therapist about any of it, and I'm damn angry at the fact that you went along with first Cole, then Ash's plan, knowing full well you were going to have to use fucking cocaine to get through any of it! What the fuck were you thinking?" Hope's angry voice is echoing around the bathroom as she reaches the height of her rant.

I can't look up at her, so I just close my eyes and lean my head back against the tiled wall. "I don't know. I guess I wasn't. I just really wanted to help the family out, especially because I was so useless during the whole kidnapping thing. Plus, how could I resist the chance to save Ash's sister from his grandmother's horrifying threat to marry her off? This was my way to be the hero, I guess."

"What a load of fucking bullshit." Hope sounds disgusted, but she can't be more disgusted than I am with myself.

"And the thought of Ash's sister having that hang over her head makes me see red."

"Well, you're not wrong there, and we need to help him with that, but we could have done it differently. I had no idea you were using cocaine to get through all those events. Fuck, Jacinta, where did you even get it from?"

"From the safe at Willow Castle," I mutter quietly, and instead of the explosive reaction I expect, she's silent, so I risk looking at her.

Her mouth has dropped open, and I think I've rendered her speechless. "I... I... But—but what?" She can't seem to form a sentence. Finally, she tosses her hands up in the air. "Seriously? I just can't with you." She walks out of the bathroom, and I take that as my cue to get to my feet and wash myself.

After getting out of the shower and cleaning my teeth, I wander back into my bedroom and look at the time on my phone. It's ten in the morning, and my rumbling stomach tells me I need some food, so I get dressed as quickly as this vicious hangover will let me. I can hear murmured voices out in the living area, and I assume it's Hope talking to Riku.

Flashes of last night come rushing back into my

mind, and I sink down onto my bed in horror. I said such horrible things. God, I was such a bitch to him. I hope he can forgive me. And Ash? Poor Ash, I made him think I didn't care about him or his sister. I have so many apologies to make. He's more than just some deal to me, and so is his sister even though I've never met her.

Taking a deep breath, I head out into the living area, and when I open my door, all eyes shoot to me. Not only are Hope and Riku here, but all of the other guys as well. I feel so overwhelmed with all of their attention on me and the horrible knowledge that every one of them knows what levels I've sunk to that I can't help the tears that start to roll down my face. I slap a hand over my mouth to stop the sob from breaking free, but before I can do anything, Jace is there, his arms wrapped around me, his soothing Southern accent whispering words of comfort.

I sag into his embrace, letting his warmth engulf me, and let go. I let go of everything that I've been holding inside of me since we first got kidnapped, since I heard my twin had been shot and didn't know if he would make it. Since I heard my mother had been killed by Julia, and that her act of giving us to Brad was actually her way of protecting us. Since I found out that maybe, just maybe, my bio dad was out there somewhere. Finally, the emotions run out, and I feel exhausted. Pulling away from Jace, I discover that we're now on the couch. Alex is on the other side of me, holding one of my hands. Everyone else is just sitting around, waiting for me to calm down. Through tear-filled eyes, I see Riku, and I hold a hand out to him. "I'm so fucking sorry. I was such a bitch."

He comes over to me and pulls me into his arms now. His unique scent fills my senses, and I instantly feel myself relax into him. "It's okay. I understand the nature of the beast. That wasn't you talking. I know it was the addiction." Frowning, I try to struggle out of his arms, shaking my head, but he holds on tight.

"I'm not addicted. I can stop at any time," I tell him weakly, and I feel him sigh deeply.

"No, Jacinta, you have an addiction. It may be only certain situations that trigger it, but you have a problem, and the first step is admitting that."

His words make my stomach roll, but deep down I know he's right. Sighing, I manage to step back from him, though I grab his hand so he doesn't take it as a rejection. "I know you're right, but saying it out loud makes it real."

"Saying it out loud is the first step to recovery." I spin around as Shane's gravelly voice draws my attention. It's his turn to pull me into a hug, and I let him. "We will be with you every step of the way if you need us, and if you want us to back off, you just have to say the word." I hear Alex scoff at that, and I hide my smile against Shane's shoulder. I don't think anything short of a bulldozer will get Alex to budge.

"I know you're right, but it's hard, you know?" I pull away and look for the other two men in the room.

Spotting Cole, I head over to him. Time to stop pussyfooting around this. The look on his face as I approach him is almost funny, but I don't smile because I don't want him to think I'm not taking this seriously. He stands like a soldier, stiff as a board, with his arms by his side, bracing for what I assume is an impact, but all I do is wrap my arms around his delicious form and put my head against his chest. "Thank you for last night," I whisper to him as his arms slowly come up to embrace me. "Thank you for stopping me from making things so much worse."

"You're welcome." He still sounds unsure, so I pull back.

"Cole, I like you. I don't know how it happened because you were an absolute asshole to me, but I feel like part of that had to do with the incredible chemistry we had and not knowing what to do with it. As you know, I'm in a relationship with more than one man, so you would always have to share me with them, but if you are interested, I would very much like to see where this goes." I know I probably sound ridiculous, bringing this up with him so formally a few minutes after puking my guts out, my eyes a bleary mess and my head pounding, but I know I have a lot of shit to take care of, and I need this chaos inside me soothed as much as can be. Before I can fix myself, I need the other rough edges of my life smoothed out.

It's amusing seeing this man completely speechless. His mouth is moving, but nothing is coming out of it, so instead of waiting for an answer, I close the distance between us and kiss him. He's slow to react, but when he does, he kisses me back with enthusiasm before he puts a little space between us.

"I would very much like that, but your recovery is more important than anything else." I feel a quick sting of rejection and start to pull away, but he holds on tight. "I'm not saying no, but I think your focus needs to be on that for now. That's more important than anything else if we want to have a relationship because I don't come on my own. I'm a two-for-one package, so you need to decide if you want Spencer in your life, because I am about to become his main parent, and he will always and forever come first for me. Like Riku said, the addiction trigger might be situational, but I can't start a relationship with you until you have it under control. My son can't have the unpredictability of an addict in his life."

My shoulders relax again as I mull over his words. He makes a good point, and I admire how he's putting Spencer first. That's all I ever wanted my mom to do for me and Jax. "Don't worry about me. I am fully aware how much Spencer means to you, and I wouldn't want it any other way." His arms drop, and I step away from him. There's a worried crease between his eyes.

"So we're good?" he asks.

"Yeah, we are." My eyes drift away, looking for the last person I need to apologize to. Ash is nowhere to be seen, but I'm sure I saw him when I first came out. Out of the corner of my eye, I see the curtains across the balcony flutter and smell a hint of cigarette smoke.

"Give me a moment," I tell everyone else in the room, and, twisting the ring on my finger, I head outside to speak to Ash, the one I probably hurt the most. What was supposed to start out as something fun, the two of us playing a part to fool his evil grandmother, turned into something just a little more serious. Alex did warn me he was very easy to fall for.

Pushing aside the curtains, I step outside into an overcast, slightly damp California day. Everything on the balcony is damp, and Ash is leaning against the wall farther down beneath the overhang so he doesn't get wet in the slight drizzle that seems to be falling.

I make my way to him, and I know he's seen me by the way his whole body gets tense, but he doesn't look at me. He just continues to puff away on his cigarette, the bright orange end of it glowing with every puff. Sliding in next to him, I bump my hip against his.

"Hi," I say to him, looking out over the LA skyline.

He grunts his greeting but doesn't stop smoking, and I grin.

"Oh so elegant for an English lord," I tease, and he shrugs. "Look, Ash, I'm so sorry. I fucked everything up, and I hope you can forgive me."

He huffs and drops his cigarette, violently stomping it out with his foot before whirling around to face me. "You didn't fuck up. This is all my fault. Please don't hate me and please don't make Edie pay for my mistakes." He sounds desperate as he steps in front of me, grabbing my biceps. "Please. If I had known how much you hated appearing in public, I never would have asked you to do this. If I had known that you were using to get through it all, I would have backed off. I thought it was a hit here or there for fun. I'm so sorry, Jacinta. Will you ever forgive me?"

"Oh, Ash." I reach up and cup his cheek with my hand. "None of this is on you. I'm a big girl, an adult, and I made these decisions. Nobody forced me to do it. I hate to admit it, but my ego got involved. When you asked me to help you, it felt good. Like for once I wasn't a burden and I was able to help. Same with when Cole asked me to help my family. Finally, I could make a contribution to them, to the people who loved me unconditionally and looked after me when my mother threw us away like old junk. So, no, you are not to blame.

How can I blame you when all you were trying to do is keep your sister safe? I will continue to help you do that. I'll have Cole draw up a press release announcing our engagement and how thrilled the Summers are that you will be joining our party, then we'll work together to find a way to get your sister away from that dragon. I promise." He sinks to his knees, a sob bursting from his mouth, and rests his head against my stomach.

"Thank you. God, thank you." He hugs me tightly around my waist, and I run my hands through his hair before pulling him to his feet.

"You may need to be patient with me. Apparently, I have a problem, and I need to get that sorted, so public appearances are out for now."

"Whatever you need, I'm all in." We're quiet for a moment as I stare into his beautiful brown eyes, and I take a deep breath. I swore from now on I wouldn't hide from what I needed or wanted, so I need to ask.

"Is this still pretend? Or are we… something?" I ask him, and for the first time, he loses that haunted look. A wry smile lifts his lips.

His hands slip from my own, and he rests them on my waist as he shuffles a little closer. "I don't know, are we? Do you want us to be?" he asks in a slightly teasing manner, but I know him well enough now. He defaults to light and playful when he doesn't want to risk being hurt.

"Look, I know that I will never be enough for

you, that your interest lies in both sexes, and I would never want to begrudge you that, but that is a conversation you need to have with other people. If this is something you are truly interested in, then you need to be monogamous within our circle."

Ash snorts and throws his head back in laughter. "Babe, that time in the closet was the first time I tried to get laid in a good six months. You shouldn't believe everything you read," he scolds, and I feel my cheeks turn pink.

"Touché." I give him that one, and his laughter stops.

"But seriously, what I feel for you is something I haven't felt in a long time, not since Alex, and I really am interested in seeing where this takes us. I will need to have a conversation with the other three, mostly to clear the air. I have no designs on Alex. I am happy for him, and he deserves what he has with Shane and Jace. I don't want to get in the way of that."

I raise an eyebrow, and his smile turns sheepish.

"I mean, if they invited me to join them, I wouldn't say no. Have you seen the three of them?"

It's my turn to giggle now. "Yeah, I know what you mean."

He raises his eyebrows in surprise. "So the three of you haven't…" He leaves it hanging, and I shake my head.

"No, not yet. I mean, there was that time in

New Orleans with Shane and Alex in the tomb, but not all three yet."

"Oh, you dirty bird, I want to hear *all* about that."

"Okay, so we're good? I don't know what the plan is yet, but whatever happens, I want you to be included, and we'll figure out a solution for Edie. I promise."

He leans in and gives me a gentle kiss, the first we've exchanged that feels genuine. This isn't for show. It's sweet and romantic, a promise of things to come, but with no pressure, which I appreciate.

"Let's go back inside. And make sure you speak to the others. I want full transparency between us all now."

"I like the sound of that." He takes me by the hand and drags me back inside to face the rest of the music.

Chapter Fifteen

Jacinta

When I push through the curtains, the sight that greets me has me wanting to turn and leap off the balcony to get away from what's about to happen. The rest of my guys and Hope are still waiting for us, but Dad, Nana, and Poppy are sitting there too, drinking coffee and talking with them all. I feel a small rush of anger, but it all disappears when my eyes meet Riku's. I can see him bracing for it, and that look in his eyes throws me back to my own childhood, to the moments where I would try to steel my spine so I could withstand one of my mother's tirades. God, I'm such a bitch. All he's been doing is looking after me this whole time, going above and beyond the requirements of his job because he cares for me.

"Ah, there you are, sweetheart. It's lucky you

two came in. Nana was just about at the end of her polite patience, ready to come and drag you in." Poppy grins and stands up, coming over to give me a hug. Ash lets go of my hand in favor of finding a spare section of wall to lean against.

"We love you," Poppy whispers into my hair as he kisses me on the temple and pulls away. He's always been an astute man, so he must know something is wrong for them to have been summoned here.

He leads me over to the sofas and helps me take a seat across from Nana and Dad. Both give me a kiss.

"Hey, honey. What's going on? Cole called and asked us to come in before we went to the office this morning." Dad's looking a little confused, but Nana has a grin a mile wide on her face.

"Does it have anything to do with the rock on your finger?" Trust her eagle eyes to catch sight of that before anyone else.

Dad's eyes widen in surprise, then he looks around at the six men like he's trying to figure out which one gave me the ring. It would be comical if the next part wasn't going to be so hard to admit.

"Yes and no. The ring is from Ash, a part of the plan to keep his grandmother off his back. She issued an ultimatum last night, and his sister was going to pay the price of his failure." Nana's glee turns to anger in an instant. Let me tell you, the woman is the most easygoing person until you fuck with her family or friends, and she's obviously decided that Ash counts as one of them.

"Howard, get Forrest on the phone. We need his best family court lawyer. We are going to get this sorted once and for all. Maybe we need a PI to investigate if Elizabeth has anything that excludes her from being a good guardian. A drinking problem or gambling? The money for the estate has to have gone somewhere, and Ash's dad has been dead for years."

"I'll call him when we are done here," Poppy assures his wife, and she nods, appeased for the moment.

"Okay, so what's the other thing you wanted to talk about?" Dad asks now that my grandparents are on Ash's case.

Before I can answer, Cole jumps in. "I'm afraid the next thing is completely my fault, and I have my letter of resignation for you. I had no idea the trouble it would cause when I asked Jacinta to help me with something, and for that I am truly sorry." He hands a piece of paper to my dad, who accepts it with a frown.

"Okay, but that still doesn't tell me what's going on. Care to elaborate?"

"When I came on with the company, there were some pretty persistent rumors being bandied around the business community—how Neighpalm Industries is in trouble, the Summers are fighting, that Harlow had led the boys astray with their illicit romance, and it was just the start of the company's downfall. All of these rumors stemmed from one person, Urie Sokolov, but it was enough to scare shareholders into selling, and the shares were being snatched up by Diamant Unlimited. I came up with a plan that would take the spotlight off all of you and put it firmly on Jacinta so we could have focused damage control efforts instead of being spread so widely and so thin." Dad's frown deepens. "I was under the impression that it wouldn't be a problem since she appeared in the gossip columns on a regular basis. She stepped down as CEO of Couture, and by drawing the public's eyes to her, they wouldn't be paying any attention to the rest of you."

Nana, Dad, and Poppy exchange confused glances. "So what's the problem? Why have you called us here?"

Cole starts to talk, but I need to put on my big girl pants and admit what I've been doing to get through it all. Wringing my hands, I look down at my lap, unable to meet their eyes.

"Since the kidnapping, all my issues that I worked on with my therapist came screaming back. The feelings of uselessness and worthlessness that my mother screamed into me. On top of that, there was the fact that I wasn't able to do anything to help Jax and Harlow, being responsible for what they went through with Peter. It was all too much. When I was out in public, I was conscious of all the gossipy whispers that surrounded me, of the people using me to get ahead in life. Of the fact that I have no real, genuine friendships… And, well, I started using cocaine to cope with being surrounded by all of this."

"Oh, Jazzy." Nana reaches over and grabs hold of my hand. "What were you thinking? Why?"

"I was thinking that I could finally be of use to my family! I could finally be the one that was saving all of you. That, for the first time in my life, I wouldn't be a burden. If I needed the coke to do that, well, it was only when I went out. I was fine any other time, or that's what I kept telling myself, but the guys have helped me see I have a problem, and I need to do something about it."

Dad stands up and runs a hand through his hair.

"Shit, I wish you'd come to see me about this." He doesn't sound angry, just resigned.

"In Cole's defense, I thought it was a good idea too. I helped fuel a rumor that Jacinta was on the outs with you, that her partying wasn't family approved. But then the Ash situation came up, and we decided that it would be good cover for both of them." I'm not surprised Hope is admitting her part in this. She's never been one to let anyone else suffer for her mistakes.

Dad paces across the room before whirling back to face us. He starts to say something when Poppy puts his hand up. "Easy now, Brad. We are partly to blame for this because we've been trying to handle it quietly. Maybe we should have shared what we've been doing with the others. They are adults, but we weren't including them as they should have been. Fortunately, or maybe *un*fortunately in this case, you raised kids who will stop at nothing to protect their family and your legacy. We should have trusted them with what was happening."

It's my turn to look confused as Dad takes a deep breath and blows it back out, nodding at my grandpa.

"We knew all about the rumors, of course, and what they have been trying to do to the company." Poppy sighs. "While they have been distracted by trying to buy us up, we've been doing the same thing. They have been so distracted they haven't noticed that a small company by the name of Incendiary Unlimited has been buying up all their shares. As of yesterday, Incendiary Unlimited, which is a nicely hidden subsidiary of Neighpalm, is the majority shareholder in Diamant Unlimited. Urie Sokolov is not going to be particularly popular with them anymore. He'll be too busy worrying about keeping himself alive to mess with what we're doing."

"Dad and I plan on doing a complete overhaul of that company and rebranding it. It has a horrible reputation with its blood diamond business, and we want to distance ourselves from any of that. We've actually been in talks with the FDOC about sending in an undercover operative to help clean out all the bad. So, really, you don't need to worry about any of that. We are on top of it even though we kept it quiet to limit the risk of it getting out."

"Again, I apologize for overstepping my duties. I should have spoken to you about what we were planning." Cole sounds contrite, and I feel so bad for him. He's now jobless, which means he will be asked to leave his apartment, and that will undoubtedly affect his ability to get full custody of Cole. I squeeze Nana's hand and nod subtly at him.

"Bullshit, Cole. This is all news to me as well, so you cannot be blamed for making choices while not knowing all the facts." Poppy shifts uncomfortably on the sofa next to Nana, and I totally get that. The tone of her voice says a reckoning is coming when the two of them are alone. "We will not be accepting your resignation. You'll just have to work hard with the new company, making it look shiny and new to the public eye, to make up for it."

Dad looks down at the piece of paper in his hand, and I can see the wheels turning before he rips it up and tosses it in a trash can in the kitchen. "Mom is right. You are an asset, and we should have been more transparent. From now on, we're *all* going to be transparent when it comes to important family business." Dad looks to Cole, then Hope, who quickly agrees.

"Right, and as for you, missy…" Nana turns her gaze onto me. "If it wasn't for you, we never would have known what was going on or who was behind the kidnapping. It was because of you that we were able to put everything together and find Harlow and Jaxon. It was because of you that Jaxon survived. If we didn't know the story, they never would have looked at Luke's parentage and worked out that Patricia was his mother. So stop blaming yourself for any of that. You are a hero, and we are forever grateful to you. You helped the family when we were all floundering."

Nana's words wash over me like a warm hug as I think back to what happened. I guess she's right, but that's not how I saw it. Maybe I just needed to hear about it from another perspective.

"But I *am* disappointed about the fact that you gave up speaking to your therapist. You know how much it helped you before, and it makes me very sad that you're letting your mother's words influence you again. Therapy can be short-term, or it can be a lifelong journey. What matters is that you put the work into what you need to be your healthiest, best self. It doesn't matter how long it takes. We will all love you and support you even if you go to appointments until the end of your days."

"Yes, I agree with Mom." Dad takes a seat on the sofa next to me and wraps his arms around my shoulders, pulling me into a hug. "This is what is going to happen. You are going to start seeing your therapist again—at least twice a week if we can arrange that. You will need to join a meeting as well." He breaks off and looks a little lost, not knowing how to go about that.

Riku jumps in to help him out. "I can organize that. There's an online option, so Jacinta can attend no matter where she is geographically."

"Excellent, because my next suggestion is that you get out of LA for a while, maybe away altogether. Don't you think it's time you had a look at some of the places you inherited?" Dad suggests gently, but I can see he's not going to take no for an answer.

"Okay," I agree, saying the only thing I can right now, and he hugs me even tighter.

"Good girl, kiddo. I don't want you returning until the thought of going out in public doesn't cause crippling fear. I want the old Jacinta back, the take no prisoners, ball busting Jacinta who laughs in the face of the paparazzi."

"You just need to learn to deal with your insecurities in a healthy way. Before, you would lash out at people like you did Harlow. When you stopped doing that, you found another way to cope with it. Your therapist will help you with *healthy* coping mechanisms."

"And you never have to go out in public alone again. I mean, you have got me after all." The guys have been quiet through the whole thing, but Alex speaks up now, unable to help himself, and it dissolves a bit of the tension when he gets a chuckle out of my dad. "Or any of us really," he adds, and my dad's arm tightens again, just minutely, before I feel him relax.

I guess having another one of his other daughters in a multi-men relationship is not easy to swallow, but he does such a good job of hiding it. I'm sure there is a conversation in the future for these guys, much like the one he had with my brothers. Poor Dad, I would almost bet money that he's going to have to have the same conversation again with the McCallisters, but that's the price you pay for having three daughters. Heaven help him if the next two are girls as well. By the time they are teenagers, they are not going to want traditional relationships if all their sisters don't have them. God, I want to laugh, but I'll wait for a more appropriate time. Maybe when Hope, Harlow, and I are alone.

"Thank you. All of you. I promise I will do everything in my power to get over this. I should have spoken up sooner. I know all of this is on me, and I don't want any of you blaming yourselves." My gaze goes to Cole and Ash specifically, because I know the two of them are beating themselves up about it. It then slides to Riku. "Riku, you'll be coming with me, right?"

Dad gives me another squeeze. "Yes, we feel that it would be prudent for you to have a permanent bodyguard. You're a very wealthy woman now and could be the target for some more unsavory ideas. Normally, I would suggest you not hide the fact that you're also in a relationship." Riku stands up and starts to argue, but Dad cuts him off. "Sit down. I will make a guess that you haven't done anything too unethical, though I see the way my daughter looks at you and you at her. It's a matter of time. But for Ash's sister's sake, for the moment, we need to make it look like she's only in a relationship with him. So you four will stay back in the States and continue on with your lives." He points to Jace, Alex, Shane, and Cole, who start to argue. "I didn't say you couldn't visit for work purposes. Maybe Jace needs to consult with Jacinta or Shane needs to photograph her estates for insurance purposes. Maybe Cole needs to visit to implement a publicity campaign for Ash and Jacinta's engagement." Dad's suggestion appeases the guys, and they settle down. "Ash and Riku will accompany Jacinta."

"I think the castle in Romania would be the best place to start. It's fairly remote and a good place for her to do some healing. It's also one of the biggest, so it may take the longest time to catalog." Poppy is looking at something on his phone. I'm assuming it's a list of my and Jax's assets. "While you're there, you can decide if you want to keep it or get rid of it, then we can either appoint an estate manager or a real estate agent."

I know I should probably kick up an argument about them making decisions for me, but it's kind of nice having it all taken out of my hands. Decision-making is outside my wheelhouse at the moment, which really highlights that I need therapy again. "Okay, that sounds good. But are we sure there's internet out there?" Poppy and Dad assure me they will make sure there is so I can do my therapy and attend NA meetings.

Nana claps her hands together in glee once the final details are agreed on. "Excellent! And while you are dealing with all of that, Hope and I will keep the tabloids busy with snippets of wedding plans, which should keep his nasty grandma off your tails until we can sort all of that out."

Chapter Sixteen

A month later

Jacinta

The snow on the peaks of the Carpathian Mountains shines brightly as the sun peeks through the clouds for the first time in days. I wrap my arms around me as I look out over the mountain range from the master bedroom balcony of the castle. Yup, the Bucătaru estate is an honest-to-goodness, gothic-style, Vlad the Impaler inspired castle, with parapets and a drawbridge and turrets. I mean, I shouldn't have been surprised considering the place back home, but this makes that look like a two-story house. There are so many rooms in this house that I don't think I've gotten to all of them in the month we've been here.

Turning from the gorgeous sight, I head over to

the fireplace and throw another piece of wood on the flames. Most of the castle is thermally heated by the hot springs that run underneath its foundation, but up here, at the top of the turret, more is needed at this time of the year.

When we first arrived, we discovered the castle had been kept in good repair by an appointed family who had worked for the Bucătarus for years. They had spent the last twenty years making sure it didn't crumble into disrepair. They greeted me like I was their own long-lost family member and have been a blessing. A couple in their fifties, Andrei and Ana Marie still take care of all of our needs. We've kept to only using a few rooms in the house —the kitchen, a living area, and a couple of bedrooms.

The wood crackles and burns, the sound comforting in the quiet room. When Ana Marie first showed me the room, I thought I'd been carried back a couple of centuries. The room has slate flooring and raw stone walls, which do little to hold in the heat. The carpets underfoot were threadbare, so that was one of the first things we replaced. The dark wood and wrought iron bed frame is so big an army could sleep in it, but the brocade curtains were moth ridden and dusty, as was the mattress, so they joined the pile in the dumpster. Within days, all those things were replaced. It's amazing what money and a family name can do, no matter where you are in the world.

This time, it wasn't the Summers' name paving the way, but I was okay with that.

A cozy writing corner is where I've set up my laptop for my NA meetings and sessions with my therapist, and I have made good progress over the last four weeks. We've really talked through the root of the problems, making plans and discussing strategies I can use if the pressure ever starts to become too much again.

I missed Thanksgiving with my family back home for the first time since I've been a Summers, but the guys, minus Cole, who spent it with Spencer, all made the trip over, and Ana Marie cooked us a feast worthy of a king.

There hasn't been much for Riku to protect me from here, and I feel guilty that he missed Thanksgiving with his family, but they have been incredibly understanding. We did a FaceTime chat with them on the day of, and I met his mother and father and got to speak to Aimi, Lacey, and Kiko. They'd informed him he was going to be an *oji* again. Kiko was wearing a shirt that said, "Best Big Sister in the World."

He's spent most of his time installing a state-of-the-art security system that rivals some of the most secure places throughout the world. I think he's been having fun in his element. He keeps calling Simon, who I've discovered is his second-in-command, and having him overnight stuff to us. He asked permission to turn one of the rooms into a security center, and he and Andrei have been all over the castle, setting up motion detectors and cameras and who knows what else.

I smile as I think back to Alex's face when he saw the castle. I swear the boys were like children in a candy store, and I felt like we were the Scooby Gang as the six of us explored the building.

Much like Harlow and the guys' house, this place is riddled with secret rooms and passages, and I don't think I've ever been as dirty as I was at the end of a day exploring all of these, but the communal baths under the castle made up for it all. Carved out of the stone grounds, the four different baths originally supplied the castle inhabitants with bathing options. The count's family had modernized the castle over the years, putting in proper bathrooms with showers and tubs, but nothing beats the thermal springs after a hard day. I asked Ash and Riku to give me some time with the guys, wanting to surprise them with the pools. They were leaving the next day to return home to their various commitments, and I felt like we really hadn't had a chance to reconnect since we'd been spending so much time making sure we all gelled together as a group.

"Ugh, I don't know about you guys, but I need to wash myself." Alex rubs a hand across his face, but all he manages to do is smear the dirt.

"Yup, I'm going to spend some quality 'me time' in the

shower." Ash winks and disappears upstairs to the bedroom he claimed for himself.

Riku leans in and kisses my cheek. "Have fun," he whispers in my ear before he disappears.

"I'll see you in the morning. Remember, your flight is tomorrow, and we need to leave early to get into the city in time for that. So not too late," he warns us, and Jace salutes him.

"Yes, Dad." The other two snicker like children, but I just smile. I love how well they all get along. Riku just flips them off and disappears in the same direction as Ash. My relationships with those two haven't progressed as far as I'd hoped, but I understand them wanting me to concentrate on my therapy and rehab before we make things more complicated.

"Want to shower together?" Alex asks suggestively, and I shake my head, watching his grin drop into a pout.

"I've got a better idea. Follow me." I turn to look back to make sure they are following me, and when I see they are, I keep leading the way to the secret entrance. The count must have closed this over years ago when he installed modern bathrooms. I could open it back up, but I like the mystery. Ana Marie had shown me when I was complaining about an aching body during my first week here.

I stop in front of the fake rock wall and count across and down until I find the right stone, punching it. There's a click, then the door pops back and slides to the side.

"Holy shit! Another secret passage." Shane sounds thrilled. He's been so animated these last few days. Usually, he's fairly reserved. He and Riku are definitely the quieter ones of my men, but there's just something about mysteries that brings out the adventurer in all of us. He's taken it upon himself to photograph every entry and exit point and make notes of all the secret tunnels. I saw him talking to Andrei about the schematics of the place, because unlike Willow Castle, there aren't any maps that show where everything is. I think he's going to have a go at mapping it out when he gets home.

"Not really a secret since this one was known about, but it's still fun. Come on." Using my phone's flashlight, I lead them down the tunnel that somehow twists downward. It's kind of like a spiral staircase cut into the rock but without the steps. Eventually, it starts to smell a little bit, and I see Alex wrinkle his nose.

"What's that smell?"

Before I can answer, Jace does. "That smells like sulfur."

The tunnel opens, and we step out into the caverns. I stop where I am, not allowing them to go any farther as I fumble around, trying to light the torch. They have all been modern- ized, so once you light one, they all catch fire, but it's fiddly getting the first one done. Eventually, I get it, and with a whoosh, the room lights up. I smile at the guys' gasps of surprise. I must admit it's pretty cool. It has a very primitive yet sexy feel to it. Although the torches light up the room, the pools are still dark. They look like puddles of blackness with little tendrils of steam curling up off them.

"There are four pools, all slightly different temperatures, and don't ask me how it works, but the water filters through something, so even if everyone was washing in here, the water was always clean. Anyway, this is my favorite one." I bring them to the back corner. It's a little smaller than the others, and it has seats carved into the rock around the edges. Ana Marie spoils me, so she went into a nearby village and got me these gorgeous jars to hold soap and shampoo and things, storing them next to the pool on a ledge. There is a shelf carved into the wall behind it, and she stacked it with large fluffy towels. I slipped away earlier and added something else to the supplies that I hope we can make use of as well.

Taking a deep breath, I blow it out and start to strip off my clothes. "Well, what are you waiting for?" I ask them, giggling when the three of them burst into movement, removing their clothes, as I push my panties down and use the steps to enter the pool. I groan at the feel of the hot water on my achy muscles. It's quite deep in the middle, so once I get in a little bit, I have to swim across to the other side. Reaching one of the seats, I turn around just in time to see all three of them naked in the light of the torches. Fuck me, I'm a lucky woman.

It doesn't take long for all three of them to join me. We don't mess around, quickly making use of all the wonderful products to clean up.

"This feels amazing," Shane says as he takes a seat next to me and rests his head back against the ledge.

"I can't believe you hid this from us." Alex is pouting again. "I could have been here every night." He comes over and stands in front of me, picking up one of my feet and massaging it under the water. A groan leaves my mouth and echoes around the cavern thanks to the immense pleasure that his thumb against the arch of my foot causes. The pout leaves, replaced by a sultry grin. "Oh, I like that. I think we should see if we can cause a symphony of sounds down here." Jace slides up next to me on my other side, and now I'm surrounded by the three of them.

Jace comes closer, slanting his mouth across mine, licking at my lips for entry. When I allow him access, he plunders my mouth, twining his tongue with mine. I reach for him, but Shane grabs my hands and stretches them above my head, lifting me out of the water enough that he can bend down and latch his mouth around one of my nipples.

"Don't you look sexy, all stretched out like an offering to the gods." Alex's hands run up my thighs as he steps closer, wrapping my legs around him. He plucks Shane's head off my nipple, and I watch the two of them kiss as Jace pulls away and grins at me.

"Sexy, aren't they?"

I stare, not sure I've ever seen them kiss like this. Why have I never seen this before? Did I make them feel like they couldn't be affectionate around me? "Why have you never kissed like that in front of me before?" I ask once they pull apart. "I've never seen any of you show passion like that. Fuck yes, it's sexy."

Shane shrugs. "I guess we didn't want you to feel pressured."

"Well, stop it. I want to see everything between the three of you and everything you want to share with me. Now, kiss Jace," I order. Alex leans over my legs and grabs Jace around the waist, pulling him toward him. Their kiss is so sexy and sensual that a shiver runs through me before Alex's hand ever reaches for Jace's cock under the water. I can barely tear my eyes away when I see his hand start to pump up and down.

A whimper leaves my mouth as Shane's tongue licks my ear, then his thumb finds my clit, circling it while we watch our boyfriends kiss.

"Hot, aren't they?" he whispers, and all I can do is nod. "Tell us what you'd like. Would you like to see us fuck?" he asks, and a shudder I can't hide runs down my spine as I nod my head. "How about you climb on my lap and sit on my dick, then I can play with your pretty titties, and you can ride my cock while we watch the two of them." His finger leaves my clit and pinches my nipple when I get lost in the sight before me.

"God yes," I breathe out, and he chuckles.

"You two should climb out so Jazzy can get a really good look at what you're doing." Shane tilts his head at the side of the pool, and Alex steps out from between my legs, grabs Jace around the waist, and lifts him out. My eyes lock on his tan body as the water cascades off it, leaving behind glittering drops against all that exposed, muscular flesh.

"Fuck!" My voice is low and breathy, and again, Shane chuckles.

"He is quite the specimen." I haven't seen Jace naked. We only had that quick and furious fuck in the elevator, and now I'm kicking myself for not getting him naked any sooner.

I wipe my hand over the back of my mouth to make sure I'm not drooling.

Alex climbs out after him, his body just as tan and sexy as Jace's, and the two of them kiss again, their cocks rubbing as they hold each other tight. I can't peel my eyes away from *them even when Shane lifts me up and slides under me, settling me in his lap, his lips at my neck and his hands cupping my breasts. His erect cock begins sliding up and down through my pussy lips.*

Captivated, I watch Alex break away. He grabs a couple of towels from the little alcove before returning and laying them flat, helping Jace down onto the softer surface. Alex reaches for the little bottle of lube I'd hidden within the bath products and drizzles some on his hand before coating his cock with it. He then spreads Jace's legs, and while he kisses him, he uses two fingers to stretch Jace's asshole. I can't decide where to look—at their mouths or where Alex's fingers are sliding in and out of Jace's puckered ring.

Jace's moan echoes around the stone chamber, the only sound apart from the quiet lapping of water.

One of Shane's hands slides down to tease my clit while the other keeps plucking at my nipples. His teeth graze my neck as he happily torments me while I watch the show in front of us. Alex switches to three fingers, and Jace's head drops back, his back arching when Alex uses his other hand on his thick dick, thrusting up and down in time with his fingers.

"Looks like Jace is ready. Are you ready to watch Alex fuck him?" Shane whispers in my ear before nipping the lobe. My moan joins Jace's as I quickly nod.

"Yes, please," I beg.

"Did you hear that, Alex? She asked so nicely. Fuck our boyfriend so our girlfriend can watch," Shane commands Alex, who uses both hands to spread Jace even wider, notching his dick at his readied hole. He pushes forward, and

at the same time, Shane lifts me and impales me on his cock. The sounds of our pleasure are loud, and it's all I can do to not drop my head back and close my eyes, but I don't want to miss a single bit of the sight in front of us.

Now fully seated, Alex wraps his hand around Jace's cock. "Fuck him hard, Alex," Shane orders as Alex draws out almost fully before thrusting in deep, grunting with the movement. He sets a punishing pace, and Jace's fingers claw at the ground as Shane leisurely lifts me up and down on his cock, whispering naughty words in my ears. The sight before me is gorgeous, and I bite my lip as I try to hold off my impending orgasm, my pussy tightening on Shane with every thrust of his cock.

Suddenly, he stops and lifts me off of him. "Stop, Alex," he demands, and Alex stops mid-thrust. They both look at us, wide-eyed, slack-lipped, and panting.

"What the fuck, man?" Alex grumbles, and Shane lifts me out of the water before dragging himself out after me. The rocks are rough on my knees, and I grimace, but Shane quickly gets to his feet and grabs a couple more towels, laying them by Jace's head.

"I didn't want Jazzy to feel left out." Shane maneuvers my body so that I'm kneeling above Jace's head, my knees on the towels he brought over. "Would you like to taste her, Jace?"

Jace's ice blond hair is sticking up at all angles, and his beautiful mismatched eyes are slightly unfocused without his glasses. He grins and reaches up and back with his arms. "Come here, sweetheart." I shuffle forward until my pussy is hovering over his mouth. "Don't be shy." Jace pulls me down and drags his tongue through my folds. I throw my head back at the sensation, but Shane cups the back of it.

"You should return the favor." He pushes me down, and Alex snags a kiss before I wrap my mouth around Jace's cock. It's sticky and sweet from the lube that Alex rubbed on it. My mind is a whirl of chaos as Alex cups my breasts and plays with them. My body feels like there's a current of electricity flowing through it, sparking at all the places they touch.

"Can you take one more?" Shane asks, notching himself at my opening. I nod around Jace's cock, and Shane slams home. My mouth opens, and Alex starts to thrust in and out again, pushing Jace deeper down my throat, but I can feel my orgasm just out of reach. Unable to move or think, I let them push me higher and higher, the slurps and skin slaps, grunts and groans, a symphony to our ears.

Shane's hands grip my ass tight as he plunders my cunt, showing no mercy. Just as Jace latches his lips around my clit and sucks hard, Shane pushes a finger into my ass, and I feel myself fly over the edge, mind and body shattering. My orgasm bursts through my body like a tsunami. At the same time, Jace erupts down my throat, and I swallow as much as I can, but I feel some dribble out of my lips. Shane and Alex last a couple more thrusts before they finish, moaning their pleasure into the air.

I'm not sure how long my orgasm lasts, but when I come back to myself, Shane pulls out, and I scramble off Jace, worried I smothered him, but he just has a dopey smile on his face. I roll next to him, and he turns his head, lazily kissing me. My body is like spaghetti, so it's all I can manage to give him those slow kisses in return. Two arms scoop me up, and *when I open my eyes, Alex is smiling down at me, his eyes full of love and wonder.*

"You were amazing. That was the sexiest thing I've ever seen." He kisses me and steps back into the water, carrying me with him. Holding me against his body, he gently washes me while Shane does the same with Jace. Once done, they help us out and dry us with big fluffy towels.

"Let's go snuggle, and maybe Jace and I can add to Shane's pile inside you." My eyes fly open at Alex's dirty words, and my mouth drops open in surprise.

The three men chuckle.

"You didn't think we were done with you yet, did you?" Jace asks me, resting against Shane.

"Oh no, baby, we've got a lot more where that came from." Shane's heated gaze tightens my nipples and makes my core tingle once more.

A knock on my door has me jumping. I'd been so lost in my daydreams that I hadn't been paying attention to the time.

"Come in."

Ash pops his head around the door as it opens. "Hey, it's lunchtime. You want to come down and have something to eat with us?" Ash has been back and forth a couple of times throughout the month, keeping up the charade that we are getting married, but I know the dragon lady has been putting pressure on him. He's getting twitchy to be seen together in public again, but he's been amazing about not putting pressure on me, which is why I'm glad I have some good news for him.

"Yeah, I'm starving. That's one good thing about not using coke anymore. I have my appetite back, and Ana Marie is the most amazing cook." I tuck my arm into his as we start the trek back to the kitchen where we take all our meals. Partly because the corridors are freezing and partly because I can't help but touch the man. The two of them have gone out of their way to drive me crazy with intimate touches and teasing kisses, and I'm close to jumping them both. "Listen, there's something I want to talk to you about, but let's wait until we get to Riku. He needs to hear my suggestion as well."

"Oh, you're such a tease." He squeezes my arm that's tucked into his.

"Not as much as you are," I mutter, but he hears it anyway and chuckles out loud.

"All good things come to those who wait."

Chapter Seventeen

Jacinta

By the time we get to the kitchen, my teeth are chattering. Although all the rooms are heated, the corridors are not, and a stone building in December in Romania is *not* a warm place to be. We've yet to replace all the moth-eaten tapestries and carpets that lined the walls and floors, all of which helped to warm things up a little bit. I'm hoping a trip to London in the near future will help with that. That's part of my surprise for Ash.

"Holy shit, it's colder than a witch's tit out there." The two of us stumble into the kitchen, which has a blazing fire in the hearth, and beeline toward the flames, holding out our hands to ward off some of the chill. Riku, Andrei, and Ana Marie laugh at us.

"It's only going to get colder," she warns me in her strongly accented voice.

"I know." Now that I'm warm, I take a seat at the large wooden table where the others are sitting, Ash taking the other place setting. The two of us dig into the hearty stew Ana has prepared. It's rich and meaty and full of vegetables. There's a glass of red wine, so I take a sip of that, letting the warmth of it all run over me. I really am going to miss this place once we leave. It has been everything I've needed.

"How did your session with the therapist go today?" Riku asks as he leans back in his chair.

"Really good," I reply, a smile spreading across my lips. "She says I've made huge progress, and she approves of me trying to go out in public again."

"Is that a good idea?" Ash purses his lips with worry, and I pat his hand.

"Yeah, I feel really good, and I don't have any of the crippling anxiety that I had before. Mind you, the medication she prescribed me is probably helping with that."

She and I both acknowledged that a little help wasn't a bad thing, so she started me on a relatively low dose. We'll see if I need more, especially when going out in public becomes a bigger part of my life again, but for now, in the wilds of Romania, I feel pretty good. Plus, I know I can pick up the phone and call her, and she'll help me. I also know that I can lean on either of these two men. They'll be there for me no matter what.

"That's really good." Riku's smile is encouraging, and it gives me the extra boost to bring up what I wanted to discuss.

"So that leads me to what I wanted to talk to everyone about. I've made some decisions." I see Ana Marie and Andrei exchange a glance. I guess it hasn't been fair to them, making them wait to find out what the fate of this place would be. When I first arrived, all I wanted to do was put it on the market, but now I couldn't part with it. I've grown attached and want it to always be in our family. I want Jax's kids to be able to come spend summers and winters here. Andrei said the lakes are good for fishing during the summer, and there's so much gorgeous wilderness to explore. Even my kids could eventually come here... sooner rather than later if Alex gets his way. I squirm on my seat when I think about what he said.

A pinch on my leg has me jumping. "You zoned out for a moment," Ash says casually while eating his food.

"Ah yes, sorry, where was I? Oh, this place. I want to finish renovating it, but it's a bigger job than I can handle, so I'm going to have to appoint more staff. Maybe I can get the two of you to do that?" Andrei and Ana Marie exchange another glance.

"Does this mean you're going to keep the property?" she asks, practically holding her breath, waiting for my answer.

"Yeah." They clap their hands and start talking fast in Romanian. "Whoa, slow down. Let me finish." They break off, but neither of them can control their grins.

"We can't live here year-round since we all have lives and businesses to run, so I was thinking maybe we can turn a small section into a catered and staffed Airbnb. That way you guys will stay employed and busy, and the castle will see life in it when we're not here. There are so many rooms, I'm sure we can work out how to do it so that when we're here, guests aren't impacted, and we aren't impacted by them."

Andrei is nodding. "Yes, how about we use the east wing for that? There's only one door coming and going to the rest of the castle from that wing, and we can lock it to keep guests out of other areas."

"How about we put a kitchen over there and a movie room and whatever else a house like this could want?" I suggest, and the others agree.

"Oh, we haven't shown you, but the east wing is where the dungeon is. They couldn't put it under the rest of the house because of the thermal pools. The guests will get a kick out of that. Maybe could even turn some of the cells into rooms," Ana

Marie says, and I exchange a look with Ash as he smothers a grin. My lovely English lord is having dirty thoughts. I mean, I don't blame him. Willow Castle had a sex room, so why couldn't this have a sex dungeon?

"Great, so before we leave, we need to hire some staff and start some renovations. I want to keep all the decor in this medieval style. I'm going to do some shopping while I'm in London, but I won't have time to do it all, so I'll leave it to the two of you to make decisions. Just email it through for approval, okay?" The older couple preen like peacocks, proud to be given such an enormous responsibility. I'm glad they are pleased because it really is a daunting task. I'm not sure what I'd do if they had declined being involved with this plan.

"London?" Ash asks, losing the smirk, and Riku raises an eyebrow too.

"Yes, London. I thought you'd like to spend Christmas with your sister. Aunt Merideth is heading to the US to spend Christmas break at our cabin with the rest of the family, but I'm not ready to return yet, so we're going to stay at her place. Jace, Alex, Shane, and Cole will be flying out because Spencer is spending Christmas with his mom before she relocates to Australia. I was thinking Edie could come and stay with us for a few days too."

"Doesn't your aunt live in a brothel?" Riku asks.

I wince and shrug. "Technically, it's a gentle-man's club. Most of the time, she lives above it, but she's recently purchased a house in the country." I don't give them any of the details since that would spoil the surprise.

"Thank you so much." Ash gives me a kiss. Ana Marie titters, and Andrei blushes red. They know that my relationship with the guys is unconventional, but they haven't been judgmental at all. I guess if their families know of the count's history, then nothing could be really all that surprising. After going through the library in the castle, I learned my grandfather wasn't the first deviant in the line. "I'm going to call Edie now. She's going to be thrilled."

"Oh, suss out what she wants for Christmas. I have no idea what fourteen-year-old girls are into now," I call after him, and he waves a hand as he leaves the kitchen.

Ana Marie and Andrei clear the table and make Riku and me a coffee before telling us they are going to the east wing to make plans.

"What about you? Do you want to return home for Christmas?" I ask my silent bodyguard as he watches the flames flicker in the fireplace. The *snap* and *pop* of the wood are the only sounds in the quiet room.

"No, I am more than content here. To be honest, I'd like to hunker down for the entire winter and not stick our heads out again until the snow thaws." I shiver at the image his words have put into my mind. I'm sure my six men could think of plenty of creative ways to keep us warm and occupied through the long cold months. If I can get this one to actually put out, that is. "Unfortunately, that is not practical, so I will follow wherever you go."

"It's not possible this winter, but maybe next. Given enough time, I bet we could make it happen despite all our schedules. I'm pretty sure Alex is hellbent on retiring from modeling."

Riku snorts. "That's because he wants to be a dad, and he thinks if he shows you he can be more than a pretty face, you'll give in and have a baby for him to look after." I feel my face heat when I think back to all of his actions. I'm not opposed to the idea, and I don't think any of the others are either. Or at least they won't be once I show them that I actually do have my addiction under control now. The thought that my and Jax's kid would be close in age is certainly appealing. Maybe I'll go off the pill and surprise Alex—after I have a chat with the others and make sure they are ready for that step too, of course.

Riku's eyes flash with desire, and he stands up. "I'm not sure what you're thinking, but if the color of your face has anything to say, it's pure filth. I don't know about you, but I am damn sure done resisting this attraction." He strides over to me, and I scramble out of my chair, my heart racing when I think about where this might be going. But all he does is pick me up and throw me over his shoulder, a squeak flying out of my mouth in shock. He strides out of the kitchen and heads in the direction of my bedroom, or that's where I think he's going. It's hard to tell since everything kind of looks the same upside down. Yup, there's the suit of armor at the base of the steps. He has three flights to go before he even gets to the steps to my turret bedroom, so I just hang on for the ride, assuming he'll get winded halfway and put me down. But I underestimated him. He's been no slouch, working out, jogging around the grounds, and lifting weights in the gym, so he hasn't lost any of his fitness. When we finally make it to my bedroom, he throws me onto the bed, barely breathless—unlike me. I'm panting hard, but it's in anticipation of what's about to happen.

"I tried my hardest to keep some distance through your recovery, but you are an impossible woman to resist. I wasn't sure if there was a space for me in what you've got going on, but you have all convinced me that not only is there a place, but I desperately want it. Tell me you feel the same way." His impassioned plea has me opening my arms and beckoning him forward.

"Yes, please." And just like that, gone is the silent man who watches and waits. In his place is a man who looks like he wants to devour me whole.

"I wanted to take this slow, and worship you like

you deserve, but I've been waiting so long." He peels off his top layers in one go, showing me his sexy, smooth, ripped chest. My mouth waters as he steps over to the fire and fiddles with it, making more heat pump into the room, before coming back to me. His hair is falling out of its usual ponytail, and it hangs down around his face, framing such an intense look of longing that I start to scramble to take my own clothes off.

"Fast is good," I rasp out as I get tangled. When I finally get free, I'm greeted with an even more mouthwatering sight. Even though I'd seen it before in his own hand and we've bathed in the thermal pools together, I haven't really had an up close look at Riku's cock. And now all I want to do is get my mouth on it.

Riku is all long, lean, and pale muscle. He stands before me like a god, his hand fisting his length. He lets it go and stalks toward the bed like a lethal predator after his prey, not stopping until he joins me on the bed between my parted thighs. With no delay, he parts my lips with his fingers and thrusts his tongue deep. I groan and thrash my head back and forth on the bed, grabbing the long lengths of his dark hair.

"Riku." His name slips from my mouth like a prayer as he feasts on me, driving me to a quick peak and stopping just before I explode. He looks up at me, his eyes feral and his face glistening with my desire.

"You're the best thing I've ever tasted," he growls before climbing the rest of his way up my body. Without messing around, he thrusts his tongue into my mouth as he thrusts his cock deep. I cry out, but he smothers the sound, and I taste myself bursting across my tastebuds. Riku is like a dancer, his hips rolling, and with every stroke, his cock hits the right spot inside me. His body is trying to wring every ounce of pleasure out of me that it can, and all I can do is wrap my legs around his slender waist and hold on for the ride. He pulls his mouth away and looks deep into my eyes, trapping me. My body is tighter than a guitar string, and as Riku slides his hand between our bodies and caresses my clit, I feel us tumble over the edge together. He stills and holds himself deep as he comes, eyes closed, my cunt pulsing around him, prolonging our pleasure.

Finally, he relaxes his body, rolling to the side and taking me with him, his arms wrapped around me, my face pressed into his chest. A finger under my chin has me looking up into his dark, love-filled eyes. He smiles down at me.

"That was worth the wait." He presses a kiss against my mouth before pulling away.

"It sure was, and now that I know what's hiding behind your cool and calm facade, I can't wait to try my hardest to push your buttons whenever I can." I grin as he tickles me, reveling in the happiness on his face.

"Brat," he grumbles, but his eyes are still smiling.

"Yeah, but I'm *your* brat." I snuggle in, looking out over the snow-capped mountains, wishing that we never had to leave our private hideaway.

Chapter Eighteen

Jacinta

London is just as cold and miserable as rural Romania, but it does have a festive vibe. We end up spending the night at the Neighpalm Hotel in Convent Garden, instead of staying at Aunt Merideth's, because we got in a day earlier than the others. Christmas Eve is only a couple of days away, but I've done no shopping at all, so I get online and arrange to have things sent to my family back in the States. This year, I bought everyone matching onesies and demanded a picture of everyone dressed up on Christmas morning. After that's done, Ash, Riku, and I bundle up and head out to shop for the guys, Spencer, and Ash's sister. The other thing I want to do is shop for the castle, but I'll wait until after Christmas to do that.

Maybe I'll take Alex and Jace with me since they have great taste.

Harrods' windows are full of Christmas displays, and when we get inside, the interior is decked out with lights, wreaths, and greenery. I beeline to the Christmas store. It's packed, so I brace myself to be inundated with all the negative feelings, but they are not there. There's no anxiety and no acidic whispering voice. It's just calm inside my head. I want to do a little dance to celebrate, but I control myself.

"You okay?" Riku asks, eyeing the crowd, and I beam at him.

"So okay," I assure him, and a slow smile stretches his lips.

"That's good, but remember, if it gets to be too much, we can leave."

"I'll let you know, but all I feel is excitement and some panic about what to get everyone."

I've arranged for a tree to be delivered to the place where we're staying, and I want to decorate it with ornaments and everything else we've picked out. We're not here long before we're approached by a staff member. In his classy suit, he looks like he may be upper management, and he's smiling at Ash.

"Lord Lavington, welcome to Harrods. Is there anything we can help you with today?"

Ash smirks at me and waves a hand in my direction. "Yes, Countess Bucătaru wants to buy

Christmas decorations. If we could have someone or a couple of someones take them and pack them up as she picks them, that would be wonderful. Everything should be delivered to the Neighpalm."

The manager finally looks in my direction, and his eyes widen minutely in recognition. "Of course, let me just find a couple of personal shoppers for you." He hurries away, and I smack Ash across the stomach.

"What was that?" I demand, and he shrugs.

"Titles always get you better service."

I grab Riku by the hand and drag him over to the ornaments. "What do you think Kiko will like? You can grab them something from here, and we'll send them to her. It will probably be too late, but she can have it for next year. Better pick something for the new baby too. Also, I saw some really nice silk scarves when we came in. Do you think the women in your family would like them? I need help, please." I'm rambling, talking a million miles an hour, but I want to get this present giving thing right. I've never had people to give gifts to before, apart from my family, and I'm kind of excited by it all. "What about your dad? I saw a nice leather wallet in the bag section when we came through."

Riku stops me and tugs me close. We're still supposed to be keeping up appearances that Ash and I are getting married, so he can't look like anything but a bodyguard at the moment no matter how much I crave his lips and arms. "Slow down, princess, we have all day. You know you don't have to buy my family anything, but I will help you if you want."

"I would have offered to fly them over, but I didn't want them to be here for the fireworks. Maybe next year we can all have Christmas at the castle. That would be fun. Oh, I need to call Ana Marie and get her to order enough stuff so we can really decorate the whole place." I pull away and take out my phone to make a note.

"What fireworks?" Riku asks cautiously, and I cringe a little, leaning in even though Ash is far enough away not to hear.

"We're going to deal with Ash's problem once and for all. But I wanted to talk to everyone when they get here this evening, okay?"

"Okay," he answers as the manager returns, followed by two personal shoppers carrying baskets.

"Kayla and Lincoln here will help you with everything you need, including the delivery arrangements. Please don't hesitate to call me if you need anything else." The manager hands a card to Ash, who takes it and passes it to me.

"She's the one you should be sucking up to. She could buy and sell me ten times over."

I roll my eyes but take the card. "Thank you," I tell the manager dismissively, then turn to the two who are going to help. "Call me Jacinta. That's Riku, my bodyguard, and this is Ash." The manager frowns, but I ignore him. "Now, let's shop."

By the time I'm done, I've spent a nice chunk of change and kept my two personal shoppers on their feet for the last few hours, but I'm happy with everything I got. All of the guys got matching hats, scarves, and gloves for the cold Romanian weather. I also got them each a bottle of cologne, having sent a few messages to people to find out what they like to wear. The only person I didn't know about was Cole, so I just picked out something I liked. Then I got them each a new watch as well. I mean, who can walk past Tag Heuer without stopping or slowing down to look at them? Ash helped me pick out some nice things for his sister, and I got her a makeover and gift voucher from Sephora. He told me his grandmother doesn't let her wear makeup, which I understand, but it doesn't hurt for her to know to apply it. She's fourteen, for God's sake. That's the kind of thing they all like. Riku helped me shop for Spencer. On top of all the guys' help, Kayla and Lincoln were invaluable, so I make sure to tip them extremely well at the end of the session.

"Ah, Countess Bucătaru, I think you made a mistake here." The judgy manager returned as I was finalizing the bill, like he wanted to take credit for all the sales himself.

"Oh?" I raise an eyebrow as he points out the tip section.

"Yes. I think you made a mistake with the tip." I

lean over and have a look at where he's pointing even though I know what he's referring to.

"Oh, I'm sorry." I had originally tipped them both one thousand dollars, but after seeing the asshole they have to work under, I change the one to a five. "After all, they did all the work." Kayla gasps, and Lincoln looks a little pale at the amount. "Merry Christmas, guys, and thanks. That money better go to them." I glare at the manager, and he swallows as Ash hands a business card to the two personal shoppers.

"Please let us know if you don't receive the tip," he tells them, and we head out of the store.

There's a press contingency waiting for us out front, and as Riku pushes through them, they shout questions at me and Ash.

"Jacinta, how are the wedding plans going?"

"Is it true the two of you are on the rocks, and that's why you've been out of the public eye for the last month?"

"Jacinta, are you pregnant with another man's baby?"

The last one almost makes me stop and laugh because it could be true, but Ash just grabs me by the arm and keeps me moving while he smiles and replies. "Jazzy and I are just here to spend Christmas with family, then we'll be right back into wedding plans, for sure."

He puts his hand on my head as I duck into the limo then climbs in after me. The door slams shut, and Riku must get into the front with the driver before it pulls away from the curb.

"Phew, I don't know about you, but I need a nap after all that." I lean my head on his shoulder, and he puts an arm around me.

"I need a cigarette and a stiff drink," he grumbles, and I pinch him playfully.

"It wasn't that bad," I argue, and he grimaces.

"It really was."

"Fine, I'll make sure it's Alex and Jace whom I drag with me on my next shopping trip."

"That will be much appreciated." He leans his head back and closes his eyes for the short trip back to the hotel.

All three of us have a nap after we grab a bite to eat. Having them on either side of me again is a surefire way for me to sleep like a log.

The guys arrive just in time to join us for dinner. Jace, Alex, and Shane greet me with steamy kisses and embraces while Cole is a little more reserved. Neither of us know where we stand, and we really haven't seen each other since the intervention. I hope he hasn't changed his mind.

"Pick a room." I wave a hand in the direction of where they are. "But don't unpack because we're moving to a new location tomorrow."

"Oooh, mysterious, I like it." Alex pats me on

the ass on the way past and winks cheekily. Jace rolls his eyes and follows him.

"Brad asked me to give you these." Shane pulls a folder out of the laptop bag over his shoulder. Handing it to me, he leans in and gives me a kiss on the cheek. "And he asked me to give you that too, and to tell you he misses you." A slight pang of guilt hits me for a moment, and I feel myself frown. Shane grins. "And then he told me to tell you not to feel guilty and he hopes you have a great time causing trouble. What did he mean by that?"

"Go put your bags away and come back. I want to talk to you all about what's going to happen."

He nods and follows after the guys, leaving me with just Cole since Riku and Ash have also made themselves scarce.

"So, how was the flight?" I grasp at a conversation starter because I'm nervous as fuck all of a sudden.

"Flying on one of your family's planes has completely spoiled me, especially that one. I'm going to hate going back to flying commercial." He picks up his suitcase. "You want to show me to my room?"

"Yeah, okay, sure." I lead him through the penthouse apartment, past the bedrooms that Ash and Riku have their stuff in despite having slept in my bed, and it looks like the other three are going to sleep in the same room. How the three of them are comfortable in a normal king-sized bed, I have no idea, but they make it work.

"This is mine, and there are a couple more that you can choose from." I wave my hand down the corridor, but he drops his suitcase and stalks toward me, frowning.

"Is something wrong, Jacinta?" he asks in that imperious tone of his that gets my hackles up.

"No, why would you ask that?" I cross my arms defensively, and he stops.

"Because you're all nervous and fidgety. Are you still having withdrawals?"

I growl at him. "No, you fucktard. You make me nervous, all right?"

"Oh really, why?"

"Because I don't know where I stand with you, and I never know what's going to come out of your mouth, compliment or criticism."

"Yeah, I can understand why you might feel that way, but shit, there's just something about you that has me messing up all the time. You're so beautiful, and maybe I just can't believe that someone like you would be interested in someone like me."

"What the fuck, dude? You were married to a Victoria's Secret model." I'm even more confused and frustrated now.

"You know what? Fuck it." He grabs me by the waist and yanks me toward him, his mouth mine. As our tongues tangle together, he steps us backward into my room and pushes the door closed, pinning me against it. His hands run up my body, lifting me so that I'm trapped between him and the wall. I wrap my legs around his waist, and he grinds his hard dick into me. "God, I haven't been able to get you off my mind. The feel of you beneath me, the taste of you in my mouth... It's like this memory that runs over and over inside my head. My brain doesn't function in your vicinity because it reverts to that time in the closet, and all it wants me to do is fuck your brains out again. Tell me yes." His voice is husky and kind of desperate, and I figure there's time for talking later. Maybe what we need is to get over the physical stuff to be able to move forward.

"Fuck yes."

Chapter Nineteen

Jacinta

Sex with Cole was just as good as the first time, but this time he fucked me face-to-face and ravished my mouth and tits while he owned my pussy. After that, we took our time on the bed, snuggling together, talking about Spencer, how much Cole's looking forward to being a full-time dad, and how I felt about being introduced as his girlfriend.

Finally, I haul myself out of Cole's arms. As much as I don't want to leave them, we have something important to discuss. "Come on." I slap his naked ass as he groans and rolls onto his front, burying his head in the pillow. "Don't you want to know what those files are about?"

I hear him mumble something, but it's muffled by the pillow, so I slap his ass again. If I take a moment to caress the round globes, well, I'm only human. Not getting any response from him, I try a new tactic, sinking my teeth into it. That gets me a yelp and a *very* quickly moving Cole. I giggle as I get dressed. His ass now has a perfect imprint of my teeth, and I can't deny how good that makes me feel.

He scowls at me and rubs the offending spot before stalking toward me with retribution in his eyes. Spinning, I race out of the bedroom before he can get to me. It wouldn't surprise me if he followed me, naked and all. He doesn't strike me as the shy type. When I get back to the living area, everyone is sitting around the table, eating.

The conversation doesn't stop as I take a seat, bless them, and Ash piles some food onto a plate for me.

"It shouldn't be too cold. It hasn't been here long," he assures me.

"We waited as long as we could, but when Ash's stomach started screaming at us, we decided we better not wait for the two of you." Alex winks as Ash flips him off.

The food is delicious, and it doesn't take long before Cole joins us. His hair is wet, so he must have jumped into the shower before coming out. I appreciate the fact that he's washed up rather than come down to the table smelling like me. Jace grins at me, not missing the flush on my cheeks.

Cole takes a seat next to Shane, who stands up

and starts passing him dishes before grabbing him a beer and me a glass of wine. It's all so domestic and sweet, and I can picture how our lives could be.

I finish my mouthful and clear my throat, taking a sip of the wine as I get my thoughts together. "I guess you're all wondering why I chose to stay in London for Christmas instead of returning to the States. Well, I'm not ready to return home, and it's time we dealt with Ash's problem." I turn to the man in question. "Not that I'm opposed to marrying you, but I want you to want it, not just be doing it for the sake of your sister."

"But I *do* want it."

"Would you have asked so soon if your grandmother hadn't forced your hand?" I ask gently, and I see him think about it before shaking his head, his eyes shining with guilt.

"I'm not upset, Ash. I wouldn't have said yes so soon either. We need to see how this whole dynamic is going to work in the long-term." I gesture to the whole table. "We can discuss something at a later time once we know we all work."

Alex crosses his arms with a stubborn set to his jaw. "I have no doubt this will work, but I'll go with the flow." The rest of us roll our eyes or scoff, knowing that won't last long. Alex is the least patient of us all.

"So we need to find a way to protect your sister, and I know you've been dealing with it through the correct channels, but I wasn't willing to wait any longer."

Ash frowns. "What have you done?"

"A couple of things. I had Jake do some private investigative work for me. He got the name of the sheik your grandmother has been in contact with, and I gave him a little call. Turns out Sheik Abdullah Amiin II was not aware of the deal. Your grandmother has been dealing with his aging father. Luckily for us, the son is in his thirties, and he's much more modern thinking. He was horrified to hear that his father was trying to buy your fourteen-year-old sister. As of now, that deal is off the table." Ash sighs with relief. "But that doesn't mean she won't find another scummy man to strike a deal with. So I looked into the judge who wouldn't rule you as her guardian. Turns out that your grand-mother is blackmailing him, and you are not going to believe the dirt she has on him."

The guys exchange blank glances, and Riku waves his hands. "Come on, you've built up the suspense. Now share with the table."

"He's a member of the Sugar and Spice Gentle-men's Club. Let's just say Aunt Merideth knows him… intimately. Apparently, when she was still a working girl, he was her biggest client despite being married. They still see each other even now, although she doesn't charge him for it anymore." I giggle as the guys at the table make all kinds of faces at the thought of Aunt Merideth and sex.

"Anyway, his wife passed away a few years ago, which is actually great news. Her finding out about my aunt was the only thing the judge was worried about. Now that the risk of that is gone, he was happy to overturn his ruling, especially when I gave him proof of your grandmother's gambling habit."

"Gambling habit?" Ash sounds shocked.

"The old bat has a problem with the ponies and the dogs. I'm afraid you're going to be even more shocked by how big a problem."

Ash groans and runs a hand through his hair. "God, what now?"

"Well, it's lucky for you that you pay for your sister to attend boarding school, because I'm afraid your estate is pretty much empty." I hand him the photos Jake had taken through the windows of the empty rooms. "She's been selling off all the furniture to pay her debts. Shit, Ash, she sold the house. I'm not sure why it was still in her name instead of reverting to you, but Forrest's English lawyer friend had a look, and it was all above board."

Ash's mouth drops open. The poor guy's face will get stuck that way at this rate. "She sold it? But... But…" He sounds outraged as he stares down at the photos in front of him. "But where is she going to live? And what about Edie? She still comes home during the holidays. Shit, how long ago was this? I just spoke to Grandmother the other day, and she didn't mention anything. I called the phone at the house, so she must still be there." He jumps to his feet, pulling his phone out of his pocket. "Fuck, I need to make some calls." I stand up and put my hand on his arm, knowing I have to share the rest before he has a heart attack.

"Sit down and let me finish." He looks like he's going to argue with me, so I give his arm a squeeze. Sighing, he sits down again. "Thank you. The new owner is giving her until after the new year to vacate the place. The new owner bought it as is, so all she has to do is remove any personal items she has left."

"Shit, I still have a lot of stuff at home, and all of Edie's things too—if the bitch hasn't sold it all. I'll have to figure out a way to get them and then arrange something for my grandmother. Where is she going to go?"

"Well, I happen to know that she made a good profit off the house. More than enough to pay off her remaining debts. She was also strongly encouraged to move into a posh retirement village that's about twenty minutes from the estate."

Ash frowns. "How do you know all this?"

"I have good people who work for me."

"That's not all, is it?" Shane asks, and I beam at my very astute boyfriend.

"No, it isn't, and I'm proud you realized it. You can have a treat later," I tease him, and he gives me a wicked smile. Maybe it will be me getting the treat.

"I bought the estate, though she doesn't know it

was me. I thought we'd have fun springing it on her tomorrow when we all roll up to have Christmas with her. Though I had to arrange to have more furniture delivered. All that was left was her bedroom furniture and a shabby lounge suite. She let go of all the staff too, so I had to make some calls to offer them their jobs back."

I pass Ash another folder, studying the absolutely gobsmacked expression on his face. "How did I not know any of this?"

"Because she kept you so busy chasing your tail and trying to keep your sister safe that you didn't have time to think about what she was doing at home. When I spoke to the butler—"

"Joseph? Why didn't he call me?"

"Because she made all kinds of threats, and most of the staff thought she still had influence. I mean, she *is* Lady Lavington. Joseph has an old nuisance arrest on his record that she was holding over his head. If he said anything to you, she would fire him. He has an elderly mother whom he supports, and he's also in a relationship with one of the gardeners, so he kept his mouth shut."

Jace shakes his head in surprise. "Wow, that woman really is a piece of work."

"You have no idea," Ash mumbles as he opens the folder containing the title and deed to the estate in his name. "What's this?" Poor thing, he sounds like this last surprise is probably the straw that broke the camel's back.

"Well, you didn't think I was going to keep it for myself, did you? That's your family home, and you deserve to do what you want with it." The money I spent is a drop in the pond that is our fortune, and when I spoke to Jax about it, he was completely on board.

Ash is speechless for a moment, then his eyes begin to glimmer with unshed tears. "I don't know how I can ever repay you for all of this."

"I can think of a few ways," Alex whispers to Cole, earning a grin from the other man.

"I'm sure we can give him a few suggestions if he needs help."

"Hang on, I'm not quite done. This is the paperwork giving you guardianship of Edie. She's your responsibility now, so it's time to clean up the playboy prince act," I scold him semi seriously because I know there's so much more to this man than the public sees. "Time to show the world what Lord Ashton Lavington is really capable of."

I hand over the last folder, and Ash takes it, but he just throws it onto the table and stands up. He pulls out my chair and helps me to my feet. Instead of hugging me like I thought he was going to, he throws me over his shoulder and walks back toward my bedroom.

"Don't disturb us until the morning," he calls over his shoulder, and I hear the rest of the guys holler and clap their encouragement.

"Now *that's* what I'm talking about!" Alex shouts.

Before we get too far away, I hear Riku remark, "Doesn't look like he needed any suggestions after all."

Chapter Twenty

Jacinta

Much like Riku had at the castle, Ash carries me to my bedroom, but unlike Riku, who threw me on my bed, Ash stops just before it and slides me down his body. When my feet hit the ground, he kisses me like I'm his savior, the air he needs to breathe. His hands tangle in my hair, angling my head to just how he wants it. We're both breathing heavily once we finally part, and his eyes widen as I push him away from me and drop to my knees.

I fumble with the button to his jeans before I get them open and yank them down. He's commando, thank God, because I don't think I could stand another layer between us. His cock is long and thick, the tip already weeping precum, so I swipe my tongue across his head, wrapping one hand around him and cupping his balls with the other.

I look up at him, unable to resist a glimpse. He's slack-jawed, watching me with a hooded gaze. "You have no idea how hard it was to stop myself from doing this back in the closet." My voice is raspy as I admit the truth to him. "All I wanted to do was wrap my lips around it."

He threads his hands through my hair, his grip tight how I like it, and I moan as he pulls me forward.

"Open your mouth for me, darling. You look so pretty on your knees. You have no idea how hard it was not to move too."

I let him guide me. He doesn't treat me like I'm fragile. Instead, he uses me just how he wants, and I'm forced to breathe through my nose as he shoves his big cock down my throat.

"Oh yeah. Your throat feels so good around me," he mutters, caressing my head while using me to take his pleasure. I hum and use my tongue when he draws back, sucking and slurping as much as I can to increase his pleasure. "Such a good girl, sucking my dick. So pretty on your knees at my feet. Look at me with those doe eyes, darling." I look up at him, and his grin is wicked as he thrusts and holds himself deep. I fight my gag reflex and breathe through my nose, but when he pulls back, tears are leaking from my eyes and saliva drips down my chin. "Fucking beautiful." He bends down and picks me up before backing up. He throws me, and I fall back with a small gasp of surprise. My legs are still hanging off the bed as he drags my yoga pants down my body and sucks hard on my clit. My moan is loud and obscene as he thrusts two fingers deep into my channel, which is sopping wet from everything I've been doing to him.

"So fucking tight," he mumbles into my pussy. "Going to feel so good on my dick." He quickly builds me to a peak, but he stops before I can explode.

"No!" I cry out, and he chuckles, dragging my top over my head and removing my bra before he finishes removing his. Ash is pale, but there's not an ounce of fat on him. He's cut like a Greek god. Damn, polo does the body good.

"God, you're gorgeous." He runs his hands up my body, cupping my breasts before giving the nipples some attention. He licks and bites and sucks until I'm rubbing my legs together to try to ease the ache he's causing deep inside.

"Enough, Ash, fuck me," I plead, and he bends to my wishes, but instead of slamming home, he lies down on the bed and pats his thighs.

"Climb aboard, baby. I want to watch you ride me." I'm quick to straddle him, rising up to place him at my core before slowly sliding down his length. We groan in tandem as my body welcomes him into mine.

"Oh my god, so good." I rest my hands on his chest and breathe as I slide up and down, trying to get him all the way in. There's tension around his eyes and jaw, and the muscles in his arms ripple as he does his best to hold still. Finally, I'm seated.

"Like coming home," he says, gazing up at me with worshipful eyes. "Take your pleasure, goddess," he encourages me, and I start to ride him, my hips undulating up and down, my body angled over his so that his cock slides past the spot that feels the best. My hair hangs around us like a curtain, and he places a thumb against my clit so that it brushes across it with every slide.

My movement starts to falter as I get closer to the edge, and he grabs hold of my thighs and takes over, thrusting into me. Over and over, he thrusts as I hang on for the ride. I try to keep my eyes on his, but they keep drifting closed as I revel in the sensations he's wringing from my body.

"Look at me, Jacinta. Look into my eyes as I own your body." Ash's voice is harsh, and as I lift my head, he flicks his thumb across my clit. A searing bolt of pleasure bursts outward as my body shudders with the onslaught. Ash bucks deep one more time before groaning as he finds his own release. Together, we ride out our orgasms, gripping one another, our breaths mingling. Finally, he pulls me down and kisses me. "You are amazing, I'm not sure how I'm ever going to repay you for what you've done, but I will spend the rest of my life trying to be worthy of you," he declares softly, and I melt against him, pressing kisses to his heart, glad to be wrapped up in his arms. I wasn't sure it would ever happen, but I finally have all of my men where they need to be.

The next day, we head out to the estate. The look on Ash's grandmother's face was fucking priceless when she realized I had bought the estate and given it to her grandson. Of course, Alex captured it on camera to preserve it for all time.

The raging argument that Ash and his grand-mother had went on for a long time. So long that when I tried to interfere, Riku just grabbed me by the arm and dragged me outside. It was freezing, but we took a walk around the estate, each of the guys taking turns keeping me warm.

"Look! I wonder if we can skate on this lake." Cole squats down to study the frozen expanse of water in front of us.

"You skate and ride horses?" I ask, leaning against Jace. It's his turn to keep me warm, not that I was the one who instituted a rule about switching off. There might have been some pouts once the others saw how much my "heater" got to cuddle while they got nothing.

"Yeah, we had a lake that froze over every winter. Ranching slows down in winter anyway, so we kept ourselves amused by playing ice hockey."

"It's all too cold for me. I've never been on skates or the back of a horse, to be honest. Now, give me a fishing pole and an unfrozen lake, and I know exactly what to do with it." I feel Jace shiver, his now shaky Southern accent highlighting why he's not so keen on the cold.

"We'll just have to fix that." Shane kisses him on the cheek and steps over to look closer at the lake with Cole. He points to something. "It looks plenty thick enough." We all turn to check out what he's pointing at—a hole.

"Why would there be a hole in the middle of the lake?" Jace whispers to me, and I struggle to hide my smile. I don't want to make him feel bad.

"That's for the fishing pole you were talking about." Alex comes over and joins us on my other side, while the other three chatter on about what fish might be in the pond.

"It's also so the fish don't die when the water freezes over." The unexpected voice behind us has us all jumping.

Ash is standing back a bit, his hands shoved into his pockets. "If the lake stays completely frozen, there's not enough gas exchange, and all the fish will die. Our groundskeepers drill a hole in the ice so that the fish can continue to live."

He sounds so sad that I pull away from my two

heaters and walk over to him for a hug. He shivers in my arms, and I hold him tight.

"I don't know how that woman became so bitter. I mean, I have never seen her any other way, but still," he whispers into my neck, and I rub his back. "Thank you. I'll never be able to repay you for everything you've done." He pulls away to look me in the eye, and I wink.

"Oh, I don't know. Keep doing some of the things you did last night, and we can call it even."

That finally chases away the haunted look, but before he can reply, another voice catches our attention—a young female voice.

"Ash!"

The lake is down in a slight hollow, and at the top, a young girl is waving her arms.

"Edie!" Ash breaks away from me and runs up the embankment toward his sister.

"Come on." Alex grabs me by the hand and starts dragging me up the hill. "I want to meet her."

I dig my heels and pull him to a stop. "You're not going to hold it against her, are you?" Alex's brow wrinkles in confusion, and I feel a touch of relief.

"What do you mean?"

"Ash broke up with you because of her." Shane steps up next to us and puts an arm around my shoulders. "I think what Jacinta is asking is if you hold a grudge."

Comprehension crosses Alex's face, and I see a

hint of hurt in the expression. "No, of course not. I would have done the same thing."

"I'm sorry. I shouldn't have suggested you would," I apologize, and Alex shrugs as Cole, Riku, and Jace follow Ash up the hill.

Alex sighs and looks between me and Shane. "At the time, I probably would have, but things are different now. I have Shane and Jace and you, and I'd like to think I've grown up a bit since then. Ash is… Well, Ash is the one that got away. I'm not sure I ever stopped loving him, but I'm super happy with what we have."

Shane growls under his breath, but we're so close together that it makes me jump. "We have talked about this. Jace and I have no problems if you want to try to reconnect with Ash, and I'm almost certain Jazzy doesn't mind. Hell, I'd be disappointed if you didn't. Look at that man." We watch as he reaches his sister, picks her up, and swings her around. "Fuck, my dick gets hard looking at him," Shane complains, adjusting himself in his pants.

"I don't know, maybe." With that surprising dismissal, Alex walks up the hill, leaving us gaping.

"He's really torn," I say as Shane grabs my hand to follow him.

"Yeah, he really is. We know how much he loves us. Don't get me wrong, if Ash wasn't a part of all of this, if he wasn't a part of this thing we've got going, then he would be off-limits, but I don't see the problem because he is."

I chuckle. "This *thing*? Still won't say harem?"

"No, I won't give Alex the satisfaction."

"Well, maybe you need a quiet word in Ash's ear. He seems to be quite dominant as well. Maybe you and him need to convince Alex this is what he needs."

Shane's eyes glimmer, and he wets his lip with his tongue. "I may just do that."

"Can you do it at the castle so Jace and I can stand in one of the hidden rooms and watch?" He stops to look at me with disbelief before it gives way to a purely wicked lift of his lips.

"You're on."

"Jazzy! Come meet my sister," Ash calls, waving his hand, so Shane and I continue up the slope toward the group. When we get there, I don't even get a chance to say anything before Edie is throwing herself at me.

"Oh my god, Jacinta, you are super amazing! Thank you so much."

Her slender arms come around me in a tight hug. She's a petite little thing, maybe even slightly underweight for her age, with a mass of long, curly black hair. When she pulls away, I get a good look at her. She's the female version of Ash, all aristocratic bone structure and plump lips with the same warm, whiskey brown eyes.

"Oh, aren't you gorgeous?" Alex takes her from

my arms and twirls her around like a ballerina. "You are going to be leaving a trail of broken hearts in your wake. You better lock this one up now, Ash. I think Jacinta's got a room for her at the top of the castle in Romania that has bars on it." Edie giggles with delight and pulls away to pinch him on the ass. Alex's mouth purses with shock.

"Alex Winters, you are one of the sexiest men on the planet. Like you can talk. Maybe Shane should do the same thing as you!"

Riku raises an eyebrow. "You know who they are?"

Edie rolls her eyes in that way girls perfect once they hit their teen years. "Of course I do. I go to an all-girls boarding school. Fashion is a major topic. I also know that Jace is the next best thing in fashion design. No offense," she says to me, looking a little guilty.

I can't help the smile that spreads across my face. "None taken, it's completely true." The two of us giggle as Jace blushes and shuffles on the spot.

"And Ash introduced you to Riku and Cole?" I ask, and she fans her face dramatically.

"He sure did. I don't know how you can stand to be surrounded by so much beefcake." Those words in that posh English accent have us all laughing.

"Can you guys give us a moment?" he asks once we get our laughter under control. The rest of the guys leave, and Ash takes me by the hand. "How about we walk to the stables? There's something Jazzy and I want to talk to you about."

"What's going to happen now, Ash? There's no furniture left in the house. What happened to it all? Grandmother said to ask you and your… trollop." She grimaces and looks guilty about parroting her grandmother, but I just shrug it off. "She's really angry."

"Well, you don't have to worry because Ash saved the house. What do you say about helping me refurnish it?" Her eyes widen with surprise before she nods enthusiastically.

"Yes please, that would be awesome."

We get to the stables. The door is hard to open since it doesn't slide well, and when we get inside, Ash wrinkles his nose at the state of disrepair.

"What happened to Sammy?" he asks, and Edie frowns.

"Grandma got rid of Sammy last Christmas. Said with me in boarding school, there was no point in paying for a groom or to feed an animal that wasn't being used."

"Sammy was supposed to be going to school with you," Ash counters.

"Grandmother pulled me out of riding lessons, so there was no need for him to be there."

Ash growls, and I feel sorry for this poor girl. It seems like a lot of things went on that she didn't share with her big brother.

"Why didn't you tell him?" I ask her gently, and she shrugs.

"I didn't want to be a burden to him. I'm young, but I'm not stupid. I know the reason he was never home is because Grandmother can be so terrible."

"Oh, Edie." Ash pulls his sister into a hug, looking guiltily over her shoulder at me. Then he pulls away and drags us over to a dusty pile of hay bales. "There are some things you should know. I don't want to have any secrets or hide things from you anymore." Edie takes a seat and puts her hands in her lap, waiting for him to continue. I sit down on one of the other bales, but Ash stays standing, pacing back and forth.

"Ash, just spit it out. I'm not a baby," Edie demands, and when he looks at me, I nod. She's old enough. Teenagers with access to the internet know a lot more than I did at their age.

"First things first, I have been appointed your guardian. Grandmother no longer has a say in what goes on with your life."

"Oh thank goodness." Tears shimmer in her eyes. "I overheard her talking about making me marry an old man, Ash!" He stops his pacing and sits down next to his sister, putting his arm around her.

"I never would have allowed it, even if I had to kidnap you. But yes, I knew about that. She's been holding it over my head as a way to keep me from being honest about myself."

She wipes away the stray tear that escaped and frowns at him. "What do you mean?"

He takes a deep breath and blurts out, "I'm bisexual, and Grandmother wouldn't let me come out of the closet. By threatening you, she was making it so I couldn't *embarrass* the family name by being queer." He sneers when he says the last part, showing how he feels about that.

"Oh no, Ash, that's awful. I'm so sorry." It's her turn to wrap her arms around her brother, and I give them a moment to comfort one another.

"So does that mean you and Jacinta aren't in a relationship?" she asks as they separate. "Is she your... beard?"

Ash snorts, and I put a hand over my mouth to smother my laughter. "Oh, she's not my beard. She's my girlfriend, but I'm not her only boyfriend."

She frowns, then her lips round in surprise. "Oh okay, polyamory. That's what it's called, right? Some of the older girls at school read books like that. Reverse harem, I think they are called."

"Yes, kind of like that," he answers, but then he looks at me. "Maybe you should explain it."

"Ha! Chicken," I scold him, and he shrugs without denying it. "Okay, well, all the men you just met are my boyfriends."

"But Alex, Shane, and Jace are like the 'it' throuple," she argues, and Ash shakes his head.

"Yes, they are, but it's because Jacinta has been keeping her involvement with them a secret for my sake. They are like me, bisexual, and Jacinta is a part of their relationship."

"What about Cole and Riku? Are they as well?" she asks.

"No, Riku and Cole are heterosexual, and I have one-on-one relationships with them."

The little crease between her eyes is adorable as she tries to get it all straight within her mind. Once it all seems to settle in, the cheeky little shit turns to Ash. "Well, why aren't you involved with all that delicious man meat as well?"

Ash's mouth drops open in surprise, and laughter bursts from my lips as Edie giggles. He's stammering, so I decide to throw him a bone. "Ash used to be in a relationship with Alex, but it didn't end so great. So maybe we just leave them be while they work out how they are going to navigate this whole complicated thing."

"Well, you'd be stupid not to tap any of that, I'm just saying." She crosses her arms, and there's a stubborn set to her jaw.

"So none of this bothers you?" I ask, unable to hold back my curiosity. I might also be feeling slightly protective of Ash. He survived his grandmother's harsh criticisms, but I don't know if he'd make it through this if his sister wasn't supportive. He looks at her like she holds the world in her hands, and I have a feeling he'd just fall apart if

Edie decided she couldn't love her brother as he is.

"No, why should it bother me? As long as you treat Ash well and love him as much as you love the others, I'm happy for him."

"You wouldn't be opposed to coming to live with us?" I ask her, and even Ash looks at me with surprise. "Well, I kind of figured it's a discussion we need to have. As much as I don't want to leave Dad's place, it really isn't practical to have all of us live there, not with Hope and the McCallisters living there too."

"You... You want me to live with you?" she stammers, looking between me and Ash.

"Yeah, of course I do, but I haven't really asked Ash to live with me yet either, so I guess I'm jumping the gun. You two might want to stay here in London, but as much as I enjoy visiting, I have no desire to live here permanently." I'm rambling with embarrassment now.

"Whatever you decide, I would love to live with you," she assures me. "If it means I don't have to go to that bloody boarding school again, I'd be happy to have a home anywhere."

"No, I'm sure we can work something out, even if we get you a tutor because we travel so much. It might be disruptive to take you in and out of normal schooling."

"Did you know that Alex has his teaching

degree?" Ash says conversationally, leaning back against the stable door.

"Seriously? I had no idea. When did he have time to do that?"

"He was doing it when we were together between modeling gigs. He knew that modeling wouldn't be forever, and I'm sure by now you realize how much he loves children." I blush because I'm intimately familiar with exactly how much he loves kids and wants his own. "So he did a teaching degree as a backup. He focused on the little ones, but it wouldn't take much to get him up to speed to teach Edie. That's assuming he finished, but maybe I'm wrong." Ash brushes off his clothes and holds out a hand for me. He pulls me up and places a kiss on my lips. "Thank you," he whispers as Edie giggles.

With a lot shared between us, we make our way back to the house. We've got a lot of decisions to make. Edie and Spencer make those decisions particularly important, ones we need to make soon, but I hope we can all at least make it through Christmas first.

Chapter Twenty-One

Christmas comes in a whirlwind of activity, food, drinks, and gift giving. Although I told the guys I didn't want them spending money on me, of course they didn't listen.

Shane gave me a blown-up photo he must have taken in Hawaii. It's of Jace, Alex, and me strolling down the beach, hand in hand, after our dinner. Jace designed me a sexy set of exclusive lingerie in bright red. Riku gave me a small taser to keep in my bag, which I completely appreciated for its practicality. Knowing that his gift was meant to give me safety and comfort gave me the warm fuzzies in a different way than the others' gifts. Cole's present is from him and Spencer—a framed drawing that Spencer did of him riding DS when he came to visit. Ash gave me a signed set of paperback novels from one of my favorite authors. It's a series I'd been reading on my kindle. I can't believe he was sneaky enough to have a look at it without me noticing.

But Alex's gift was the one that had me laughing the most. He gave me a book of baby names and a pregnancy test. Could he be any less subtle? I had just finished processing that when he disappeared and came out with a big box. When he put it down on the ground, it shuddered like there was something in it.

"What's this?" I ask, and he tries to control how excited he is but fails miserably.

"Open it. It's from all of us," he insists, but Shane pulls him back onto his lap and shakes his head.

"Yes, but it was your idea." He kisses our boyfriend soundly, but Alex is too impatient to sink into it as usual.

"Hurry, she's been waiting."

"Huh?" A small yip has me reaching for the paper and tearing it back before the top of the box pops open. A little white puppy sticks her head out. "Oh my god, she's adorable!" I reach in and scoop the tiny thing into my hands, bringing her out. Edie is instantly by my side, talking to her and scratching her head.

"Alex suggested that maybe what you needed to help with your anxiety was a puppy. We spoke to your therapist, and she said it was a great idea. We could have her certified as an emotional support dog, so you can take her everywhere with you,"

Riku explains, getting down with us and cooing at the puppy as I rub her nose against mine.

"Oh, and wait!" Alex tries to scramble off Shane's lap, but his firm lover wraps his arms around him and holds him tight, allowing Jace to bring out another gift box.

"We picked out some cool accessories and things for her. She's up to date on vaccinations and worming treatment, and Harlow said she'll do the spaying when it's time." He passes the box to Edie who opens it up and starts digging around. I put the wiggling puppy down when Edie finds a rubber chicken and squeaks it for her. The puppy barks with delight and runs her tiny, stumpy legs toward it only to tumble over in her haste.

"You need to think of a name for her." Cole's leaning over the back of the couch, smiling. "I'll bet Spencer will ask for one now too."

"I'll think about her name for a few days. I want to get a feel for her nature." I shuffle across the carpet on my knees until I get to Alex and Shane, then I lean in, putting my arms around both of them. "Thank you," I whisper into Alex's abs. "It's the nicest present anyone has ever given me."

"Well, while you're down there…" Alex nods in the direction of his dick, but Ash reaches over and slaps him on the back of the head.

"Dude, my sister."

"Rain check," I promise him.

Edie and the guys were thrilled with their gifts

from me, and I can't wait to take Edie for her makeover. We FaceTime with everyone back home, which was a noisy and long affair, and I was thrilled to see the smallest baby bump developing on Harlow's stomach. Of course I made her lift her shirt to show me.

Edie was a little overwhelmed, but Nana had her coming out of her shell, and I can see that she's going to be another one my family adopts as their own. She already has a date with Dad to go riding when we eventually return.

And that was the big question of the day. When are we returning? Soon, but I'm not quite ready yet, and it's with this in mind that I make the next suggestion.

"I'm a little sick of the cold. How does everyone feel about South America for the new year?"

"Yes!" Alex shouts in tandem with Jace.

"Are you sure?" Riku assesses me with his serious gaze, and I shrug.

"Yeah, I mean, why not? We need to deal with the property down there. We might as well."

"I think what Riku means is that there could very well be coke in that house as well." At least Cole is diplomatic enough to whisper that while Edie is distracted by Alex and Jace. It's not that I plan to keep my addiction a secret from the people who are important, or will be important, in my life. It's just that I need to take each step on my own time. I've been working on confronting my problem and the roots of it, and being open and honest about it to other people will be the next step I take once I've worked up the courage to do it.

"Colombia is well known for its drug trade," Shane says just as quietly.

"I'm fine, I swear. It wasn't that I was addicted to the coke for the coke, but for how it made me feel when I went out. I didn't use it when there was no chance of me running into anyone, and I think I've pretty much worked through most of that anyway. I'll keep up with my therapy and my NA meetings just to be safe," I say to the men I've grown to love. It costs me nothing to make this promise, and I mean those words. It's not bravado or denial or coke-driven confidence. I've honestly made genuine strides that let me say these words with a real belief that I can and will follow through.

"Then I say let's go," Ash says, nodding to Edie, "as long as she can come."

"Ash, I said it before, but I'll say it again. We are not leaving her behind, ever," I assure him and then sigh. "I was pushing this conversation off because, well, it's a complicated one, but I think we need to talk about our relationships going forward. Hey, Edie," I call out, and she stops her banter with Alex and Jace to look at me.

"Do you want to head upstairs and pack anything you want to take with us? We may not be coming back here for a few months. Oh, and can you keep the puppy with you for the moment?" I ask, and she jumps up, bending over to pick up the toy poodle.

"Sure, but I don't need a distraction. Just ask me for some privacy next time." She's smiling as she walks away, and Riku shakes his head, smiling after her.

"That girl is way too astute for her own good."

"So, what is it you wanted to talk about?" Shane asks, wrapping a strand of my hair around his fist and tugging me toward him for a blistering kiss.

"Oh yeah, I can get on board with this. Orgy!" Alex starts to strip off his shirt, and I pull away from Shane.

"For fuck's sake, Alex. My sister could walk back at any time." Ash throws his shirt back to him, but I don't miss the way he also takes a good, solid look of Alex's abs.

Alex puts his shirt back on with a pout. I swear the man who's obsessed with having kids is nothing but a big one himself.

"What's next?" I ask, and the six of them exchange a confused glance.

"What do you mean?" Cole's the one who asks.

"Well, eventually, we all need to go back home, sooner rather than later. Cole needs to go back to work, not to mention Spencer, as do all of you. Riku is fine with me, and I guess Ash now needs to start thinking of his life as a guardian to his sister and committed partner in a relationship, and need to give Edie some stability. But there are too many of us to move into Dad's place or your apartment. And then there's another question. Do we want to live together, or are you guys happy just spending time together and not necessarily living together? We've never talked about it, and I guess I feel like I need to know where we stand."

They all seem to mull over the question, and it's Jace who finally speaks up. "What about you? What do you want?"

"Well, I love you all. I hate the thought of us being apart, but I want to figure out something that works for everyone." I'm not looking at them, and I realize that you could hear a pin drop in the room because it's so quiet. Fuck, what's the problem now? As I look at each of the men for a clue, I think back to what I just said. Oh! I guess I've never come out and really said *it* to any of them even though it's how I feel, even for Cole.

"You love us?" It's Shane who finally breaks the silence, the others practically vibrating with anticipation for my answer.

"Well, yeah. I mean, of course I do. I know it's soon, and I completely understand if it's not how you all feel too." I quickly rush that out so they don't think they have to say it back to me, but then I shore up my strength. I'm not going to apologize for my feelings. "Life is too short to waste on maybes and what-ifs and obeying social niceties. I love you all and can't wait to start a life together. I want us all to live in one house and make decisions together and have babies." I look at Alex with that comment. "As soon as we possibly can. I don't want to wait anymore. God, with what I inherited, none of you ever have to work again if you don't want to. You can all be kept men, and we can just enjoy life." I finish my uncontrollable rant, and for a moment it's still so quiet that I feel my heart sink. Crap, maybe they don't want it? Maybe they are all happy with their lives the way they are?

Ash is the first to move, but it's like he unpaused them all. They come at me with their own words of love and reassurance, which is music to my ears, and for the next ten minutes, I'm swept up in kisses and hugs and individual declarations of love from each of them.

Alex is last, and he just throws me over his shoulder and starts for the staircase.

"Where are you going?" I hear Riku demand from behind us.

"Babies," is all Alex says, and I laugh and smack him on the ass.

Louder than my giggles, Ash calls out, "My sister is still around."

"Dude, she's always going to be around. We'll have to soundproof the bedroom or get her and Spencer some noise-canceling headphones."

He doesn't stop, so I start to wiggle. "Put me down, you doofus. I have to have my implant removed."

He stops and slides me down his body. "You

mean all this time I've been trying there's been no chance?" He sounds a little devastated.

"No, sorry. I thought you realized that when I told you about the birth control in Hawaii."

He wrinkles his nose sheepishly. "I was hoping maybe you'd forgotten to take it. Kind of like how Harlow got pregnant."

"Yeah, no, that's why I have an implant. But hey, practice makes perfect, right?" His pout clears, and he bends down to throw me over his shoulder again, but I hold up my hands. "Nope! I have to make some calls and have Forrest let the law firm in Colombia know what we're doing. Plus, we still haven't made any decisions about where we'll live when we return after the new year. *And* Ash's grand-mother will be here soon for Christmas lunch."

"Ha, I'm surprised the old bat is even coming. I refuse to hide what we have anymore." He crosses his arms, and I look around the room. The rest of the guys are in agreement, even Ash.

"Well, that's fine. She's got nothing to hold over our heads anymore," I agree, cringing at the thought of how uncomfortable lunch is going to be, but we're all she has. It would have been rude not to invite her, especially since we practically shoved her out of the house and into the assisted living place. "Why don't you all go pack while I make phone calls? The kitchen staff is hard at work on lunch, and I have the chauffeur going to pick up Elizabeth. We have nothing to worry about until she gets here, which, if I've timed it right, should be just as the meal hits the table. That way there's no awkward small talk beforehand. We can all keep food in our mouths to avoid conversation."

Jace laughs. "I'm not sure it will be as easy as that."

Cole shudders. "No, that woman is a menace. I anticipate we'll be having the most uncomfortable Christmas ever."

"I'll make it up to all of you, I promise. It just didn't feel right booting her out and leaving her on her own."

"That's because you're a really good person." Riku kisses me on the forehead, which he knows I love, before heading up the stairs to pack.

"Yup. He's right. I would have let her suffer," Alex agrees as he grabs Shane and Jace by the hands and drags them away too, with Cole trailing behind.

Ash comes over to me and draws me into his arms. I rest my head on his chest, and his heart beats steadily into my ear. "They are all right. She hasn't deserved any kindness, but I do appreciate it for Edie's sake."

"You guys will always be my priority, so if she's too much of a cow, we'll just ask her to leave. I had to at least try."

"I know, and that's why we love you too." With that parting remark, Ash heads upstairs, and I sit down on the couch to make my phone calls.

Before I can, my cell rings. On the screen is Thomas's name. "Hey, big bro, how are things?" I answer, and he chuckles.

"Ah, Jazzy, it's so nice to hear your voice. I can't tell you how worried we've all been. Seeing you so happy at Christmas was the best present you could have given us." A little lump forms in my throat when I think about how worried they all must have been.

"I promise I'll do better."

"I'm sure you will, and I'm sure your guys will make sure you do. Or at least they better. You have six brothers who will dole out some punishment." I giggle and roll my eyes at the protective big brother routine.

"Yeah, yeah. Anyway, is everything okay? How are Harlow and the baby doing? What about Kai? Veronica is due at the end of January, isn't she? He must be starting to freak out."

Tom scoffs. "Hardly, the dude is cool as a cucumber, but I cannot wait to be rid of that woman. It's time she paid for her crimes. Thankfully, the doctor limited our visits to once a month since Thanksgiving. Her blood pressure gets too high when we're there."

"That sucks. I'm sorry."

"Look, that's not what I was calling for. I'm sorry to be the bearer of bad news, but Matthew Shaw has disappeared. They think he's fled to South America to escape trial. I'm so sorry." My stomach rolls with annoyance and a hint of fear. How the fuck did this happen?

"Well, that's fucked." I sigh, and he grunts his agreement.

"Jake is having one of our agents that works down there keep an eye out for him, but for now, he's in the wind. The other news is that Urie Sokolov has also been spotted in South America. He fled there once the Diamant Unlimited execs realized they no longer had any control over their own company."

"Shit, we were going to head to Colombia tomorrow. We're all sick of the cold and wanted something warm for New Year's. I was just about to call Forrest to have him make the arrangements."

"Well, he was last seen in Argentina, so that's nowhere near Colombia. I think you'll be fine, but I'm going to send Riku an email with Sokolov's file so he can familiarize himself with what he looks like just in case. With the private plane and the funds we have, Forrest can make sure your arrival and transportation is as quiet as possible. There's no need for any fanfare, and if we do this as stealthily as we can, there's no reason to believe that Urie would hear about your arrival in South America."

"Okay, thanks." It's comforting that Thomas is being so pragmatic about this. If he had started freaking out, I might have lost my nerve to go there. Sure, my brothers can be overprotective at the best of times, but I still trust their instincts. If Thomas says it's okay, then we can do this and stay safe.

We talk about family stuff for a little longer, but then he hangs up so I can make the rest of my calls, putting what he just shared with me out of my mind. Christmas Day is not for worrying about attempted rapists and treasonous Russian criminals.

Chapter Twenty-Two

C hristmas lunch turned out to be perfect because when the chauffeur arrived to pick up Elizabeth, she refused to get in the car, so our meal was full of laughter and affection. The only thing missing was having Spencer and my family around, but we'll see them in the new year.

We actually discussed what we were going to do for housing, and a decision was reached. We're going to build something on Dad's land because they are all in agreement that they are happy to stay close to my family. While the construction is happening, we're going to try to find something to rent nearby. Nana is working on that for us, and the guys are going to start looking over house plans or at least writing a list of what we want and finding an architect to help us out. While I was talking to Nana, she mentioned that Parker McCallister is a qualified architect, so maybe I'll just ask him to draw us up some plans. Might as well keep it in the family, so to speak.

My phone calls were successful, and the law firm in Bogotá is expecting us to arrive in Colombia two days after Christmas. From there, we'll travel to Cartagena, a seaside city where the Bucătaru estate is. The groundskeeper will be expecting us and will help with anything we may need.

It's with great enthusiasm that we're all up bright and early on Boxing Day. The flight from London to Bogotá is about eleven hours, so I'll sign some paperwork with the lawyers who will meet us at the airport while the plane refuels, then we'll fly on to Cartagena, where two hired cars will be waiting to take us to the Bucătaru estate which sits about twenty minutes north of the city. It's going to be a long couple of days. Ash and I spend the morning giving the staff instructions on furnishing the place, and then we kill some time shopping for the Romanian castle. Poor Cole, Shane, and Riku were bored out of their brains, but Ash, Jace, and Alex had fun helping me pick things.

Edie's eyes are wide with amazement as we board the plane late afternoon. "Holy shit, this is amazing. Some of the girls at school were rich, but this is next-level rich."

"You have no idea," Jace mutters to her as we say hi to James, Chris, and Jilly before he makes his way into the back of the plane.

I snicker with laughter. He's become accustomed to it now, but he was just like Edie the first time. I introduce the staff to Edie as Jilly tucks her arm into hers and drags her off for a tour of the plane.

"Jilly has prepared a meal for you. It will be served just after takeoff," James tells me as the steps are wheeled away and he closes the doors. "Then it would be best to sleep most of the way there. We should land in Bogotá just after five AM. I'll wake you all about an hour before landing in case anyone wants a shower or anything."

"Okay, I'm sure the guys might watch a movie, but that sounds great. The lawyers aren't meeting us until about eight AM, so we can have breakfast and refuel while we wait for them."

"Excellent. You know the drill. If you need anything, just call out," he says before joining Chris in the cockpit.

Takeoff is smooth, and dinner is delicious. Edie and the guys do get in a movie, but I snuggle up on a couch with Dolce and pull out my bag of yarn and my needles. It's been so long since I've had a chance to knit. I want to create something for the babies coming into my life, but Dolce is getting a cute little jacket first. I've got some hot pink feathery wool that's going to really pop against her white coat. I was worried about traveling with her, but I did some research and realized that it's not as difficult as I thought. I put some puppy pee pads down in the shower of the master bedroom and will take her down there for a chance to wee during the flight. She's crate trained too, so once I put her in there, she will let us know if she needs to go. She's such a smart floofy ball. I am so totally in love with her.

When we finally arrive in Colombia, it's early morning. The sun is starting to poke its nose over the horizon, and the temperature is expected to be warm today, certainly a contrast to London.

Once the lawyers arrive, they are shown into the plane's conference room. Only Riku accompanies me to the meeting, the others letting me deal with this on my own.

"Thank you for making the trip out here for me. I appreciate it," I tell the two gentlemen, gesturing for them to take a seat at the table.

"It's our pleasure." Miguel, the older brother, and Emilio, the younger of the pair, exchange glances. "Yes, but I can't tell you how surprised we were when we were contacted by your lawyers and apprised of the situation. We had thought the Bucă-taru line ended with the count."

"What was going to happen to the estate?" I ask. According to the trust lawyers, it was going to revert to them after a certain amount of time. Or that's how I understood it.

Emilio shrugs. "The caretaker is doing a good job, so we would have just continued the way it is now."

That seems kind of weird to me, but who am I to argue with them? Miguel pulls some paperwork out of his bag before I can dig into that thought. "If you would sign these, they are just documents transferring the deed into your and your brother's names. Your lawyer has looked them over and sent you correspondence okaying it."

Having seen the email from Forrest, I don't hesitate to sign on my and Jax's behalf.

"The caretaker's name is Diego Blanco. He lives at the estate and will be able to answer any questions you have, but don't hesitate to contact us if there is anything you need," Emilio offers as they both stand up, and I shake their hands.

Riku is a quiet presence at my back as we watch them go down the steps, but as soon as they are in their car, he wraps his arms around me. "Was it just me, or did they seem shifty as fuck?"

I lean my head back against him. "Yeah, they did give off a bit of a creepy vibe, but Forrest assured me the documents were on the up and up. I guess we did kind of appear out of the blue. Neither the count nor Dragos knew about us, so it really isn't surprising that they are a little shaken. It was only announced to the world a few weeks ago during the press conference, so I guess they are still adjusting to the news."

"Jacinta." Jilly's voice has us both turning. "If you're finished with your business, the guys are ready to get this bus in the air again."

"Yeah, let's go. I can't wait to see what I've inherited."

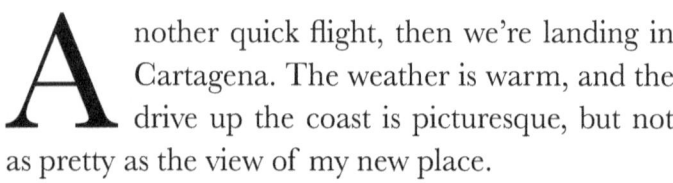

Another quick flight, then we're landing in Cartagena. The weather is warm, and the drive up the coast is picturesque, but not as pretty as the view of my new place.

"Holy crap!" Edie, who claimed the spot next to me in the car, leans forward as we drive up the long, winding driveway. "This view is spectacular."

The estate is perched on a hillside that looks over a pristine white beach with what appears to be a fairly decent surf break rolling in. There are a few surfers sitting on boards, patiently waiting for the next wave.

Ash pulls the car to a stop in the driveway of a sprawling multi-level Spanish colonial mansion with orange roof tiles and white rendered brick. The gardens are a riot of palm trees and green foliage that look like they haven't been tended to in years.

The other car pulls in next to us, and we all get out to look around. I've got Dolce under my arm, holding her tight when she wiggles to be put down. I wouldn't want to lose her in the overgrowth. "Looks like it needs some work," Ash comments, putting a hand up to shield his eyes against the sun.

"Hopefully it's just some maintenance to the

gardens. Maybe the inside is okay." Jace tries to reassure me as the front door opens, and a man steps out onto the veranda. His face is in the shadows, but he looks to be tall and fit, wearing shorts and a T-shirt, and his skin is deeply tanned.

It's quiet for a moment, I guess he's studying us, before an American accented voice calls out, "Hi there, you must be the new owner. I'm Diego. Come on in." He steps forward, and I finally get a look at him.

He's probably about my dad's age, with a few wrinkles around his blue-green eyes, which are framed by thin spectacles. His long bleach-blond hair is down to his shoulders, and it has that messy, just got back from a surf look to it. He's smiling at us. Behind me, one of the guys gasps quietly, but I ignore it.

"Hi, I'm Jacinta Summers, and these are my boyfriends." I introduce everyone, and I've got to give the guy credit, he barely flinches when I announce my relationship. But I wouldn't have cared if he did. I refuse to hide it from anyone no matter what they think.

"Well, it's great to meet you all. I can't tell you how shocked I was when the lawyers contacted me and told me the news. I can't believe an heir was found after all these years. Come in, please, and I'll show you around." He waves his hand at the door, and we all move forward.

Diego gives a quick tour of the house, pointing

out the game room, theater, library, and gym. When we return to the sprawling open-plan living area, he shoves his hands into the pockets of his shorts. "You've had a long flight, so I'll leave you to get settled in and explore the rest at your leisure. I've hired a chef and a housekeeper for the time you're here. If you need anything, I live in one of the guest houses at the back of the property. If you want to stretch your legs, there's a path that leads down to the beach. There's a boat house of sorts down there with jet skis, surfboards, and SUPs if you want to use them. I look after them all myself, so I can assure you they are all in top condition."

"Are there any secret passages or rooms in this place like the rest of the count's properties?" Alex asks eagerly, and Diego's eyebrows jump.

"You know about them?" He looks at me, his eyes filled with surprise.

"They are my boyfriends. I have no secrets from them."

"Then yes, there are a few, mostly underground, not within the walls of the estate. I can show you those later if you wish. For now, I'll let you rest. I'll see you around." He waves goodbye and leaves, though it seems a little reluctant.

"Okay, so I guess we better find some rooms for us?" I put Dolce down, and she wiggles off, sniffing and wagging her tail in excitement.

"I want a view of the ocean!" Edie shouts and

heads back in the direction of the stairs that lead up.

"Hey, I do too," Alex complains, but I grab him when he starts to head off after her.

"Maybe not too close to her room though, okay?"

He frowns in confusion, and Jace laughs, grabbing him by the hand.

"Because we tend to get a little loud when we fuck," he says quietly in case Edie is still within earshot.

"Oh yeah, okay, good call." They both hurry after her.

"I'll start unloading the bags," Cole says, and Riku and Ash volunteer to help him, which leaves me with Shane.

Shane's quiet as I step up to the huge, bi-fold doors that lead to a veranda with a spectacular view of the rest of the property, overlooking the ocean. "This is gorgeous. I bet you can take some great photos here," I say to him as he wraps his arms around my waist, hugging me from behind.

"I brought my waterproof case, so maybe I can get some photos of us using the equipment later in the week."

"That would be nice."

"Jazzy, babe, did Diego seem familiar to you?" he asks after a few moments.

I feel my forehead wrinkle in a frown. "No, I

don't think so. Why? I mean, I guess I really didn't look at him that closely."

"Babe, come sit down." He leads me to a sofa, and we sit down together, our bodies angled so that we can look at each other while we speak. "I might be wrong, but I don't think I am. I probably look at people differently due to my profession, but I would stake my reputation on this. I'm almost a hundred percent sure that Diego is actually Dragos. Think about what he'd look like with short black hair and no glasses. He's basically the spitting image of what Jax will look like in twenty years."

I feel my heart race at his words, and I jump to my feet and start pacing back and forth across the tiled floors, mulling over what he just said, trying to picture it in my head.

"Do you really think so?" I ask him, and he nods.

"Yeah, babe, I really do."

"Why wouldn't he tell me?"

"I guess it's probably as much of a shock to him as it was to you. Remember, you've known for a lot longer. Maybe he just wasn't sure how to tell you. Not to mention, he's obviously using a different identity. It couldn't have been easy being the son of Count Bucătaru. Maybe he's hiding in plain sight too."

"I need to know. I'm going to find him. Watch Dolce for me?"

"Whoa, hold your horses," he says as the other guys return with our bags.

"Why are we holding our horses?" Cole asks, dropping the bags he's holding onto the ground.

Probably realizing how much I need to get on the move right now, Shane says, "Riku, can you go with Jazzy? I'll explain to the others."

"Thank you." I hurry in the direction I saw Diego go, hoping that Riku keeps up.

Chapter Twenty-Three

Jacinta

"Hey, slow down! What are we doing? Where are we going?" Riku catches up to me as I exit the house. Looking around the property, I try to decide where he went.

The backyard is gently sloped downward, away from the house, and it's filled with vegetation, but I can see a few buildings in the distance. I take a wild stab that one of them is the guest house, find a trail that's well traveled and not as overgrown as the rest of the backyard, and head in that direction.

"Shane thinks Diego is actually Dragos," I call over my shoulder, and I hear Riku curse and the thud of feet as he runs to catch up with me. In his hand is his pistol, and he pushes in front of me to lead the way.

"What are you doing?" I ask, a little surprised at seeing the weapon.

"If he is your biological dad, we don't know if he's friendly or not."

"If he wanted to hurt us, I think he would have laid a trap for our arrival."

"Maybe, but let's just be careful anyway."

It doesn't take us long before we reach the tiny replica of the main house. There, sitting on the patio, with a beer in one hand and a cigar in the other, is the man Shane thinks is my father.

"You can put the weapon down. I mean you no harm," Diego says to Riku. "Why don't you pull up a chair, and I'll get you both a drink. I guess we need to have a conversation."

I snort. "You think?"

A wry grin crosses his mouth. "Jesus, you remind me of your mother when you say that." I feel myself grimace, and he rubs a hand across his jaw, wincing. "Yeah, I guess we have a lot to talk about." He gets up and goes inside. Riku doesn't put his gun away until he returns with two more beers in hand. "Come on, I won't bite."

He hands us each one, and Riku finally holsters his weapon. The cigar smoke drifts around us as he takes a couple of puffs while we find a seat.

"Are you Dragos Bucătaru?" I ask him, not wanting to wait anymore.

"Yes, Jacinta, I am your father."

Holy shit. I giggle hysterically at my very own

Star Wars moment. Jax is going to be bummed he missed it.

"While Jacinta gets her brain under control, why don't you explain to us how you ended up here?" Riku suggests. "You've obviously seen the news and know that you have kids, so why didn't you come forward? What are you doing in South America when you could be living back in the US?"

Diego sighs. "I guess you know by now what kind of man my father really was." He's not asking a question that requires an answer, so neither of us speak, letting him continue on.

"As a kid, I idolized my father. He was everything I wanted to be when I grew up, and not having a mother, he was really my only parental figure. But by the time I was a teenager, I had started to realize the kind of man he truly was, and I was sixteen when I really learned how depraved he was. He started inviting me to his sex parties and offering me drugs. For a week or two, I indulged. I mean, what sixteen-year-old wouldn't take a little advantage of a free opportunity to party? But then I invited Brad and Chuck to join me, and they both freaked out. It was their reactions that made me rethink what I felt about Dad."

He stops to take a sip, avoiding our eyes like he's worried he'll find judgment if he looks at us. "After that, I tried to stay as far away as possible. I didn't want to be involved with his illegal dealings. I spent all my time at the Summers' place, but then he introduced me to Carmen. He told me she was an old friend of the family and asked me to show her around LA. It wasn't long before I found myself head over heels in love with her, but I didn't want her caught up in my father's lifestyle, so I made plans for us to run away together. I was going to raid the vault and steal enough money for us to live off of until we could find jobs and establish new lives. I didn't even tell Chuck and Brad, just made our excuses as to why we couldn't visit Chuck out in Connecticut."

"We know most of this," I say harshly, wanting to get to the bit that's still a mystery. I know he can't understand the baggage connected to my mother's memory, but hearing him talk about her—loving her, wanting a life with her—just makes me a bit… unsettled. I don't want to think about what could have been, what my life could have been, if they had actually succeeded in his plan.

"And you know that Carmen wasn't actually an old friend but one of my dad's girls?"

"Yes, just tell us what happened when Julia shot you."

"Well, Julia and Dad were waiting in the vault when I went down to steal from it. Dad and I were arguing when Julia grabbed a gun and aimed it at us. She made demands. She wanted my father to marry her and make her the heir to his fortune, but he just laughed in her face. Told her no two-bit whore was going to ever inherit his kingdom. It was the weirdest thing. I expected her to throw a tantrum or something like that, but she just... smiled and said 'We'll see,' and pulled the trigger. I couldn't believe she actually hit him because she was coked out of her head, but when he collapsed with the hole in the middle of his forehead, I turned and ran. I heard the gun fire again and felt a blinding pain in my back, strong enough to make me stumble and hit my head. I blacked out. When I came to, the vault was closed, and Julia was gone."

"Okay, so what happened next?" I lean forward in my seat, finally getting the answers to one of the questions that has plagued me since we found only one body in the vault.

"There's another way out of the vault, but it's carefully hidden, and if you don't know it's there, you'll never find it. It leads to a small tunnel into the back of the walk-in freezer. When I came to, I used this exit to leave. It was late at night, and there was no staff around, so I got in one of our cars and just drove. I had a bullet wound in my shoulder, and I needed it removed. My father's connections spanned far and wide, so I made a call to the South American lawyers you met earlier this morning. They arranged for a private plane to pick me up at the Mexican border and transport me here, where I've lived ever since. They are the only people who know I'm alive."

"That explains how shifty they were this morning," Riku says, his beer sitting untouched because he won't drink it. Instead, one hand is braced on his knee while the other stays close to where he tucked away his gun.

"I had no idea Carmen was pregnant, and I had no intention of returning to the States. She had betrayed me, and my father was dead. This was my way of getting a fresh start."

"Why here?"

"When Pablo Escobar was shot in the early nineties, my father had taken over his substantial drug network, but unlike Pablo, who was flashy and indiscreet, my father was smarter. When he disappeared, gangs in the area tried to take a piece of that network. It started to become messy. I decided that being the Bucătaru estate manager was a good cover, so I took over his business holdings here under that guise. I phased out the flesh business and scaled back the drugs, only dealing with supplying enough to keep all the cartels happy and off my back. We have a good arrangement. I'm not a good man, like Brad or Chuck, but I'm not filthy like my father was."

"And that's why you never came forward when the twins' origins hit the newspapers. You're protecting them." Even though I think I have to agree with Riku, there's still a little bit of skepticism within me.

"Yes. As far as I'm concerned, Dragos Bucătaru died that day. You are the only living heirs to that fortune. I want nothing to do with any family legacy. Though I wouldn't be opposed to getting to know you." His voice lifts in hope as I think about everything he told us.

"I can't keep this a secret from my family. Jax deserves to know," I tell him flatly, not entirely sure how I feel about all of this.

"I understand. I trust Brad, and I'm sure his children are just as trustworthy. But if we could keep it a family secret, not breaking this outside the Summers, I'd appreciate it. I wouldn't want any of my enemies in South America getting wind of you being my child."

I stand up. "Yeah, look, I've got a lot to think about. Thank you for being honest with me." Without a backward glance, I head back up to the main house. I hear Riku and Diego murmuring to each other before Riku hurries to catch up to me. He wraps a comforting arm around my shoulders.

"Want to talk about it?" he asks, and I shake my head.

"Not at the moment."

"Okay, but we're here if you need us. Remember, getting it out is a good way to keep it from festering and turning into some kind of poison. The negative feelings will gain power if you let them, and we will support whatever you need to do to take care of yourself."

"I think I'm going to go to a meeting and call my therapist," I tell him as we get back to the house. Dolce leaves the little bed someone has put out for her and comes running up to me, so I scoop her up in my arms. The guys are nowhere to be seen, and I appreciate them giving me space for the moment. "Just give me until lunchtime, then come find me. I'll be okay, I promise."

His brow is wrinkled with worry, but he agrees, giving me a gentle kiss before allowing me to leave. I wander up the stairs in search of a bedroom where I can wallow in my thoughts for a while, finding the master suite. It's a complete opposite of the one at the castle. This one is all airy and light and beachy, with gauzy curtains surrounding the orgy-sized bed, which makes me crinkle my nose. Hopefully, it's been replaced since the last time anyone came here.

I throw myself on it, careful not to hurt Dolce, and she curls up for a little nap, exhausted by everything that's been going on. I run my hand through her soft white fur and gaze out the window at the tranquil view, so different from the one in Romania. No matter how hard I try, I can't seem to form any coherent thoughts about how I feel. Grabbing my phone, I settle back on one of the pillows and call my therapist. I still have her on a twenty-four-hour retainer, so she gets paid very well to answer my calls whenever and wherever.

My therapist is able to help me get my thoughts in order, and after lunch and reassuring my guys I'm okay, I head back to the guest house to talk to Diego a little more.

"We're going to go into town to grab some supplies," Alex says as I walk out the door.

"And do a little sightseeing?" Edie sounds hopeful, and Alex ruffles her hair.

"Of course." She beams at him, and I smile. They seem to have formed quite a nice friendship, which is great. I want her to get along with all of my guys, but it's especially important that she and Alex develop a relationship in case he and Ash ever reignite the romance between them.

Cole steps up next to me, tipping my chin up with a gentle touch. "I'm going to hang here and call Spencer. So if you need me, I'll be around."

"Thanks, I might need a hug when I come back."

The air is hot, and I swat at a couple of bugs as I walk down the path once more. I might see if Edie wants to have a swim with me this afternoon. The infinity pool is on the side of the house with another superb view. I can see it now—Edie and I trying to work on our tans while Alex cannonballs into the water, with Riku smiling on the sidelines and Shane getting involved to keep the peace. Yes, I might be trying to distract myself from my impending conversation, but a little distraction is a much healthier "remedy for my anxiety than coke, so I'll give myself a moment to daydream.

This time, my nerves are just as big as they were before, but I think it's more due to excitement. Brad is my dad, and Diego or Dragos or whatever he wants to be called will never replace him, but I'm keen to get to know this man who's biologically responsible for Jax and me. I should probably call Jax and tell him everything, but I know he'll be on the next flight out the moment I do. I've already sent the plane back to the States just in case. Jilly and the guys will be on standby, ready to bring him down as soon as I tell him.

Diego isn't on the front veranda this time, so I knock on the door and wait for him to answer. When he does, he's no longer wearing his glasses. His hair is tied back, and I can't believe I didn't see the resemblance before. I guess I'm kind of staring because he chuckles and invites me in.

I follow the man into his little living area. "Can I get you a coffee or something cold?" he asks.

"Actually, coffee would be great."

He goes behind the little counter that separates his kitchen from his living area. "How do you take it?"

"White and two sugars, please."

Diego chuckles. "Does Brad still have it that way? I assume that's why you do."

"Yeah, he actually does. Listen, what do I call

you? It's all confusing in my head. Do you want to be Diego or Dragos? I'm not ready for the other D-word, and I'm not sure I'll ever be. Brad is my dad, and right now, I just know I'm not comfortable with anyone else taking on that title."

His smile drops, and he puts the coffee pot down as he looks at me. "Dragos is dead, and I'd like to keep it that way. Diego works, and I'm hoping one day you might do me the honor of calling me Dad too—if Brad doesn't mind."

"No, he probably wouldn't. He's just that good. Okay, Diego works for now."

"So what can I do for you?" He finishes setting up the coffee machine and starts it up. It hisses and steams, and it's not long before the coffee is dripping through, filling up the jug. He grabs two cups from a cupboard, putting two teaspoons of sugar in one and one in the other.

I wriggle in my chair a little before blurting out, "I guess I just wanted to get to know you."

Those must be the right words because he beams at me. "That sounds wonderful. I feel the same way." So, once the coffee is done, he pours me a cup, and we spend the next three hours just talking about our lives—the hard stuff and the good. We don't hold back from one another. I think we realize that this has been a hard journey for both of us, and only complete transparency is going to cut it going forward. He was devastated to hear what a horrible person Mom turned out to be, though I assure him that Dad more than made up for it.

Finally, a knock at the door has us both jumping, having lost track of time. "That's probably one of your guys coming to check that I haven't buried you somewhere on the property. I'm actually surprised they lasted this long, especially Riku."

I stand up, knowing he's most likely right. "I've really enjoyed this. Maybe I could come back tomorrow?"

"I'd like that," he tells me, and I give him a quick hug, which I think surprises him, but eventually, his arms come up, returning the gesture.

"Oh, I'm going to tell Jax tonight, so he'll probably be here tomorrow too."

"I look forward to meeting him." Diego smiles and lets me out, waving at all six of my men who have made the journey down.

Alex has Dolce on a leash, and she's having a great time sniffing everything. He hands the leash to Riku and steps up onto the porch. "I'll catch up in a minute." We leave him with Diego, the two having a quick and quiet conversation, and when he catches up, he's wearing a smug, satisfied smile. When I look back, Diego appears slightly bewildered, but that's to be expected. We've all felt like that after a conversation with Alex.

"Everything okay?" Shane asks as I join them, and we start our trek back up the hill.

"Yeah, actually. Everything is good, really good," I assure him.

"Edie wants to go for a swim, and she threatened to come and get you herself, so we thought we'd save you the drama," Ash explains from behind. The track's not wide enough for us all to walk abreast, so I'm surrounded, with Shane holding my hand, Alex with Jace, Cole in front, and Riku and Ash bringing up the rear.

"We bought some steaks in town. We're going to grill, and I'm going to make some salads." Oh, I could go for some of Jace's cooking. His declaration has my stomach ready to growl. Now that the nerves are a bit settled by my conversation with Diego, I'm ready to resume my regular life which means paying attention to how hungry I am.

"And I'm going to make cocktails because we're in paradise," Alex singsongs, skipping ahead, having reclaimed the puppy.

"How was Spencer?" I ask Cole, and he grimaces.

"Not happy. He misses me, and his mother is paying no attention to him because she's getting ready for her move to Australia."

"Why doesn't he fly down with Jax?"

"Jax is coming?" Shane asks.

"Well, I'm pretty sure he will when I call him and tell him everything that's happened."

"Yeah, I would too." Riku doesn't sound surprised.

"Do you think Jax would mind? He's a handful."

I laugh. "He needs to get used to it. He's going to have two of his own soon. Honestly, I bet they'll all come. Maybe not Merideth, but I bet every last dime of my fortune that my whole family makes the trip. Don't forget, Diego and Dad were friends. He'll be looking forward to his own reunion, I'm sure."

Alex stops and turns to look at us. "You know what that means?" he says, and I shake my head.

"We need to have our orgy tonight! Can't have one once the family is all here."

Laughter and shouts fill the air as we all react to his words, and it makes my heart feel so full. I didn't think I was the kind of person who deserved to have this kind of joy, but moment by moment, my men are proving that assumption wrong. Maybe Jacinta Summers is the kind of girl who does get a happy ending after all.

"There you are! I was ready to come looking," Edie complains as we step onto the veranda.

"Just give me a moment to get changed and make a call, then I'm all yours," I tell the teenage girl, giving her a kiss on the cheek. Cole echoes the same, grabbing his phone and heading inside.

"Okay." She smiles happily, taking Dolce from Alex and cooing at her.

"I won't be long," I assure them all as I walk away to give my brother some life-changing news.

Chapter Twenty-Four

Jacinta

As predicted, when I give my brother the news, he gets off the phone as quickly as possible so he can make flight arrangements, though it'll be a day or two before they can leave. Harlow has a prenatal appointment, her first one, tomorrow, and they don't want to miss that. Once he hangs up, it just takes a few quick calls for me to figure out the rest of the family is coming too, so I take care of the other arrangements—like hiring cars—then get changed and go back outside to meet Edie and the others.

Dinner was a casual, relaxed affair with lots of shouts and laughter in the swimming pool. Alex disappeared after dinner, reappearing later with a triumphant grin and a smudge of dirt on his face.

"Where have you been?" Edie asks him, wiping a thumb across his cheek to remove the dirt.

"Exploring the secrets underground," he explains, which earns him a pout of his own. Oh shit. Alex has mastered that sad lower lip, but I think he's got nothing on fourteen-year-old-girl pout. He's going to have to up his game if he doesn't want his throne usurped.

"Oh, but I wanted to come too!"

His eyes widen, giving him that deer in the-head-lights look that the rest of us usually get when he turns his pouts on us. But then resolve stiffens his shoulders. "Tomorrow. Why don't you head up to bed? We can get started early once everyone is rested," he coaxes her a little suspiciously, but luckily, she doesn't catch on. Not long after, she says goodnight, the excitement of exploring tomorrow winning over staying up late.

"What are you up to?" Shane asks our boyfriend, who taps a finger against his nose.

"Wouldn't you like to know?"

"Yes!" we all chorus, but there are smiles on our faces and laughter in our voices. Alex is just too ridiculous and adorable to get mad about him keeping a secret or two for a short while. The joy on his face from knowing something we don't is kind of infectious, and I'll take anything that makes my guys happy.

"Well, let's clean up, then I'll show you." He starts gathering the dirty dishes, and the other guys stand up to give him a hand, clearing away the rest of the meal. I chuckle at their enthusiasm and how quickly it happens now that they have motivation.

I sit back and drink the delicious cocktail Alex made me, thinking of the way Ash and Alex argued while he mixed it. It was good-natured, playful banter between two people who can't help but try to push each other's buttons. The sexual tension between them is off the fucking charts, and Jace and Shane seem to encourage it.

Finally, they are done, and we follow Alex downstairs into the garage. "When I spoke to Diego earlier, I asked where the hidden underground entrance was. I also asked if he had been down here. He told me he had, but he hadn't explored everything because he didn't have the codes to get into the doors with the keypads. That was in the book he had given your dad, and he didn't care enough to keep guessing."

I gasp, realizing why he had that big smile on his face. "I have the codes in my phone!"

He claps his hands. "I know, so let's check out what's down here."

"Hang on a minute." Riku leaves us standing in the garage full of vintage cars. There must be at least twenty cars down here, and the boys ooh and ah over them while we wait.

"Can we take these for a drive while we're here?" Shane caresses the vintage burgundy Rolls Royce Phantom almost as reverently as he does my body.

"I'll ask Diego if they have been maintained. If so, then I don't see why not."

Riku returns, holding his gun again. "I'm sure no one is down here, but…"

"Better to be safe than dead, right?" Cole says as Alex lifts an old can of spray paint. The click of the secret door is deafening in the quiet garage.

"The old bastard really liked his secret shit, didn't he?" Jace mutters as we all peer through the doorway. The automatic lighting kicks in as soon as Alex steps forward, illuminating the passage with an eerie, blue-tinted light.

"This tunnel apparently leads to two exits. One somewhere down by the coast, in a cave where a souped-up motorboat is ready for a quick escape. The other is farther into the property where there's an escape route in case we can't use the main drive-way. There's a car parked there too."

"Wow, Diego really saved us some time." Ash sounds impressed by Alex's interrogation skills.

"See, my nosiness pays off."

Alex leads the way down the corridor, followed by Riku and his weapon. The rest walk behind, but it's a little creepy, and I find myself reaching behind me for a hand. A warm one hits mine, and when I look back, it's Cole's.

"I'm here." It's not those words that make me feel better. No, it's the press of his hand, the warmth of his closeness, and the sound of his voice that makes the churning in my stomach come to a rest. Who would have thought this would develop between us? A few weeks ago, he and I couldn't even be in the same room without almost throwing down.

"Here's the first keypad!" Alex calls back, finally stopping. "The other rooms are all empty. Diego said they had drugs and guns in them when he first arrived, but he sold all that off and refuses to use his house to store those products anymore. He has an underground bunker elsewhere on the property."

"Holy shit. You two really talked. I can't believe he gave you this information." Jace stares wide-eyed at Alex, who shrugs.

"He also promised that if I told anyone or hurt Jacinta, he'd kill me in my sleep, followed by the rest of you. He might not be the count, but he is definitely not vanilla either." Alex shudders before gesturing to the keypad. "Do your thing."

"I can't believe my bio dad threatened you," I mutter as I pull out my phone and bring up the codes.

"Oh, your Brad dad did too," Jace shares helpfully. "After our trip to see you in Romania, he had the three of us and Cole for dinner one night. He and Howard and your brothers put the fear of God into us."

"Yeah, we got that conversation via satellite," Ash says, and Riku chuckles, nodding.

"Well, okay then. Guess I'm not surprised they

were so… thorough. I wonder if I'll get the same talk from your families." I tilt my head in question. We haven't talked a lot about their families. Have I been neglectful? I forget not all are as wonderful as mine.

Alex scoffs. "Hardly, my parents don't give a crap."

"My mom and dad love you and are thrilled I'm in a relationship even if it isn't traditional." Riku holds his gun up, waiting for me to input the code. "Heck, Aimi would steal you away if she had the chance and thought you'd be interested. Her wife's already had to give her the lecture about how not everyone gets a harem, and that's just how life is."

Shane takes his turn to share because of course we've now decided to have this conversation in the middle of a secret basement exploration. "I don't have parents, and you won't see my brother unless he wants money."

"You have the seal of approval from the only person I care about, but she will be very upset if she doesn't get to explore down here," Ash warns.

"What about you two?" I ask my remaining boyfriends as Alex wriggles with impatience beside us. Thankfully, he realizes the importance of this conversation, so he keeps his mouth shut.

"I have almost as many siblings as you do. My parents love a big family, so they are not going to care either way. Though they will insist on us coming out to meet them as soon as we can—all of us. They'll want to get to know Jacinta, of course, but they'll also be interested in the men who will be an important part of their grandson's life."

"As long as I don't have to ride a horse," Riku grumbles, and I snicker. I'll get him on one, one day.

"Jace?" I ask, and he grimaces.

"My sisters will be judgy and bitchy, but once they see how happy I am, they'll come around."

"Please, they'll just be jealous of all the amazing dick you're getting." I clear my throat, unsurprised by Alex's contribution. "Sorry, dick *and* pussy," Alex corrects and blows me a kiss. "Can we do this now?"

I press the numbers into the pad. Unlike the vault at home, none of these have biometric scanners, so the door clicks open as soon as I hit the last number.

"Let me go first." Riku pushes through, gun at the ready, and as he steps over the threshold, the room lights up. "Holy shit." His words are practically a whisper, but they seem to thunder back to us.

"What?" Alex follows after him as we all wait more patiently. "Yes, I fucking knew it!" Alex crows, and it's enough to pique our collective curiosity, so we follow after him.

"What the fuck?" Jace's shocked exclamation has me giggling when I catch sight of the room's contents. I don't think he's ever seen a sex dungeon before, not that I have, but I'm not surprised after I heard all about the one at Willow Castle. I was very surprised when the castle in Romania didn't have one. The seven of us look around the room. I never went up to the one back home since I didn't need that mental visual of my brothers and Harlow using it, but this one seems to be very well stocked.

"I'm not using this room until I know all the equipment has been deep cleaned," Shane says, examining a paddling bench. "Then this will do very nicely."

The guys spread out to examine the room, but I grab Riku by the arm. "Will you come check out the other locked rooms with me?"

"Sure, lead the way."

The two of us go out into the hall and head back down the tunnel. It's about twenty yards farther down that we get to another keypad. We follow the same procedure, with Riku waiting, weapon ready, while I take care of the passcode. The door swings open, and he steps in, triggering the automatic lights. I gasp in horror when I see what's inside this room. It's a cell block with barred rooms. I follow close behind as we walk the length, looking in each individual cell, my fingers crossed behind my back in hope that we don't find a dead body. I sigh with relief when they all turn up empty.

"Why would the count have cells under his house?" I ask, a little dazed. I know he was a bad man, but this takes it to a new level.

"Maybe the playthings for the other room were

kept in here," Riku suggests dryly, and I shudder at the thought.

"Let's lock this one back up. We don't have any need for it."

We exit, and I slam the door, reactivating the lock. There's one more keypad on the opposite wall another twenty yards or so down, so once we make our way there, I plug in the code. When this door swings open and the room illuminates, it's a little like déjà vu. Just like the vault under Willow Castle, this one contains guns, drugs, and treasure. Gold bars, jewels, and antiquities fill the shelves, pallets, and wall space.

"Holy shit." Ash's voice has me jumping, though Riku's reaction is a little more dangerous. He whirls around, his gun pointed in the direction of the voice. Ash jumps and holds up his hands. "Hey, it's just me!"

Riku huffs out a breath and lowers the weapon, tucking it into his waistband. "You're lucky I didn't shoot you."

"Look at this. This is freaking amazing." Ash goes to grab something, but I hold out a hand. "Let's not put fingerprints on things just yet."

"Oh, good thinking." He snatches his hand back, a contrite look on his face.

I snort, looking around. "Not my first treasure vault. Okay, the guns and drugs have to go. We'll tell Diego he can deal with those. As for the rest, well, I guess if we ever run out of money, it will be here if we need it. Come on."

"Don't you want to look through it?" Ash looks longingly at the treasure like he's Gollum and it's the ring to rule them all.

"I guess if you want to catalog, we can, but not tonight. Anyway, I can guarantee most of it will have been stolen or collected by ill-gotten gains."

Grumbling, they follow me out of the room, and once again, I slam the door shut. I am seriously getting sick of finding shit. I just hope the rest of my houses are normal.

The next day, I return to Diego's guest house, and we talk some more, including sharing what we found in the tunnels, which he promises to deal with. He has men who will be discreet, and they'll use the tunnels to ensure the dangerous stuff, like the drugs and guns, has no risk of falling into the wrong hands or being seen by the wrong people.

Jax and the rest of the family arrive late afternoon, having left as soon as Harlow's appointment was done. Unfortunately, there's one little piece missing from our family reunion. Hayden refused to let Spencer come since it would take time away from their remaining days together before her move. So, even though we are incomplete, it's still a big moment for our family. There is quite an emotional reunion between Dad and Diego in particular.

Over the next few days, Jax and Diego get to know each other, and Dad and Diego catch up on each other's lives. Dad tries to get Diego to return to LA, but he refuses to make that big of a change. He's happy with his life here, but he gives in a little bit, because Dad wouldn't give up until he got his old friend to agree to some visits in the future.

On New Year's Eve, we head into Cartagena and celebrate in style. Diego booked out a restaurant for all of us, so we have food and cocktails and watch the fireworks explode over the ocean. The streets are full of revelers, and it's fun and relaxing. The next day, it's time for us to return to real life. Cole is champing at the bit to see Spencer, and I can't deny that I want to see him too. I was already fond of his son, but now that Cole and I are committed to trying a relationship, there was this *click* inside me. Those maternal instincts are firmly switched on, and I can't wait to get some hugs from his little man.

Most of the family head home after emotional goodbyes with Diego, who promises it wouldn't be another twenty years before they saw each other again.

It's just me and the guys left when a commotion in the garage has Riku pulling his weapon from its holster. The shouting comes toward us, growing louder, and we all move out of the way as Diego comes into view, followed by four men. They are walking in pairs, each partnership holding a limp man suspended between them.

The men are thrown on the floor at my feet, and I stare at my biological father in confusion.

"I wasn't able to protect you for the first part of your life, so I thought I should make up for lost time." One of the men groans and rolls over. I don't recognize him, but Riku's eyes widen in surprise.

"That's Urie Sokolov."

"Yes, it is. He will be found in a hotel room, which will be booked by my men under his name, this afternoon. Conveniently, he will have five kilograms of coke on him, enough to put him in jail for a long time," Diego says conversationally.

Ash nudges the other lump of meat, because these two have been beaten within an inch of their lives and can't be described as anything else. This one is fully unconscious, and when Ash manages to roll him over with his foot, I gasp. "That's Matthew Shaw! What the fuck?"

"Yes, it is, and I should cut off his hands and dick for what he did to you." Gone is the kind and quiet man I've gotten to know over the last few days, replaced with the crime lord he had to become to survive. "But I am pretty sure that would upset you, so he will go on a flight back to the States to await trial for his wrongdoings. I'll make sure that his judge will throw the book at him. Who knows? He might just wind up with coke on him too, so even if he gets off on the sexual assault charge, they can't overlook the cocaine trafficking."

I blink a couple of times before throwing my arms around him. When we met, I just wanted answers. He owed me no other penance, nor did I expect him to make up for my mother's shortcomings. I thought we could get to know each other as friends, then become family with a little more time. I didn't expect him to treat me like this... like his daughter. I'm overwhelmed by the feelings bubbling up inside me, but in this case, it's a good thing. All I can feel right now is a sense of belonging and love. This just feels right, like he was always meant to be another shield at my front and guard at my back. It's okay, I realize, to feel this way about him. I know Dad would be proud of me for making room for another special person in my life, especially knowing what Diego has just done for me, and just like that, I make a decision.

"Thank you, Dad," I say, and his arms immediately wrap around me in that tight kind of hug that only a father can give.

"Anything for you and Jax."

When we break apart, I notice the guys have all drifted away. I'm assuming they are in the car. Diego says something in Spanish while snapping his fingers and pointing to the two beaten men. His guys pick them up and haul them away. There's no fanfare about it, which is fitting. These two assholes don't deserve to be a big deal. They deserve to be quietly caught and serve the time they have earned.

"I guess we better get going. You promise you'll come up when their baby is born next month?"

"Yes, my identity as Diego Blanco is well established, so I can come and go as much as I want. Plus, it helps that my daughter, son, and best friend have a private plane at their beck and call." He escorts me out to the car.

"Well, I'll see you then, and again, thank you for everything."

He smiles and waves to the guys in the car. "If any of them give you any trouble, just let me know."

I give him a kiss on the cheek, taking one last moment to appreciate the ease between us now. "They won't, but okay."

I climb in the back next to Cole, who puts an arm around my shoulders.

"Why do I get the feeling that your dad just offered to *take care* of us?"

I look back as the car makes its way down the driveway, my dad getting smaller and smaller until he's out of sight. "Because he did. You all better watch your backs. I've got two dads now, and neither would hesitate to bury you in a shallow grave."

"They'd probably do it together," he grumbles before kissing me hard.

When he pulls away, I sigh and lean into him for the trip to the plane. "I don't know about all of you, but I'm ready to get home. I want to start making plans for our house and get life back to normal."

"Sounds perfect," Ash says from the driver's seat.

"I can't wait to see your house and the tigers and the horses and Willow Castle and the zoo." I smother a smile as Edie rattles off a list of every single thing she's excited about for our future. Edie and Ash are going to move into Dad's place on my and Hope's floor until we can find a rental big enough for all of us. Just the thought of our future, all of us being together in one place, making a home, has my cheeks straining with a smile. I seriously can't wait to begin the rest of my life with these guys.

None of us knows what the future has in store, but this princess finally has faith that it'll be her happily ever after.

Epilogue

"I can't believe it took me so long to convince Tom to tell us where she was," Harlow complains as our limo pulls up in front of a small castle hidden away in the south of Ireland.

"It was only because the baby is coming soon that he finally caved and gave me the information. Well, that and some seriously bendy sex positions that I surprised even myself with, but that's neither here nor there."

Harlow grins as I wrinkle my nose and gag a little bit. "Ew, I don't want to know those details."

She scoffs, but it's playful, the easy back and forth that sisters should have. It's been both a long and short journey for us, but we love each other, and I know my life is more complete because I have her in my life as my sister. "And *I* didn't want to know details about your foursome with men I basically consider brothers, but you were happy to share many details of Jace's, Alex's, and Shane's talents."

I smirk and shrug. "Fair enough. Sex talk with each other is off the table. Agreed?"

"Agreed, but Hope is still fair game."

"Oh, absolutely, and I am almost certain she is getting it from someone, but I can never see anyone coming and going from her room. I had my money on Parker McCallister, but the tension between them is still awkward."

"Well, one mystery at a time. Once we sort this one out, we can turn our attention to Hope," she says, then sighs. "I guess we should get out."

"Fuck." I focus on the weather outside. It's mid-January, and it's absolutely freezing. The wind is howling, and sleet is pelting against the windows as we climb out of the car and rush over to the door as quickly as pregnant Harlow can manage it. Thankfully, there's a portico, so we're sheltered from the inhospitable weather as I lift the huge door knocker and bang it against the wooden door a couple of times.

I stomp my feet and rub my gloved hands together as Harlow grumbles under her breath. "Someone better open this fucking door soon, or there's going to be hell to pay." She digs around in her pocket for the spare key Tom gave her. We wanted to give Maxine some control of the situation, so Tom advised us to let her have a chance to welcome us in first, but if she doesn't answer, we're using that key.

Finally, just when we're about ready to handle it ourselves, the door opens. Standing in the doorway, outlined by the light behind her, is our friend Maxine who has been missing from our lives since September with no explanation as to why. She never even reached out about Harlow's pregnancy.

She sighs when she sees us. "I was wondering how much longer I was going to get away with this. I guess you two better come in."

"Well, shit has happened in our own fucking lives too, but you'd know that if you'd been around," Harlow snaps, not pulling any punches, but her anger drains away when we step closer and the rest of Max's body becomes easier to see. My mouth drops open in surprise, because our friend Max looks to be about six months pregnant.

"Oh, Maxy Max, I think you've got some splainin' to do," Harlow quips as we step into the warmth of the house and close the door behind us, locking out the freezing weather.

She sighs. "Yeah, I guess I do."

With that, the three of us settle in the living room, ready to hear the story of how our family has yet another baby on the way.

Woohoo! And that's Jacinta done and dusted. But don't dismay, I will return to the Neighpalm World in 2023. We've, of course, still got Max and Hope's stories to come, and who knows maybe a sneaky peak at what Harlow and the gang are up to with zoo openings, and baby arrivals and building new homes.

PS. If you liked the sound of the cocktails Hope and jazzy drank in the first chapter I've left the recipes on the next page.

Thank you for reading!
I hope you enjoyed the book. It would be super awesome if you could leave a review wherever you bought it, because I love to hear what you thought of the story.

Want to keep up to date with new books coming soon? Sign up to my newsletter here
Newsletter

Another way to do that is to join me Facebook group. I drop teasers and giveaways in there all the time. Here's the link
Lexie's Ladygarden

Visit my webpage and check out reading orders and what else I've written.

Afterword

www.lexiewinston.com

Zombie Brain shots
Ingredients
1 part Vodka
1 part coconut creme or piña colada mix
Edible fake blood*

Edible Fake Blood
$\frac{1}{2}$ cup light corn syrup
1 tbsp cornstarch
.25 cup water
15 drops of red food coloring
1-5 drops of blue food coloring

Instructions
Mix all ingredients for the edible fake blood - for easy use, pour into a squeeze bottle for decorating. Combine all ingredients except fake blood in a blender and blend until combined. Drizzle fake blood over shot glass.

Mad Doctor
Ingredients
1.5 ounces vodka

¾ ounce Sour Apple Schnapp Liqueur

¾ ounce Sour Apple Mixer

Ice for shaking

Instructions
Combine vodka, liqueur, and mixer in cocktail shaker and fill with ice.

Cover and shake for a good 30 seconds. Strain into serving glass.

Drop in a cube of dry ice for the smoke effect and a candy eyeball for garnish.

Black Magic
Fill a shot lass ¾ full with black sambuca. Swirl in Baileys to create a swirly effect

Acknowledgments

I'm glad that Jazzy got her happy ending despite the struggles through out. I've read a few reviews where people weren't happy with her drug use especially after her mom, but I think it's unrealistic to not believe that good people make mistakes, specially following trauma..

Fiction would be pretty boring if I wrote my female characters with the same flaws and the same problems as each other.

Anyway, thank you for reading. Next up for me is a Galaxy Circus novella that has a little Rocky Horror Picture Show vibe to it. You can preorder A night Most Wicked here.

Thank you to all the normal crew this book wouldn't be possible without you all.

Thank you…..

Michelle for your invaluable editing.

Jess for squeezing me in for a proofread.

Emma for all the late night and early morning chats.

My alpha and beta teams for being super awesome as usual.

And of course my friend Grace who attempts to keep my needy ass sane.

Thank you to everyone who reviews and recommends it and thank you to all of you who take the chance and preorder the next one as soon as you've finished the last. You guys are the reason I can keep writing this story.
Until next time. Happy Reading
Xoxo

Lexie

For so long now I've been a solo operative, not having to worry about anyone but my target and myself. I even have a code name that is whispered throughout the underworld.

The Phantom.

And people know to be scared if they get on my radar.

But the director of the secret agency I work for is also my dad, and I'm still his little girl despite how many kills I have under my belt. He's decided that I need to have a team to back me up.

I strongly disagree.

But we made a deal. If he wins, I have to join a team of his choosing and work a sex trafficking case with them, leaving the Phantom to retire. But if I win, he never brings it up again and I get to stay a ghost.

I'm going to hand this team their ass, because the Phantom is not a team player

Get it now